GEM, HIMSELF, ALONE

GEM, HIMSELF, ALONE

P.D. WORKMAN

ISBN: 9781988390567 (IS Hardcover)

ISBN: 9781988390550 (IS Paperback)

ISBN: 9781774680308 (IS Large Print)

ISBN: 9781988390512 (KDP Paperback)

ISBN: 9781988390529 (Kindle)

ISBN: 9781988390536 (ePub)

pdworkman

ALSO BY P.D. WORKMAN

YOUNG ADULT FICTION:

Medical Kidnap Files:

Mito

EDS

Proxy

Toxo

Pain

Between the Cracks:

Ruby

June and Justin

Michelle

Chloe

Ronnie

June, Into the Light

Tamara's Teardrops:

Tattooed Teardrops

Two Teardrops

Tortured Teardrops

Vanishing Teardrops

Breaking the Pattern:

Deviation

Diversion

By-Pass

Stand Alone YA novels

Stand Alone

Don't Forget Steven

Those Who Believe

Cynthia has a Secret

Questing for a Dream

Once Brothers

Intersexion

Making Her Mark

Endless Change

Gem, Himself, Alone

MYSTERY/SUSPENSE:

Zachary Goldman Mysteries

She Wore Mourning

His Hands Were Quiet

She Was Dying Anyway

He Was Walking Alone

They Thought He was Safe

He Was Not There

Her Work Was Everything

She Told a Lie

He Never Forgot (Coming soon)

She Was At Risk (Coming soon)

Kenzie Kirsch Medical Thrillers

Unlawful Harvest

AND MORE AT PDWORKMAN.COM

To those who have been victimized and alone.

PROLOGUE

GEM HAD A SPECIAL gift. He knew from the time that he was little that he wasn't the same as everyone else.

It had to be kept secret.

But it made him different, able to do things that no one else could. When he looked at the other people around him, he saw their limitations. How they were bound by rules he didn't have to follow.

But he was special.

———

Gem stared down at the grave marker, trying to make out the letters of Honey's name through a blur of tears. He took a glance around to make sure that no one was observing him. Gem didn't cry. He wasn't a baby. But knowing that Honey's thin, tortured body lay under the ground beneath him caused a stab of pain in his chest so bad that he thought he might have a heart attack and lay his own body down right there on top of hers.

But he didn't.

The doctors had patched him up, drilling screws into broken bones, dripping antibiotics and other chemical cocktails into his veins, and putting him on a diet intended to restore the weight he'd lost. They had wanted to keep him in hospital, but Gem was strong enough to leave. He wanted to move on. His heart pulled him south, following Honey, even though he knew he would never see her pretty face and shining blond hair again.

He knelt there staring at the temporary grave marker and the little pot of violets he had placed beside them, feeling the rocky soil beneath his knees and smelling the freshly-cut grass. He had followed her there, away from his origins and from Raphael's shop, to where he didn't know anyone. It was a fresh start, where he would have no rep, good or bad. He and Honey had talked about what they would do when they got out of there. Where they would go, the jobs and lifestyles they would have. They would go together, or at least keep in touch. They wouldn't forget what they had shared.

He had known even while they talked about it that it was impossible. It would never happen. They were throwaways and would never be able to rise above the street life. They would either end up behind locked doors or under the ground.

Like Honey was now.

Even with his gift, he hadn't been able to save her. He had been able to kill Raphael, but he had been too late to save Honey's life.

I

GEM

CHAPTER ONE

GEM HAD HEARD THEM coming. The Rippers, one of the local street gangs. Teens and young adults. Boys. A mix of racial profiles. There were a few girls associated with them, but only as girlfriends and groupies; they weren't considered members of the Rippers.

Gem had been keeping an eye on the gang since he had moved into the neighborhood. Getting a feel for them and letting them see him, making it known that he was available.

It had started with one of them following him. One set of footsteps echoed behind him. He took a glance over his shoulder, but couldn't make the boy without being obvious about it. Another set of footsteps joined the first as Gem went around a corner.

He looked around, back and forth, watching for more of them. It wasn't very long before he was flanked; then he saw Thrasher approaching from ahead of him.

Gem faced the gang impassively, waiting for them to make the first move.

"So you been hanging around a lot lately," Thrasher commented. The leader of the gang, he was one of the oldest, his scarred face chiseled and his eyes like ice.

"Yeah," Gem agreed.

"You trying to get into a gang?"

Gem shrugged. "You looking?" he countered. It wouldn't do to look too eager. He kept his answers brief, studying each of the gang members and assessing them. They hadn't immediately grabbed him and didn't look like they were going to beat him down just for being in their territory, so he was already ahead of the game.

"That depends. You got references?" Thrasher demanded.

"No." Gem hadn't been in a gang before, so he didn't have anyone to stand up for him. In a new city, there wasn't even anyone who could say that he wasn't a snitch or a troublemaker.

"What's your name?"

"Gem."

"Gem what?"

Gem shook his head.

"Where ya come from?"

Gem considered his answer carefully, considering how much he wanted to reveal. "North."

Thrasher chuckled. "You don't waste words, do you?"

Gem shrugged again.

"You didn't know anyone up 'north'? Nobody to speak for you?"

"No."

Thrasher put a cigarette in his mouth and let it hang there, not lighting it. "You don't make it easy. How do we know you ain't a rat?"

"I'm not."

"How old are you?"

"Eighteen."

Thrasher laughed and shook his head. He had eyes. With Gem's slight build and baby face, no matter how he tried, he couldn't pass for an adult. "Good answer. How old are you really?"

Gem wasn't sure he was willing to reveal the truth. After considering, he swiped his ragged blond hair away from his eyes and amended his answer. "Sixteen."

Thrasher's eyes flickered over him. Gem felt like Thrasher could see right through him. "Maybe. I doubt it, but it'll do for now."

"You ain't letting him in, are you?" one of the others piped up. A darker boy, tall and gangly. The rest of the gang had remained respectfully quiet as Thrasher conducted business. Thrasher half-turned to see who had interrupted him.

"Maybe he'll take *your* place. I ain't making a decision yet, just getting information."

Gem took a step backward. No point in prolonging the interview if Thrasher wasn't ready to make a decision yet. "I'll be seeing you around, then."

"Yeah. We'll let you know if we want you."

Gem nodded and moved on. He could wait. If the Rippers wouldn't take him, he'd find another gang for protection.

Thrasher consulted his lieutenants on various gang matters over a six-pack and a couple of lines of coke at his apartment. The TV played away to itself in the background. Smoke hung heavy in the air.

"That new guy looking to get into the gang," Thrasher started. "Gem. The blond kid."

"Something weird about him," Bishop suggested. "The look in his eyes creeps me out."

Thrasher nodded, grinning. "I finally got a line on him. Someone who went to school with him for a while. Said he's nuts. Certifiable."

"Then he's out."

Thrasher swigged a drink. He pursed his lips. "Don't jump to conclusions. From what I gather, he's still pretty savvy. Sometimes it's not a bad thing to have a nut job in the gang to do your dirty work."

The boys were silent, considering the statement. Bishop frowned and scratched his sandpaper jaw. "You wanna take that chance? Having someone that unstable in the gang?"

"Like the rest of you are so stable? He's probably no crazier than some of the others. So far, there are no complaints around the neighborhood. He keeps a low profile."

Bishop shrugged and wisely voiced no further protest.

———

Gem talked to himself in a low whisper, huddled in the dark alley where no one could see him. The air was cold, and the ground was hard and littered with gravel and glass.

"The Rippers are gonna take me. Long as I pass the initiation. Thrasher said I checked out. Don't know what he found out. No one knows anything. I'll get through the initiation, though. No problem. I can manage that."

He nodded and let out a long breath, trying to dispel the anxiety. "It'll work out. A gang's good protection."

Gem yawned and stretched. "Better knock off and get some sleep."

———

The next night, he watched the beat-down by the Rippers from up above. He wished he could go for help, but all he could do was stay and watch to see what happened. Someone must have seen what was going on and called the police after the Rippers took off, because the cops went straight to the alley as if they knew where Gem's unmoving body was lying. Neither got close, to begin with. The junior officer hung back, and the older, graying cop turned away while he called in on his radio for an ambulance.

"Is he breathing?" he asked the younger officer.

The younger cop steeled himself and bent over Gem's form, looking for the rise and fall of his chest and feeling for a pulse. He drew his hand away, fingers sticky with blood, trying to hide how violently he was shaking.

"Weak pulse," he advised, "but he's alive."

"Where are your gloves?"

The rookie looked at him blankly.

"You've got gloves, haven't you? You want to get AIDS?"

The rookie suddenly realized his mistake and looked down at his hands. "Oh yeah," he wiped them on his pants, embarrassed. "I wasn't thinking."

The older cop nodded. "Be more careful. Always look out for

yourself first." Then he prodded at Gem with his foot. "He's in pretty rough shape. I don't know if he's going to make it."

"Shouldn't we do something?"

"Like what?"

"I don't know. Something."

They were both silent for a few minutes, waiting for the ambulance.

"What happened to him? This is Rippers territory, isn't it? He's nowhere near the boundary. Couldn't have accidentally wandered into it."

"Initiation. Rippers tend to go a bit overboard jumping their boys in. They've been known to kill initiates."

Not this time. Gem wasn't going to give up. Gem had been through tough times before and survived. He wasn't going to get killed by a stupid jumping-in.

An ambulance pulled into the lane, lights flashing but siren off. A medic got out at a leisurely pace. "What've we got?"

"Ripper initiation."

"Great." The medic bent over Gem's body and examined him. "Well, they did their usual thorough job. Let's get him on the gurney."

Gem's form was loaded unceremoniously into the ambulance. The ambulance's driver stepped out for a smoke before starting for the hospital.

———

Gem woke up in the hospital, sore and fuzzy-headed. His body pulsed with pain. For the first little while, he just drifted in and out, and couldn't remember what had happened. He thought he was in the hospital after being rescued from Rafe's shop. Then he remembered the gang. He had survived the initiation. Or at least the first stage; some of the gangs had several levels of initiations to pass. He wasn't sure about the Rippers' practices.

He'd been there for a while, aware of his surroundings but not ready to move, when a cop walked in and looked down at him. Paunchy. Graying at the temples. "Well, you're awake."

Gem said nothing. In trying to focus on the cop and to read his name bar, Gem realized that one of his eyes was swollen shut. His vision through the other didn't seem to be as clear as usual.

"I guess that means you're the newest member of the Rippers, huh?"

Gem shrugged. Just the slight movement of one shoulder sent pain coursing through his body. So that was it; that was the full initiation. The cop wouldn't say he was in if there were more to it. He'd be trying to get Gem to back out, to stay away from the Rippers and live an honest life.

The cop stared down at him. Gem felt exposed and vulnerable lying there. "Do you have a name?" the cop demanded.

"Gem."

"Gem? Like a diamond or something?"

Gem nodded. "Yeah, Gem."

"That's your street name. What's your real name?"

Gem didn't answer.

"I'm Pagetti."

Gem still didn't reveal his full name.

"You got folks around here? Or are you a runaway?"

"I don't have any folks."

"Foster care, or what?"

"Am I in trouble for something?"

Pagetti didn't have anything on Gem, or he'd be using it. He wasn't going to be able to trace Gem's identity. Not like Thrasher had, putting the word out on the street. He'd have to try another method, like fingerprints, but he didn't have any cause.

"That's what I'm trying to determine. Have you been in trouble before?"

"None of your business."

"I think it is. Are you on probation? Any outstanding warrants?"

"No."

"You want to charge the guys who beat you up?"

"No."

"Why not?"

Gem carefully composed his answer, taking his time responding. "It was... a misunderstanding."

"It was an initiation," the cop said flatly, "and they could have killed you."

"They didn't."

"Not through any lack of trying."

"I'm tired," Gem said, ending the conversation.

"You can answer a few more questions."

Gem shut his eye and ignored any further attempts by the cop to get him to answer anything else. Eventually, Pagetti left him alone.

———

Sitting with Thrasher in his broken-down old couch, Bethany stared off into space, oblivious to him. He played with the ends of her long, blond hair, studying her face. She was young. And she was pretty. More than he could say about most of the girls who spent time with the Rippers. And he knew that unlike most of the gang groupies, she actually had some brains.

"Hey, what'cha thinking?" Thrasher prodded.

She looked at him, focusing in on his face. "That new kid. The blond. Is he gonna get into the Rippers?"

"Gem?" Thrasher yawned and stretched. "He might. How come?"

"Nothing. I saw him today."

"Today? No way."

"I thought I did." Bethany's brows drew down.

"Uh-uh. We jumped him in last night. He's in the hospital if he didn't kick it."

"I was sure it was him..." She shook her head, puzzled. "Must have been someone else."

"It was somebody else," Thrasher assured her. "Or else it wasn't today. Maybe it was yesterday."

"I suppose..." Bethany gave a little laugh. "Who can keep track?"

CHAPTER TWO

GEM HAD TRIED TO get out of the hospital several times. He figured he should be able to be up and around, but the nurses and his body had other ideas. He could barely make it past the hospital room door. The last nurse to pick him up off the floor, a fierce little woman, told him that next time he wandered off, she'd put him in restraints. As small as she was, he knew he was still too weak to prevent her.

Too weak to walk out to the street, too weak to protect himself, too weak to be back out there yet. He lay back in bed, trying to get up enough energy for his next attempt.

———

Nurse Rachelle saw Officer Pagetti approaching Gem's room and motioned for him to stop and talk to her.

"How's he doing?" Pagetti asked.

"Well, I don't think he's going to be staying around here for long."

"He's recovered that fast?" he asked in surprise. The boy had appeared to be in pretty bad shape.

"No, but he's been trying to check himself out. So far, he can't make it to the door. But I know that kind of determination. I'll bet you he's gone in a day."

"Well, I'd better make my questions count today. Has he had any visitors?"

"No. Nobody."

"What's his condition? Is he going to be okay if he skips out of here?"

"Mmm. Not great. He might start bleeding. He might get an infection. He's going to be mighty sore and weak for a while. I certainly wouldn't recommend being out on the street in that condition. But I know these kids."

"Okay. We'll see how this goes."

Pagetti went into Gem's room. The boy was asleep. If anything, he looked worse than he had the day before. His bruises had darkened, and his eyes had sunk deeper. There was a thin sheen of sweat on his face. Pagetti hesitated to wake Gem up, but he trusted Rachelle's judgment. If she said Gem would be gone tomorrow, she was right. Pagetti shook Gem to wake him.

Gem opened his eyes and, after a moment, focused on the cop. "What do you want?" His voice was dry and hoarse.

Pagetti held out a cup of warm water from the table beside the bed. "I want to talk a little more."

Gem eyed the water. "How do I know you ain't trying to poison me?"

Pagetti chuckled. "Because then I couldn't question you."

Gem didn't smile. He continued to stare back suspiciously. Pagetti shook his head, disconcerted to realize that Gem was serious. "Drink it or don't, I don't care. I'm just here to talk."

Gem shook his head. Pagetti put it back on the table.

"So, I couldn't find any outstanding warrants or missing persons reports on you. But then, it's not so easy when you don't have a full name. Where are you from?"

"None of your business."

Pagetti could see that Gem wasn't going to give him any identifying information, so he switched tactics. He sat down in the chair beside the bed, closer to Gem's eye level. "So you figured you'd join the Rippers, huh?"

Gem shrugged and didn't deny it. His face was drawn and gaunt with pain. Like Rachelle had said, not someone who should be back out on the street again so soon.

"Who recruited you?"

"No one."

"Oh, come on. I can't go out and arrest someone for talking to you," Pagetti cajoled.

"I don't have to tell you anything," Gem retorted. His jaw was clenched, and he stared a challenge at Pagetti.

"I'm not threatening. You can lose the attitude. Let's just chat."

Gem shook his head. "I only talk to my friends."

Pagetti took a pointed look around the hospital room. "You don't seem to have a lot of friends around here."

"So I don't talk."

"Why don't you tell me about yourself?"

"I got nothing to say."

"How about sports? Are you a football or baseball fan?" Pagetti tried to find some way past the barriers.

Gem closed his eyes and settled back. "The doctor says I gotta sleep," he snapped. He turned his face away.

"You know you're in for some shock with the Rippers," Pagetti said. "It's no place for a young kid like you. You've got no idea how tough it's going to be."

There was no response from Gem.

But Pagetti hadn't really expected one.

———

Gem finally hunkered down, his arms wrapped around himself. He was sick and sore, but he was away from the hospital and back to the safe anonymity of the streets. The streets had their own dangers, but he was prepared for those.

It was a cold night, a brisk wind blowing, and Gem huddled down in his coat and held himself tightly. He knew he was going to be stiff in the morning.

———

Gem might have passed his initiation, but it soon became clear that he wasn't yet a full-fledged member of the gang. He had recovered from the beating, and he sat at a party, outwardly one of the gang. But the Rippers were aloof. They didn't talk to him like he was one of them. He was still an outsider. Not entirely trusted. Sort of on probation. He was going to have to do something to impress them. Something big.

Gem turned his head, feeling that he was being watched. Bethany was looking at him from across the room of revelers. Their eyes met for a long moment. She was one of the prettiest girls he'd ever met. Her long, blond hair reminded him of Honey's. Gem felt a hot flush rising from his neck up to his ears as she looked at him. Self-conscious, he looked away.

Sykes elbowed him in the ribs, urging, "Go for it."

Gem startled and looked at Sykes. What had he missed? "What? Go for what?"

"Bethany. Go; have some fun." Sykes leered.

Gem's face burned, even more embarrassed that someone had noticed the look that passed between them. "I thought she was Thrasher's girl."

Sykes tipped back his head to take a long swallow from his bottle. "Nah. She doesn't belong to Thrasher. You want to spend time with her, she's game. Just give'er some dough to help pay for her apartment. Other than that," he grinned, "do whatever you like with her. Although," he added as an afterthought, "Thrasher gets ticked off if she gets real bruised up."

Gem glanced at Bethany again, uncertain. He wasn't the type who attracted a lot of girls. He had embarrassingly little experience where the opposite sex was concerned. It was a state of affairs he was eager to change.

"Go on," Sykes pressed again. "At least go talk to her."

His heart pounding so loud he was sure Sykes could hear it, Gem got up and strolled over to where Bethany was sitting, trying his best to look cool and casual. "Hey."

"Hi."

"I'm Gem," he introduced himself awkwardly.

She smiled and nodded, patting the seat beside her. "Yeah, I know."

———

The bedroom was warm enough to be comfortable without blankets. Gem lay there a few hours later, soaking up the heat, totally relaxed. Bethany stirred beside him, yawning and stretching her body like a cat.

"How old are you, Gem?"

Gem tensed and looked at her, the feeling of well-being evaporating. Had she brought him there just to dig into his past? "None of your business."

"I don't really care; I was just... curious."

Gem wondered if he'd been so inept that he'd tipped her off. He didn't think he'd fumbled or been overly clumsy. But maybe she could still tell.

Then again, maybe it was his smooth, undeveloped body. Plenty of guys Gem's age were shaving already. And had hair on their bodies. But his body seemed to be one of the slower ones. Although he talked in a deep voice, it was by conscious effort and not because his voice had really changed. He could usually pass for older than he was, but he hadn't fooled Bethany.

"I'm sorry," Bethany said frankly, stroking his arm with one finger. "I hate it when people ask me how old I am."

"How old *are* you?" Gem countered.

She studied him for a moment, her eyes closing halfway. "Fifteen," she said finally.

"Me too." Not really, but it was close enough to be the truth. He wouldn't mind being the same age as she was.

"Cool," said Bethany.

They both laughed a little and relaxed again.

CHAPTER THREE

GEM WALKED AT A normal pace down the busy sidewalk. He was careful not to run or look suspicious, and he kept to well-populated areas. It would be harder for the cops to track him in a crowd.

His vigilance paid off, and Gem managed to avoid the police for another hour. Rather than searching the street for him, they had just put the Rippers' hangouts under surveillance and waited for him to show his face. Gem got to the pool hall and was ambushed at the door.

"Stop right there and spread 'em," a harsh voice ordered.

Gem turned around to look at the owner of the voice. A fist contacted his chin with a crack and Gem went over backward, landing on the concrete with a crash that jarred his bones, still tender after his initiation.

"Did I tell you to turn around?" demanded the square-faced, cleft-chinned cop whose name tag said Riker. "Belly down and lace your hands behind your head!"

Gem's head spun, and he wondered if he were going to black out. The punch had taken him off-guard. He hadn't expected to be assaulted without even a warning.

"Do it!" Riker insisted, kicking him in the leg. "Hands behind your head!"

Gem groggily rolled onto his stomach and put his hands behind his head. Riker patted him down, clipped the cuffs over his wrists, then pulled Gem to his feet.

"You'd better have a helluva story, kid. That's all I can say for you."

The world tipped drunkenly around Gem, and he wasn't able to stay balanced on his own. Riker and his partner, Gordon, held on to him and kept him on his feet.

The cops dragged him to their car and took him to the police station.

———

Gordon was the strong silent type and Riker the one taking charge.

"What's your name?" he demanded at the booking desk.

Gem's legs were a bit steadier, but he still held on to the counter to keep the world from tilting over and dumping him on the floor. "Gem."

"Your full name," Riker snapped. "You're under arrest for armed robbery."

"Gem Johnson."

"Date of birth?"

Gem gave it.

"You're a minor," Riker observed. As if he hadn't already figured that part out. "Who are your guardians?"

"No one."

"You in foster care, or what?"

"No."

"Runaway, then. Fine. Do you have a lawyer?"

"No."

"You'd better call legal aid. What's your address?"

"Don't have one."

"Phone?"

"No."

"Any outstanding warrants?"

"No."

"He's got previous charges, though," the booking officer said, printing off Gem's rap sheet. He handed it to Riker. Gem watched

Riker's eyes go back and forth over the words. Riker's expression grew grimmer. Gem wondered how much the printout revealed about his past.

"Well, we've got you dead to rights this time," he growled. "You're not slipping out of it."

That's what *he* thought.

Gem said nothing, biding his time.

They took him to an interrogation room. Gem sat down, wishing they'd unlock his hands. His chin was stiff and throbbing, swelling up. He looked around the bare room. Green painted walls. Bare table and chairs.

"Where were you at four o'clock this afternoon?"

"At a movie."

Riker glanced at him, raising his brows. "Alone?"

"No. With a girl."

"Who will happily corroborate anything you say."

"If you can find her," Gem agreed. "I never met her before."

"Are you in the habit of going to the movies with girls you never met before?"

Gem shrugged. "There's girls hanging around the theaters. You pay for their ticket, they'll... hang out with you."

"And provide some extra services when the lights go out if you buy them a soda," Gordon spoke up. "Yeah, I've heard the hookers have been hanging out at the x-rated films on hot days lately."

Gem shrugged. "She was real nice."

"I'll bet she was. Did you buy her a soda?" Riker demanded.

"It *was* hot out."

"And did she thank you properly?"

Gem ignored Riker's insinuating tone. "She said thank you."

Riker smoothed a page in his notepad. "Did she give you a name?"

"Cheyenne."

"Well, that's a little more unique than Krystal or Candy, anyway." Riker scratched it down. "Can you describe her?"

Gem considered. "Long red hair. Tall. Dressed in black today."

"Black in this heat? And how much did you pay her to lie to us for you?"

"I didn't pay for anything but her ticket and refreshments."

"Yeah, you wouldn't happen to have the ticket stubs, would you?"

"They were in my pocket."

Riker left to retrieve the brown envelope of Gem's personal items. With a sneer, he dumped out a handful of change and crumpled papers, among which he found a couple of ticket stubs for the three o'clock matinee.

"Well, nice to meet someone who respects our work well enough to at least try to establish an alibi. Now let's talk about where you really were at four o'clock. You were busy robbing a drug store at gunpoint. And firing off shots at the customers for kicks. There was a witness outside who saw your face after you stepped out and took off your ski mask. And the witnesses inside all described what you were wearing. Your goose is cooked."

"It wasn't me," Gem maintained. They wouldn't be able to do anything to him. He had faith in himself and his gift.

"We'll see about that."

———

The witness looked over the boys in the photo array. "Number three," he said immediately, reaching out and tapping it. No hesitation or dithering about.

"Bingo," Riker said smugly. Any doubts he had about Gem's fabricated alibi disappeared. He went back to the interrogation room.

"You were identified," he told Gem.

"I still didn't do it." Gem seemed completely unconcerned by the revelation.

Riker smirked and shook his head. "Tell it to the jury."

"It's not going to a jury. Check my alibi."

"A phony alibi isn't getting you anywhere."

Gem sat back in his chair, folding his arms. "It's not phony."

———

Gordon called Evans, the officer listed on Gem's rap sheet for the last charge that had been dropped—a murder.

"I'm calling about a case you handled last year," he said after introducing himself.

"Sure, what can I help you with?" Evans sounded friendly, eager to help out a fellow officer.

"We've arrested a kid named Gem Johnson."

"Gem." Evans's sigh carried all the way down the line. "Good luck convicting him of anything."

"What's the problem?"

"His alibis. He's always got strong witnesses to say he was somewhere else."

"You couldn't discredit them?" Riker was skeptical.

"Let's talk specifics." Riker heard a long squeal as Evans leaned his chair back. "We arrested him for the murder of his pimp. There was a witness—someone who knew him. But Gem had a dozen witnesses who swore he was locked in a room with them the whole time. And the officers investigating the case were the ones to release them from that locked room, everyone including Gem."

"He was a male hooker?"

"He was a child unlawfully confined in what turned out to be a sex shop. Even if we'd been able to make the murder charge stick, it was probably justifiable, with the torture the vic was putting those kids through."

"So the witnesses had reason to protect him. He was one of them."

"But we couldn't break the stories of any of them. My own investigators said the door was locked and Gem on the other side. Even the pimp's employees agreed that Gem and the others were securely locked away and couldn't possibly have done it."

"So, it wasn't him." Riker stated the obvious.

"I'm convinced it *was* Gem." Evans sounded frustrated. "He was so blamed cocky about the whole thing."

"Or he was innocent."

"Even an innocent person knows he can be convicted in error. Gem knew he had an alibi. He knew he couldn't be convicted."

Riker considered this. "The alibi he's claimed this time is also a hooker."

"I wonder if it's one of his old friends. Send me as much identifying information as you can. I'll cross check it against the murder file and see if it was one of the other kids in the shop. Anything to help break one of Gem's phony alibis!"

"Have there been others?"

"Yes. Nothing as serious. But he's always got something cooked up. If I didn't know better, I'd say that kid can walk through walls or teleport himself."

Riker rolled his eyes. "Thanks for your offer. I'll send you the info on the girl as soon as we catch up with her."

"Sure. I hope I can help."

———

Riker strolled in front of the plaza looking for a redhead. A blonde with lurid makeup scowled at his uniform. "What are you doing here? No one's doing anything illegal."

"I'm looking for a girl named Cheyenne."

"She's not here."

"She's not in any trouble. But she may be able to help a boy who is."

The blonde shook her head and walked away. It took Riker another half hour of walking around to spot the tall redhead dressed in black sequins.

"Hi, Cheyenne."

She stopped and scowled at him. "Am I supposed to be impressed that you know my name?"

The girl had looked good from a distance. Closer up, she looked tired, her makeup smudging in the heat.

"No. But I need your help for a few minutes."

"Sorry."

"There is a boy in a lot of trouble. He says he spent some time with you earlier today. All you need to do is say no. Then I'll leave you alone."

She looked at him for a moment. "Gem?" she asked tentatively.

"Yes. Gem."

She scanned her surroundings, looking for anyone who might be paying attention to her conversation with a cop. She didn't need potential johns avoiding her or her pimp getting angry with her. "He was a nice guy. Acted like I was a real person instead of just…" she gestured to her outfit, "just this."

"What time did you see him?"

"Three o'clock show."

"And what time did you split up?"

"Between four-thirty and five."

"You were with him the whole time? He never left for a refill? To go to the john?"

"You don't go to the john in a place like that," she laughed.

"Did you separate at all in that period?" Riker persisted.

"No."

"You're going to have to come in for questioning."

"Oh, come on," Cheyenne complained, "all we did was watch a movie together!"

"I doubt if you even did that. But if you're going to stick to the story that he was with you, we have to get your statement."

"What if I don't?"

Riker smiled. That would suit him just fine. "Then we take him down for armed robbery and a number of other charges."

She shook her red head deliberately. "I can't let that happen to him. He was a nice guy."

"So nice you agreed to lie for him."

"I'm not lying. Other girls saw him with me. The ticket guy, the ushers, they all saw him too."

"Doesn't mean he was there the whole time."

She rolled her eyes and huffed. "Ask some of the others who were there," she insisted. "It's not just me."

Riker nodded. "That's exactly what I plan to do. And you're going to help me."

———

The next day, Gordon talked with the theater staff while Riker worked with Cheyenne to track down and interview the other prostitutes who might have seen Gem at the theater.

"Do you remember seeing this boy yesterday?" he questioned the man in the ticket booth, holding up a photo of Gem.

"I don't allow underage kids in there," he snapped back, not looking at it.

"I'm not here to bust your chops about it. He says he was here. I say he wasn't."

The man motioned for the picture. Gordon slid it under the glass to him.

"I hate to disagree with a cop, but..."

"You saw him?"

"Yeah. With one of the girls. The... redhead, I think. I thought he was lucky to get in with her; she doesn't usually go for the young ones."

"What show?"

"Afternoon matinee. Three o'clock."

"Did you see him come out?"

"After the show? Can't say I noticed."

"During the show?"

"No. No one leaves without security knowing it. We don't want any trouble—guys hanging out in dark corners, all worked up, people sneaking in and out the back door. No, we're careful here. I would know if someone left in the middle of the movie."

"Can I talk to your ushers and security?"

"Head of security is just around the corner. He'll direct you to who was on duty yesterday."

Gordon went in to see him. The head of security listened to his request and nodded. "Yeah, the regular usher didn't show up, so I had to stand in myself."

"You see this kid?"

The guard took the picture and studied it carefully. "Sure, I remember him. Got in a ruckus in the middle of the show."

"He *what?*"

"The guy behind him was complaining about the kid making too much noise. Kid said he was just whispering to the girl. I suspect they were doing more than just talking, but he was behaving himself when I shone my light on him. I told him to shut up, or I'd turn him out."

"About what time was this?"

"Halfway point. About quarter to four."

"Are you sure he couldn't have snuck out after that?"

"Why would he sneak out? Usually, they're sneaking in. I kept an eye on him the rest of the show to make sure he didn't make any trouble. He never left his seat."

Gordon swore in disbelief.

———

"Oh, there's Gracie," Cheyenne said. "I think she was around. Gracie?"

The girl was younger than Cheyenne. Closer to Gem in age. She looked Riker over vaguely before turning to Cheyenne.

"What's going on?"

Cheyenne didn't answer. Riker took out Gem's picture. "Have you ever seen this boy?"

Gracie squinted at the picture.

"Where's your contacts, honey?" Cheyenne asked in a motherly tone.

"I lost them."

After looking around covertly, Gracie slipped a pair of glasses out of her purse and put them on. She looked at the picture again. She brightened and took the picture from Riker. "Is that Gem? How did you know I knew Gem?" She looked at both of them.

Riker was startled. "You know Gem?" he repeated.

"Sure, I know him from back in—from before." She hesitated. "What's this about? Is Gem in trouble?"

"You never said anything yesterday. Didn't you see me with him?" Cheyenne demanded.

Gracie motioned in embarrassment at her glasses. "I can't see faces without these. Unless we're real close. I couldn't even describe the guy I was with last," she said with a laugh. She looked back and forth at them. "So, what's Gem in trouble for?"

"Are you one of the kids from the same shop as Gem?"

"Oh... you know about that?" Gracie thought for a moment before revealing anything further. "Whoever killed Raphael saved my life. And the others' too. That place was a rat hole. Honest, the rest of us woulda been dead in a few more weeks. The doctor said so. But Gem didn't kill Rafe. He's like a brother, and I'd lie for him if he needed me to, but I didn't need to. He was locked up with the rest of us. He couldn't have killed Rafe."

"Just like he couldn't have committed an armed robbery yesterday because he was with your friend," Riker said, turning to glare at Cheyenne.

Gracie took off her glasses and put them away. "Yeah, I guess. Gem's pretty good at keeping out of jail."

With that, she started to walk away.

"Gracie, you get yourself some new contacts," Cheyenne called after her. "You gotta be able to see what's in a man's eyes."

Gracie waved her hand. "I can still tell. I'll get new ones soon."

CHAPTER FOUR

G EM HAD BEEN IN custody for a few days when he decided it was time to call a lawyer and get himself sprung. He called legal aid, and they sent him a young lawyer fresh out of law school.

He had a round face and didn't look like he belonged in a suit. "Hi, I'm Henry."

Not even old enough to warrant a 'Mister.'

"Hi."

"So I'm told you were charged with armed robbery, among other things," Henry said rapidly.

"I didn't do it," Gem said flatly.

This seemed to fortify Henry slightly. He nodded. "Well, then, let's see about getting you out of here. You don't have an alibi for the time in question?"

"Yeah, I do."

Henry checked himself. "Really? Didn't they look into it?"

"You tell me."

Henry nodded and wrote it down on his legal pad. "I'll find out. What evidence do they have against you?"

"Witness picked me out of a photo lineup."

"Did the others in the lineup fit your general description?"

"No idea. I didn't see it."

"Yeah, I guess. Is that it? One witness?"

"Yeah," Gem shrugged, "far as I know."

"I'll go talk to the investigating officers and see if they have enough to proceed."

———

Henry was nervous talking to the officers, even though he knew he had every right to do so.

"Hi, I'm Gem Johnson's attorney," he told Gordon, wiping his sweaty hands on his pants and then deciding not to shake hands.

"Legal aid?"

"Yes, but I don't see what that has to do with it," Henry bristled.

"Nothing. Just wondering if parents had happened to show up and hire someone."

"Oh. No, I am legal aid."

"So, what can I do for you, Henry?"

"I was wondering about the progress of your investigation. I understand my client has an alibi."

"Well, at first blush..."

"You found it to be false?"

"Not yet. But we expect to be able to shortly. It's obviously fabricated."

"Why is that?"

"For one thing, his alibi is a hooker. For another, we have witnesses who put him at the scene."

"More than one?"

"One who saw his face. The others described his build and clothing."

"And picked him out of a lineup?"

"No, only the one picked him out of the lineup."

"And did this hooker corroborate his story or not?"

"Yes. He may have paid her, or it might have been a favor for a mutual acquaintance, who we have identified."

"So it's his witness against your witness."

Gordon looked uncomfortable. "To be honest, your client's side is looking slightly more favorable. There have been a few more witnesses say that they saw him elsewhere."

"I see. And how about forensics?"

"Nothing to confirm that it was him."

"So what exactly are you holding him on? One witness who's been contradicted?" Henry's voice rose a few notes.

"He's a flight risk. He's got no roots here. If we let him go, he'll run."

"You can't hold him just because he's indigent."

"He's been charged. We're allowed to hold him."

"Let's ask a judge if you have enough to go to trial."

"You'll have to talk to the attorney prosecuting the case."

"Why don't you give me his contact information?"

Within a few hours, Gem was released.

———

Thrasher saw Gem walking along the street gazing in the shop windows. "Hey, Gem. You bust out, man?"

"They let me go."

"I thought they had you cold!"

"They could never get me on anything," Gem said with disconcerting self-assurance.

"Is that so? You did do the job, didn't you?"

"Yeah. Sure."

"How'd you get off?"

Gem shrugged.

"There's something about you, Gem. What is it?"

Gem gave a sly smile and didn't enlighten Thrasher. Thrasher shook his head and lit himself a cigarette.

"You coming with us tonight?"

"Where?"

"Partying. We got a big thing going on in a warehouse, should be a lot of fun."

Gem shrugged. "Sure. Sounds good."

They reached the apartment building that some of the Rippers lived at and which had, therefore, become a central meeting place for them. Bethany was coming back from running an errand and flashed a smile aimed at Gem in particular.

"Hey, Gem."

"Uh—hi."

"Have a good time." Thrasher leered and walked away. Gem looked at Bethany.

"Are you coming in?" she asked.

Gem nodded and followed her to her apartment. Dietrich, one of the other Rippers, was hanging around Bethany's door, and his expression fell when he saw her with Gem. They all looked at each other awkwardly.

"I'll talk to you later," Gem said to Bethany, with as much dignity as possible.

Bethany looked at him, with gratitude in her eyes. "Okay, Gem."

"You're an okay guy," Little D said.

Gem made a quick exit.

———

Rico greeted Gem like an old friend. Gem was finding that the drugstore holdup and subsequent release from police custody had had the desired effect of solidifying his membership in the Rippers. Everybody was treating him like someone special now, instead of shutting him out of their conversations.

"Gem, hey man. Where've you been? Glad you're gonna join our party."

Gem nodded. He held out his hand to Rico with a couple of pills he had stolen from the drug store. Rico raised his eyebrows.

"Cool," he said appreciatively, and popped them. "You make a good haul at that drug store?"

"Yeah. It was a good hit."

"I hear you were pretty slick."

"With a good plan, I can do anything."

"You think so?"

Gem nodded. "Anything."

Rico considered this thoughtfully. His face started to flush. "Right now I'm gettin' high... but let's talk about this again."

"Sure."

Gem watched Rico wander away again, the pills obviously kicking in already. Must be good stuff. Gem popped a couple himself and waited for the party to get hopping.

———

Later, Sherwood looked down at Gem where he lay on the sidewalk and gave him a kick. "Looks like someone doesn't know his limit." He kicked Gem again, harder. "If you don't want to get rousted, you'd better get up!"

Gem stirred, curling up protectively.

"Gem! Man, that's a weird name. Gem, get up or get canned."

Gem groaned. "Lemme 'lone."

"If you want to get rousted."

Sherwood tried one more kick to convince Gem to get up. One of Gem's wiry arms snaked out around Sherwood's leg and jerked sharply, toppling him to the ground. Gem threw himself on top of Sherwood, fists flailing.

"I said lemme alone!"

Sherwood was somewhat drunk himself and his reactions slow. He looked into Gem's eyes and saw the crazed recklessness. Gem was higher than a kite. Sherwood tried to grasp Gem's wrists to hold him still, but couldn't bring the smaller boy under control.

"Somebody wanna give me a hand?" he demanded, wrestling with Gem.

A couple of the others lent a hand and hauled Gem off of Sherwood. They held Gem down until he stopped fighting and lay there breathing heavily, cursing under his breath.

———

Bethany opened the door. He looked in and tried to see around her. "Hey, Bethany."

"Hi Gem, how's it going? Come on in."

"I hoped you'd be alone…"

"Yeah." She stepped by to allow him in. "There was a party, and I think most of the guys are sleeping it off."

He nodded. "Yeah, I was there earlier."

She smiled welcomingly. "I'm glad you came by."

———

An hour later, they lay together, Bethany rubbing his back. "Are you okay, Gem?"

"Sure, why?"

"You seem different tonight. I don't know what it is… you're really quiet."

"Sorry." He shifted around and rubbed his forehead. "Got my mind on other things."

"You wanna talk about it? I'm discreet, you know. I'm a good listener, and I won't tell anyone."

"No. It's nothing."

"If it's distracting you, talking might help…"

He smiled. "Thanks, Beth. Really, I'm okay."

"If you're sure."

———

Rico clasped hands with Thrasher and looked around before speaking to make sure there was no one to overhear them in the busy bar. "I think we could use Gem for something big."

"Like what?"

"I dunno. This drugstore rip-off was sheer art. And he was bragging he can do anything."

"So, what are you suggesting?"

Rico got red around his ears and neck. "I dunno… couldn't think of anything big enough."

Thrasher laughed. "Well, the biggest thing would be a hit, wouldn't it?"

"I thought of that, but what hit? We can get away with that already, long as we're careful. It's gotta be something bold."

Thrasher scratched at his scrubby beard. "Yeah, I see what you mean. We'll have to figure something out. Something good."

CHAPTER FIVE

H EY, GEM. YOU LOOKING for an apartment?" Joey asked as they hung out at Thrasher's place.

Gem considered. "I dunno. You're looking for a roomie?"

"Yeah. It ain't much, but you know, somewhere to crash."

Gem didn't know whether to accept the offer or not. He scratched his temple, thinking. "I gotta have privacy," he said.

"And you get that sleepin' in alleys?"

Gem nodded. "Yeah, I do," he said steadily.

"Well... the bedroom's got a door. Come see, if you like."

"I'll take a look at it."

Joey took him to the apartment and stood around while Gem sussed out the rooms, considering.

"This your room?" Gem asked, gesturing to the one that was obviously occupied.

"Yeah."

"You wanna switch?"

"Why?"

Gem didn't give anything away. "I like yours better."

Joey studied Gem, trying to divine his motives. Then he shrugged. "Okay, whatever you want. I'll switch with you."

"I'll think about it," Gem said. "I'll let you know."

———

Riker watched the scene on the closed-circuit set. One of the other officers had set up the camera to monitor activity on the street corner a block away. On the screen, a young man approached the hooker standing on the corner and talked to her. When he handed her his money, Riker revved the engine and raced up to them.

"Caught red-handed," he said cheerfully, getting out of the car.

"You're a cop?" Gem asked the girl in surprise.

"No!" The pretty black girl scowled at Riker. "You trying to get me in trouble or something? You're gonna get me messed up."

"Well, stay off this street. Residents are complaining." He looked at Gem, frowning, then remembered who he was. "Gem Johnson. Well, maybe I couldn't get you for robbery, but I got you for soliciting."

"Do I know you?" Gem demanded.

"You get brought in so often a couple hours in an interrogation room makes no impression on you?"

"Oh... Riker. Right?"

"Yeah. Now you..." He motioned to the hooker's closed fist. "Let's see the cash."

The hooker started to smile. "Now this is funny," she said. "You're really gonna love this."

"What's funny? Let's see."

She opened her hand for him. Where Riker expected to see a wad of cash, there was a half-roll of cough drops. Riker stared, then looked at her other hand, which was empty.

"What're you trying to pull here?"

"I stopped to talk," Gem offered. "She was hoarse and coughing. I gave her cough drops. You gonna arrest me for drug trafficking or something?"

"Put up your hands," Riker told the girl. She obeyed, and he checked her pockets and sleeves for the money.

"Cough," he ordered.

She coughed experimentally, and then in earnest. She was definitely congested. In disbelief, Riker went to his car and ran the video back. He watched again as Gem approached and exchanged greetings with her. The girl was coughing as she talked. Then out came Gem's hand from his pocket, handing her something unidentifiable. Money or a roll of cough candies, it was impossible to tell which. Riker straightened up and looked at them.

"You're lucky this time," he conceded. "But you keep in mind, I'm watching you, Johnson. I'm gonna get you on something, sooner or later." He looked then at the girl. "Go find another corner to ply your trade. Preferably, not on my beat. Or better yet, go home and put something on your chest. Quit spreading your germs."

After exchanging farewells too quietly for Riker to hear, both kids went their separate directions.

Thrasher lit a cigarette and leaned back against the headboard, closing his eyes and savoring the soothing nicotine. "Tell me what you think about Gem," he suggested to Bethany.

Bethany looked at him frowning. "What do you mean?"

"You've entertained him. Your thoughts. Anything at all."

"He's a nice enough guy... kind of strange, though."

"In what way?"

"I don't know. He forgets things. And he acts differently, sometimes."

"Different than what?"

"I don't know. Himself. Sometimes he's really intense. And then another time he's laid back. It's weird."

"Drugs, you think? High and low?"

"No... I've seen him high, but that's different. This is... different. I can't explain it. I've even asked... but he says it's nothing."

"You think he's schizo? Split personality?"

"Maybe," Bethany said doubtfully. "He seems okay otherwise. Other than being forgetful. Maybe it's just ADHD."

Thrasher nodded.

"What do you know about him?" Bethany countered.

Thrasher considered his answer. "You'll keep your mouth shut?"

"Don't I always?"

Thrasher scratched his chin. "He's been in the nuthouse. At least once. But my sources ain't so good. Missing lots of details."

Bethany thought about that. "Oh. What was he in the... that place... for?"

"I can't get anything solid. Some kind of breakdown or meltdown. I dunno. I want to get something concrete, so if you can get anything for me..."

"Yeah, okay. But he doesn't tell me much..."

Thrasher shrugged, blowing smoke away from her. "Just if he says something."

———

In the cool of the evening, the Rippers had thrown together a casual game of football. But some of the boys seemed to have forgotten it was just a friendly game. Gem had already taken a few knocks from the bigger, heavier boys before he was tackled by Cairns with a bone-crunching blow that threw him headlong into a big tree that marked their sideline. The ball bounced off the field of play, and the action stopped as everyone waited for Cairns and Gem to untangle themselves and rejoin the game.

Cairns got up, crowing about his tackle, but Gem was slower to rise. When he did, it was obvious from the way he held his arm against his chest that it was injured—probably broken. His face was white as a sheet, and his dark eyes burned with fury.

"Hey, I'm sorry, man," Cairns said, laughing. Not looking the least bit sorry.

Gem lunged for him. Sherwood and Thrasher jumped in to hold him back before he could do himself further damage.

"Cool it, Gem," Thrasher advised. "You're hurt. Go to the clinic."

"I'm gonna kill that—"

"You're not killing anyone today. You're crippled. Go get your arm looked at," Thrasher insisted.

Gem shook himself loose from their grips and stormed off.

"Hey," Sherwood called after him. "You want a ride or something?"

Thrasher shook his head. "Let 'im go. Give 'im time to cool off." He turned to Cairns. "And if I was you... I'd watch my back. There's a lot more to little Gem than you think..."

Cairns just shook his head, laughing.

———

Thrasher's words were prophetic.

It was Bernard, Cairns's roomie, who squealed to the cops. By the time the police got there, Bernard was half-hysterical, ready to spill everything he knew. As they waited for the coroner and homicide officers, he ranted about the football game, the tackle, the near-fight, and the threat on Cairns' life.

"And did you see Gem shoot Cairns?" Molner asked when Bernard finally started to slow down.

"No, I heard, though."

"You recognized his gunshot?" Molner questioned wryly.

Bernard looked confused. "No, man... Cairns woke up. I heard him say, 'Gem' before the shot."

Molner nodded, looking around the room. "You heard him say that from the next room?"

"Yes!"

"You sure you weren't a little closer than that?" Molner suggested, pointing to the rumpled sheets on the empty side of Cairns's bed.

Bernard reddened around the ears, shaking his head violently. "No way! Me? I'm straight!"

"Yeah, sure. You sure you're telling the truth about what he said? You know it was this Gem?"

"Yeah. For sure."

Molner nodded. He didn't believe a word of it, but he figured Bernard probably had a pretty good idea who the perp was, even if he were lying about the circumstances. "We'll put the homicide boys onto it."

———

Homicide called Riker the next day when they looked at Gem's rap sheet, and Riker was more than happy to help to close a noose around Gem's slim neck. Gem had already been located and pulled in.

"So we meet again," Riker said cheerfully, joining Gem in an interrogation room. The walls were puke green. Riker always wondered whether the color had been picked by an interior decorator, by a psychologist who thought that green was calming, or by the cleaning staff because it best camouflaged stains from drunk detainees.

Gem looked Riker over. "Yeah, I guess so."

"So who've you got for your unbeatable alibi this time?"

Gem took a moment to answer, a slow smile spreading across his face. He gave a short laugh. "You are."

"What are you talking about?"

"The cops. You're my alibi. I was in the drunk tank."

Riker stared at him. "When?"

"I was... self-medicating." Gem indicated his cast. "Your boys in blue picked me up. Maybe nine or ten o'clock."

Riker could think of nothing to say. He couldn't believe that he was going to lose another chance to put Gem behind bars. He walked out of the room. The homicide cops who'd been watching through the observation window were scrambling on phone and computer to verify the alibi. Both came up with the same answer.

"He was in a cell at ten-thirty."

"What time was Bernard's 9-1-1 call?" Riker demanded.

"After midnight."

He swore. "What about the time of death? Maybe he didn't call at the time of death. Maybe he got home and found the body at midnight."

"No go. Others heard the shot. And the corpse was warm when the first patrolman got there. No rigor."

Riker groaned and put his hand over his face. "This can't be happening again!"

"He's not our perp."

"He's guilty."

"Nope, not this time. Not of this murder."

Riker slammed his hand down on the table, swearing.

———

Bernard was smoking on the sidewalk talking to Rico, when he went rapidly pale, looking at something beyond Rico. Rico turned around and saw Gem. "Gem?" he said in astonishment. "I thought the cops got you."

"Yeah, thanks to big mouth here," Gem sneered, indicating Bernard.

"You killed Cairns!" Bernard protested, outraged.

"So?"

"Why'd they let you go?"

"Because I had an alibi. Just like I'll have when I kill *you*."

Bernard swallowed and backpedaled. "I was upset. I don't blab to cops."

"You did. Maybe *I'll* talk too."

"Talk to who?" Rico interjected, confused.

Gem met Bernard's eyes, raising an eyebrow questioningly. "Maybe Bernard has a secret he'd rather everyone didn't know."

"What secret? What are you talking about?" Rico demanded.

Bernard shook his head. "Gem don't know nothing. He's just pullin' your leg. Ain't that right, Gem?"

Gem studied Bernard with a self-satisfied smirk. He nodded, chuckling. "Yeah. I know Bernard would never do nothing to jeopardize our friendship."

"Yeah, that's right."

Rico studied them. "I dunno what's going on here... but I find things out. I always find out sooner or later."

Gem grinned at Bernard. "He always finds out," he repeated.

CHAPTER SIX

RIKER WAS GROWING MORE and more obsessed with finding out how Gem did what he did.

He was almost starting to believe that it was supernatural. Maybe Gem *could* walk through walls or teleport himself. It seemed like the only explanation. How else could he murder someone while locked in a room or a cell? How could he commit armed robbery when so many witnesses saw him elsewhere?

The secret must lie in his background somewhere. So far, all Riker knew was that Gem had been trafficked by a pimp who had then been killed. What happened before that? He was a runaway, presumably. Had a family somewhere. Where had he come from? What could his family and friends tell Riker?

Gem's secret was in the past. Somewhere along the line, he had learned the skills he was using now. And somewhere along the line, someone knew about it.

———

Gem curled up on his old, musty mattress and whispered to himself so that no one outside the room could hear him.

"Everyone else is so limited. So stupid. I can do anything, and they can't get me for it... But I have to be careful. That cop's out to get me now. Maybe I should move on... No, he can't get me on anything. Doesn't matter how hard he tries... But what if he makes up his own evidence? It happens, and then maybe I wouldn't have an alibi... He wouldn't do that. If he was going to do that, I'd be in jail already. He woulda just ignored the evidence. No, Riker's a clean cop... He could change. He was pretty mad about the drunk tank thing..."

Gem yawned and drifted off to sleep.

———

Gem's memories of childhood were scattered and sketchy. Usually, he didn't try to recall them. He didn't want to. Sometimes an event would bring back a brief flash of memories. Sometimes it would be a person who reminded him of someone in his past. Sometimes it would be a word or two. It might be a vivid nightmare, and he couldn't tell whether it was memory or imagination.

He dreamed he was in the old apartment. The one they eventually were evicted from because it was condemned and had to be bulldozed to the ground. Gram was there in the dream, and a bedraggled woman who might have been Gem's mother. Had she ever lived with them in that apartment? Gem wasn't sure. He couldn't have been older than two.

His mother, if that's who she was, was screaming obscenities at the top of her lungs. It must be his mother. Gram left the apartment, slamming the door so hard it made the walls of the apartment shudder. Gem's knees were too weak to walk. He crawled to the dark closet to hide from the silence that suddenly enveloped the apartment with his Gram leaving.

His mother's yelling was frightening, but her silence was terrifying. Gem could hear her walking through the apartment, shoving furniture around and opening and slamming drawers and cupboards.

Gem shrank back in the closet, screwing his eyes closed and making himself as small as possible. Her footsteps got closer and closer. Tears started to run down Gem's face, but he kept his sobs silent so she wouldn't hear him crying.

It was no use.

She opened the closet and dragged Gem out.

The sobs in his chest became audible as he protested and tried to get her to stop. He couldn't form words. His chest was so tight he thought he would burst.

She dragged him into the bathroom. Gem screamed as she pushed his head towards the toilet. Icy water closed around his face and ears. Gem closed his mouth and held his breath.

But he couldn't hold it forever.

Cold, foul water filled his lungs, and then blackness blocked out his vision.

———

Gem awoke in the dark, gasping for breath. "Drowning, drowning," he choked, panicking.

Looking around, he tried to calm himself. "It's okay. It's just a dream. Not drowning. It's just a dream."

He lay back down, drinking long breaths of cool air into his tight lungs.

"Just a dream," he repeated like a mantra. "Just a dream. Not real. Just a dream."

———

But he was fated to dream all night. He awoke into a dream back in the old apartment, surrounded by kind cops. Gram was there, watching him with beady black eyes from across the room.

"My daughter is not well," she said to the officer in charge.

"Obviously not," the cop replied. "A sane woman could never do this to her babe."

Gem was wrapped in a towel, held with his head resting on a uniformed shoulder, his hair pasted wetly to his face and a sour taste in his mouth.

"The boy is okay. We got to him in time." This from Gram.

"It was only by luck. He can obviously not be left with her."

"Well, he won't be. She's gone. Taken off. I doubt if we'll ever see her again."

"Someone from Social Services will be by to ensure that suit-able arrangements are made."

"He'll stay with me."

"A social worker will talk to you about it. And I think that a doctor should look at the child."

"Gem will be fine. He was just a little shaken up."

Gem drowsed against the other cop's shoulder, feeling safe.

———

Riker looked at the names and numbers he had gathered so far. Somehow he would piece together Gem's checkered past and discover his secret.

He started with the director of the self-styled 'rest home' that Gem had spent time at.

"I'm calling concerning a previous patient of yours," he said after introducing himself.

Decker, the director, hummed and hawed for a moment. He had a high, nasal voice. "I can't divulge privileged information," he reminded Riker.

"His name is Gem Johnson."

"Gem. We treat some... very troubled individuals here."

"I gather your facility is for wealthier individuals," Riker said, wondering just what kind of background Gem had initially come from.

"Well, generally speaking, that is true. But with the over-crowding in government-run facilities, there was a grant to move some patients out of the most crowded institutions into private facilities and to pay for their care."

"And Gem Johnson came here under that grant?"

There was a significant pause before Decker answered. "I couldn't comment on that."

"He came to you at the time the grant was given."

The doctor cleared his throat.

"Can you tell me something about his treatment there?" Riker tried.

"Sorry, I can't."

Riker considered his options. "Is there a particular specialty that your facility treats?" He asked with as much tact as he could muster.

"We do a lot of work with personality disorders."

"Personality disorders like..."

"We've had a few Multiple Personality Disorders," the doctor said slowly, "also bipolar disorder, generalized anxiety, paranoid schizophrenia, Borderline Personality Disorder, unexplained dementia..."

"Was Gem treated for all of those?"

There was a long silence. Eventually, the doctor answered. "Obviously, I can't tell you what any patient might have been treated for. There are some patients that we have a very difficult time even coming up with a diagnosis for. They don't meet the qualifications for any particular diagnosis."

"If you couldn't diagnose him, how could you treat him?"

"In some cases, if you cannot properly diagnose, you have to try a broadband treatment. Address the symptoms."

"Would that be medication or therapy?"

"Both."

"Did Gem leave your facility because he was cured?"

There was a period of silence as the doctor considered. "Cure is a fraught term when dealing with mental illness. We prefer... stabilized."

"And that means he was supposed to stay on his medication," Riker guessed.

"I couldn't tell you that."

"He wasn't cured; he was stabilized. Isn't that what you said?"

The doctor made a noncommittal noise.

"Who was he released to?" Riker asked.

"I will give you the name of a social worker who might know more."

CHAPTER SEVEN

GEM TOSSED AND TURNED restlessly, dreaming wild, frightening dreams.

Gram was holding him and rocking, humming a song to herself. Gem squirmed. She was holding him uncomfortably tight. Gram tightened her grip when he tried to free himself. Gem struggled harder. Her grip loosened for a moment, but she just wrapped the blanket tighter. Gem could barely breathe. He started to scream.

Gem clawed at the blankets, trying to free himself.

"Gem, what's wrong?" It was Bethany, in bed beside him. "Are you okay?"

Gem took a deep breath and tried to control the sobs, pulling the sheets of the bed back up around himself. He breathed deeply.

"Just a dream," he murmured.

"Oh," Bethany put her arms around him comfortingly. Gem held on to her until he fell back asleep.

He was in school. The teacher was mocking his reading skills— or lack thereof. The class howled with laughter. Gem, his face hot with embarrassment, tried to make himself as small as possible. He buried his face in his folded arms on the desktop, trying to stifle the hot tears that threatened to brim over. Choking back sobs before anyone could hear them. The teacher walked over to him.

"Get your head up," she ordered, "and read it again."

Gem shook his head, still turtled down. He could taste the tears now and feel them dribbling over his arms. The teacher grasped his shoulder roughly and tried to force him up.

Almost before he knew what had happened, Gem had sunk his teeth into her. Dug them in hard, wanting an escape from her tyranny, wanting to hurt her, wanting to punish her. And then he was flat on his back on the floor, his ears ringing.

Gem moaned, rocking back and forth. Bethany held on to him, stroking his hair. "Wake up, Gem. It's just a dream. You're just having a bad dream."

Gem awoke enough to hear her and push the dream back to his subconscious.

"Sorry," he apologized for waking her up. He drifted back into the dream, or into a different one.

"I won't have that animal in my class! I will not put up with his misbehavior any longer!"

"We'll take care of it, Miss Preet. He can be put in another class."

"He drew blood! If a dog did that to me, I'd have him put down!"

"Why don't you go get that looked at? I will take care of Gem."

She went her way, still muttering and complaining to anyone who was listening. The principal walked over to the troublemaker's desk, where Gem had been left. Gem covered his aching face with both hands, trying to keep from crying again. His pants were wet. He felt as if he was soaked in shame.

"Tell me what happened, Gem," the principal said, his tone less harsh and accusing than Gem had expected. Almost as if he were concerned about Gem.

The floodgates opened, and Gem couldn't stop the tears, could hardly breathe because of the sobs. The principal put his hand on Gem's head to comfort and calm him.

"There, now. You're okay. Just tell me what happened."

Gem left his seat and threw his arms around the sympathetic listener, unable to quell the heartrending sobs. The principal held him gingerly, mindful of his wet trousers, and let him cry it out.

Bethany held Gem as he wept uncontrollably. She didn't know

whether he was awake or still dreaming. She just knew he needed to be held. Eventually, he stopped and lay still and quiet sprawled next to her.

Gem heard the principal say aside to his secretary as he was taken out of the office, "That child is very troubled."

———

Gem was sluggish in the morning, feeling worse than when he went to sleep. His head ached, and he felt sweaty and nauseated.

"You had a pretty rough night," Bethany observed.

"Don't usually dream like that," Gem mumbled, trying to decide if he was going to have to get up.

Bethany kissed him on the cheek. "Because you have a fever," she told him. "You're sick."

"I am?"

"Yeah. So you just stay in bed. I'll play mama today and take care of you."

That sounded awfully good. "Okay," Gem murmured, snuggling down deeper into the covers and closing his eyes. "G'night."

CHAPTER EIGHT

GEM STOOD BY THE window. The temperature in the apartment was like an oven. He was restless to get out but didn't have anywhere to go. He gazed down at the sidewalk, where he saw Thrasher talking to an unfamiliar man. "Who's that?"

"Who?" Joey asked. He joined Gem at the window. "Oh, Sunny-boy. He's Bethany's boyfriend."

"Bethany's boyfriend?" Gem repeated, frowning. "I thought she just hung out with the gang."

"She's *owned* by the Rippers. Until Sunny pays us the money he owes."

Gem felt the blood draining from his face. He fought hard to ignore the tightness in his chest and keep his voice steady. "She's a hostage?" He swallowed hard.

"Some hostage!" Joey laughed. "We cover her rent; all she has to do is turn a few tricks."

Gem felt sick. He turned and walked out of the apartment. Joey called after him, but Gem pretended not to hear him and kept going.

Gem walked the few blocks through the blistering heat to Bethany's building. He hesitated outside her apartment door. Then he mustered up the courage to knock. Bethany opened it a few moments later. She looked tired, but smiled at him pleasantly.

"Hi, Gem. Come on in."

He walked in stiffly and eventually perched on the edge of the couch. Her apartment was comfortable; the air conditioner humming away out of sight. Bethany sat down beside him, looking disconcerted by his mood.

"What's up?" she asked, head cocked.

"I'm... I'm sorry," Gem ground out.

"Sorry? What for?"

"I just found out that you are... held hostage here. Before I thought that you... just liked company." It sounded lame in his own ears. Had he really believed that she hung around with the Rippers and kept them entertained of her own free choice?

"I *do* like company." But he saw something in her eyes. Something that she had been able to keep hidden from him before.

"I didn't know," Gem persisted, his voice breaking a little. "I didn't know about Sunny and the loan and everything. I'm not that kind of guy! I'm not a John or a perv."

Bethany just looked at him, letting him go on.

"I honestly thought you only went with guys if you liked them."

It was stupid. She wouldn't believe him. She'd think he was just another scummy guy taking advantage of her.

"Why are you so upset about it?" Bethany asked in a flat, unemotional tone. "I actually do like you, but what does it matter?"

Gem couldn't answer. He swallowed, tears leaking down his throat, trying to keep his composure.

"If I really wanted to, I could take off," Bethany pointed out. "There's no handcuffs. No bars. No locks that I don't have the key to. I'm saving my money, and maybe one day I'll take off. But right now, I choose to stay here."

Gem took a deep breath. "Where I was... there *were* locks."

Bethany's eyes met his searchingly as if trying to read the truth. She took his hand and held it firmly. Her hands were cool and dry, but Gem's were sweating. "Who locked you up?"

"A man. A slimy pig who didn't deserve to be called human."

"A pimp."

Gem nodded, breathing through his mouth, having a hard time catching his breath. She squeezed his hand.

"The Rippers locked me up twice," Bethany confessed. She bit her lip. "Not Thrasher, he hasn't been leading the gang that long. The guy before him. Neil. When they first brought me here, and then once after the cops picked me up. They chained me up. It wasn't for long, but it was still... you know, sort of scary."

Gem nodded.

"I still get scared, feel trapped sometimes," Bethany admitted. "But I know I have the money to skip town if I have to. I don't mind so much if I'm with a guy that I like. And if I'm with someone I don't like, I just sort of blank it out, you know?"

"Yeah." Gem knew.

"It's just sometimes in between, thinking about it." Her voice trailed off.

They were both silent for a few minutes, swallowed up by emotion.

"How long were you locked up?" Bethany asked softly.

"I don't know. I lost track. Months."

Bethany looked horrified. "Months? When I got locked up, it was only for a couple of days."

"But how long have you been here?"

Bethany frowned. "A few months. It's not the same, though. And I do know the difference."

Gem looked around her apartment critically. It wasn't a bad place. Better than anywhere he'd lived, and she had it to herself. Most of the time. Would it be worth turning a few tricks to have a place like that? Not an endless parade of men night and day. Just a couple of the Rippers now and then. Gem almost always found her by herself.

Gem shook his head, trying to erase the thoughts and memories. He wasn't Bethany, and he didn't have to decide. She said she'd made her own choice. He didn't have to think about it or be a part of it. He'd just stop coming to her apartment until Sunny's debt was paid.

The thought gave Gem pause. "Just how much does Sunny owe?"

"I don't know. Gotta be a few thousand, or he would have paid it back with his winnings sometime."

"And borrowed more 'cause he was on a streak. You can't trust gamblers."

"I know."

"Do you think you could find out how much?"

"I guess." Bethany shrugged. "Why? What are you thinking?"

"I'll tell you when I know for sure."

Gem knew he was going to have to do some careful planning. The cops were already out to get him. He was going to have to have the best alibi he'd ever had. And it had to be something he hadn't used before. Something they couldn't get around, no matter how hard they tried.

———

As soon as he heard they had a warrant out on Gem, Riker had to be there to see the boy brought in. Riker was almost giddy. They had him this time. It might not be enough to put him away for as long as Riker would have liked, but it was undeniable. Gem had no defense this time.

They had him as clear as day on an ATM security camera. Face, profile, back; they had it all, and time stamped too. They could see the whole drama like the exaggerated acting of a silent film. Gem coming up behind Bernard at the ATM. Bernard turning to see who it was, terrified. Gem with his arm tight around Bernard's throat—his arm healed and cast off now—whispering threats in his ear. And that stupid, careless kid jabbing his piece into Bernard's throat right in front of the security camera. There was no actual violence done. But the use of the gun to threaten someone was still a crime. They could send him away for it. Maybe pad it out with some other charges.

A beat cop in the gang's territory managed to track Gem down and bring him in. Riker played the surveillance video for him. Gem just sat there in silence.

"Well, Johnson? What do you have to say for yourself now?"

Gem shrugged. "I got nothing to say."

"No alibi?" Riker persisted.

"No."

Riker's heart leapt. It wasn't much. Not when they knew Gem had committed murder and armed robbery. But it was a start. They got Capone on tax evasion, didn't they?

"I want a lawyer," Gem said.

"You got one, or you want legal aid?"

"Legal aid."

"I'll call them for you. It's not like anyone can get you off this time." Riker couldn't stop smiling, happy as a kid in a candy store.

Gem rolled his eyes, leaning back in his chair with his arms folded across his chest with the tough and unconcerned posture of a hood. He had no answer.

———

After his lawyer had gone, Gem overheard them saying that the juvie facility was under lockdown, and no one was going in or coming out, which meant that Gem was staying in the city lockup. Special arrangements would have to be made. Gem watched Riker huddle with a cop out of Gem's hearing. Riker watched Gem the whole time he talked to the cop. The cop escorted Gem to the cell block.

"They want the kid to get special treatment," the cop sneered. He glanced over the log book and planted his finger on one of the cells in the diagram.

"Put him in there."

The other cop dutifully wrote down Gem's statistics and took him into the cell block. They walked past a row of occupied cells and stopped in front of an empty one. But then the cop unlocked the cell across the corridor from the empty cell and pushed Gem into it.

Gem surveyed the surly occupants of the cell as the door locked behind him.

Special treatment, indeed.

Put the kid in the cell with the worst offenders. See how long it takes them to break him down.

But they didn't know about Gem's past. Or his mission. He

could survive one more night of abuse behind locked doors for Bethany's sake.

They weren't going to do anything to him that hadn't been done before.

———

"Hey, Riker, where's the video machine that you had yesterday?" Dimitri questioned.

"Still in room B. Why?"

"Central sent us the surveillance video from the bank holdup. Someone thought the perp was wearing gang colors. They're hoping we can identify him."

"Put it on; let's take a look."

Dimitri took the video into the interrogation room and put it in. Riker watched the flickering screen for a few seconds and frowned in disbelief. "It's Gem Johnson. I've already got him in a cell."

"You what?"

"What a stupid kid! Gets caught on camera twice in one night! He certainly kept himself busy!"

"Are you sure it's him?" Dimitri said doubtfully.

"Watch my video," Riker put it back in and pressed play.

They both watched it in silence. Dimitri shook his head. "It could be the same kid on mine, but it's hard to tell. The clothes are different, and you can't see his face in mine."

"Oh, it's him. I know this kid. His build, the way he moves. You can see his profile for a second." Riker pointed at the screen. "We couldn't get him on armed robbery before, but we knew he'd done it."

"Well, if you've still got him here, why don't we talk to him?"

Riker nodded. "I'll fetch him."

———

Riker went with the officer on duty to the cell Gem was in. He spotted Gem sitting on the floor with his back against the wall, face buried in his bent knees. Riker focused in on the others in the cell. A nasty-looking bunch of men.

"I gave specific instructions he was not to be jailed with any adults."

"I didn't put him in here," the officer said immediately.

He opened the door, calling Gem's name gruffly. Gem didn't move. The officer shook his head and went into the cell to retrieve him, one hand resting on the butt of his gun. "Come on, kid."

He grabbed Gem's arm and pulled him to his feet. Gem shuffled out, head down. Riker studied him. Gem's face was bruised. He moved gingerly. Riker took Gem by the arm and escorted him to the interrogation room. Gem flopped into the chair, winced, and readjusted several times, searching for a comfortable position.

"I told them to put you in a cell by yourself," Riker said guiltily. This kid had already been through a rough enough time at the hands of men like the ones in that cell.

Gem hardly raised his head. "Sure, boss," he said flatly.

His eyes were gray and dead. The taunting Gem that Riker had met before was hidden miles below those veiled eyes. This was the Gem who had been rescued from Raphael's shop. Distant and untouchable, blocking out the pain.

"Do you want to see a doctor?" Riker suggested.

"No."

"You want a coffee?"

"Yeah. Sure."

Riker left him alone for a moment to get a cup of undrinkable coffee. On his return, Gem didn't appear to have moved a muscle.

"Here you go. Are you sure you're okay?"

"Yeah."

Riker let him drink half the cup before pursuing the interrogation. "I've got another video for you to watch."

Gem shrugged. Riker played the short video clip of the bank holdup and Gem watched it without a flicker of expression.

"Well?" Riker prodded.

"What?"

"That was you."

"No."

"I recognize you! Don't try to snow me."

"I wasn't there."

"Where were you, then?"

"What time?"

There was a timestamp on the video, which Riker pointed to. "Six-thirty. Right before closing time."

The ghost of a smile passed over Gem's face. "I was having a chat with my buddy Bernardo."

Riker thought his heart would stop. There was a timestamp on the other video too. Riker was afraid to put it in. Gem's eyes livened up a little, looking more like himself. Riker stood up and switched videos again. The timestamp was the same in both videos. Six-thirty. Gem's face was clear on the video with Bernard. In the video of the bank, the perp's face was hidden by a baseball cap. Gem couldn't be the boy in both videos unless he'd somehow managed to tamper with the timekeeping system in one of the cameras.

Riker left the room and looked for Dimitri. "What was the take in that bank heist?" he demanded.

"A few hundred thou'. What's wrong? Your guy didn't confess?"

"Not only that. Your video and mine were recorded at the same time."

Dimitri snickered. "Then I guess he's not the one on my video."

"Unless he managed to hack into the security system somehow..."

Dimitri shook his head. "Give it up. You can't stick him with both. As a matter of fact, you'll be lucky to stick him with either, now."

"Why? I've got his face clear as day on my video."

"Because all his lawyer has to do is bring the other video into evidence. The kid knows it exists because you showed it to him."

Riker swore angrily. "He's not getting off the weapons charges. The bank heist video never shows his face. We'll deny it's him."

"Good luck."

———

Gem told his lawyer he would plead out on the weapons charges and pay fines. Riker wanted him to do time, but the prosecutor was happy to let Gem cop the plea.

Riker heard later that Gem paid in cash.

———

Thrasher was reluctant to allow Gem to pay Sunny's debt off, but in the end, he accepted the money for Bethany's freedom.

"If he borrows from the Rippers again, he can't use Bethany as collateral," Gem said.

"I dunno that she'll want to go back to Sunny after this," Thrasher said with a shrug. "I wouldn't. And I think her and Little D are getting pretty serious."

"Dietrich?"

"Yeah. I guess 'cause he's younger like her. Or maybe it's that shy country boy look of his."

"I didn't know she had a special guy," Gem said, depression settling in.

"No," Thrasher agreed. "She's pretty discreet."

CHAPTER NINE

HE SAT IN THE pub by himself. The bouncer had considered refusing him entrance, but had probably decided that by himself, one boy wouldn't cause problems, but an angry banger returning with a group of Rippers might be more than they could handle. So he was allowed to sit peacefully with his thoughts as he had on other occasions. His eyes were on the TV, but the fact was, he didn't even know what it was showing. He was startled by a tap on his shoulder. Turning, he saw Bethany there, looking uncertain.

"Hi, Bethany." He forced a smile.

"Hey, Gem. Want some company?"

"Sure." He looked around. "You want a booth? More private than the bar."

"Yeah, that'd be good."

They found a quiet corner to sit in.

"How did you know I was here?" He hadn't told anyone where he was going.

"I've seen you here before. It's where you come to be alone, isn't it?"

"Yeah, it is."

"Do you mind me coming?" Bethany asked tentatively.

"No."

"You're in your quiet mood again."

He smiled. "Sorry, I don't mean to shut you out."

"It's okay. I don't mind doing the talking. I'm just observing."

He nodded and gazed at her in silence.

"Gem…" There were suddenly tears brimming in Bethany's eyes. "No one's ever done anything like this for me before."

"Sunny's debt, you mean?"

"What else would I be talking about?" Bethany wiped the corners of her eyes. "And you didn't even tell me what you were up to!"

He shrugged, looking away from her in embarrassment. "I didn't know if it would work. Didn't want to get your hopes up."

"I can't believe you did that! Thrasher wouldn't even tell me how much it was."

He considered for a moment, wondering if he should tell her the truth or keep it a secret. "Ten grand and change," he said finally.

"Ten thousand dollars? Where did the Rippers get money like that to give Sunny?"

"Drugs, mostly. I gather it wasn't all at once."

"And where did *you* get that kind of dough?" Bethany demanded.

"I came into some money," he said wryly. "I still have some left over. You want to help me spend it?"

"How much do you have?"

"Enough to have some fun."

Bethany's eyes sparkled. "Enough for new clothes?"

He looked her over. "Enough for new clothes. New car. New digs."

Bethany raised her eyebrows. "Well, what are we waiting around here for?"

He swallowed the rest of his drink and stood up. Bethany stood up too. She didn't head directly for the door, and he looked back at her.

"Gem…?" Her voice was soft. "What was the first thing you did when you got out of that place?"

He frowned, considering. "Had a shower," he said finally, dredging up the answer.

Bethany nodded. "That's what I just did. Funny."

———

Riker put his photocopies in front of Gordon. "I got a bunch of stuff on multiple personalities," he commented.

"Okay... why?"

"It's one of the things the doctor implied that Gem Johnson was being treated for."

"So, does it help us?"

"Maybe. Now, it says that people with MPD or DID—that's what they call it—usually went through severe abuse as children, so I'll keep looking at his background for any detail on that. It also says that they are often very intelligent and may go to great lengths to give the impression that their various personalities are actually separate people."

"Yeah?"

"Yeah. So maybe he does have it, and these alibis are an elaborate attempt to prove he's two—or more—people."

"Maybe."

"I'm getting closer, Gordon. All I have to do is figure this kid out, from the inside, and then I can nail him. Once I find out his secrets, he won't be able to get away with anything."

———

He was in good spirits. Bethany was having a blast spending his money. She had bought several new outfits, gadgets, and junk. They carried her bags back to her apartment. He looked around as he put the bags down.

"Do you want to keep your apartment? Or you want something new?"

Bethany looked around speculatively. "I don't know. What are you going to spend your money on? You haven't bought anything yet."

He shrugged. "I don't know yet. I can't think of anything I want."

"Nothing?"

"Maybe a car. Maybe a new place. I don't know."

"There must be something you really want."

"I already got what I really wanted." He gave her a shy smile and blushed.

Bethany flushed as well. They both laughed in nervous embarrassment.

"I don't feel like I owe you," Bethany mused. "I think I should, but you don't make me feel that way."

"You don't owe me. You should never have been trapped here to begin with. I just made it right."

"Why?"

"I couldn't stand... seeing someone else go through that."

Bethany rubbed her feet as she settled into the couch. "So what kind of a place would you get if you got a new apartment?"

He put his head on her shoulder and closed his eyes, envisioning. "Clean," he said with a laugh.

"No rats," Bethany agreed.

Before long, Bethany's 'I' and 'my apartment' became 'we' and 'our apartment.'

He didn't correct her. It was comfortable.

CHAPTER TEN

GEM DIDN'T SEE BETHANY for a couple of days. He was kept too busy with gang business. He met up with Thrasher, who mentioned having seen her.

"I guess Bethany was properly grateful for your intercession," Thrasher commented.

Gem frowned. "What do you mean?" he asked, hearing the heavy innuendo in Thrasher's voice.

"You didn't seem to have any trouble getting around Dietrich. Bethany's going around saying you two are shacking up."

Gem's jaw dropped. "What?"

"She said you were buying a fancy new apartment and moving in together," Thrasher said with a snicker. He took in Gem's reaction. "I take it she was getting a little ahead of herself."

Gem nodded. "I'd better find her."

Gem tracked Bethany down at her apartment.

"Oh. Hi, Gem." She smiled. "How are you?"

"Yeah, fine," Gem said impatiently, "we gotta talk."

Bethany motioned him in. "What's up?"

"What's this I hear you're telling everyone about us moving in together?"

"Well, I thought when we got the new place..."

"I'm not moving in with you."

Bethany looked surprised. "But when we were talking, I thought..."

"Sometimes I get carried away," he growled. "I don't want to move in together."

"Why not? If we're both getting new places... Oh." Her face fell. "I get it. We're not, are we? That was just talk too."

"I'll still get you a place if you want."

"Oh, so I'll be your on-call mistress? How's that any different from what I just got out of?"

Gem was offended. "You think I would do that to you?" he demanded. "After what I went through? Someone told me you and Little D were sweet on each other. I figured *he'd* move in with you."

"Is that what this is about? You think me and D should be together instead of you and me?"

Gem shook his head. "I don't care. Stay with D if you like, or don't. But I can't move in with you."

"Why not?"

Gem shook his head. "I can't explain it. I just can't."

"You're afraid of the commitment? It doesn't have to be forever. Leave when you like, or tell me it's time to leave. I won't be hurt."

"It's not that. I *can't* commit to you, but that isn't it. There's other things. Things I can't talk about." Gem was aware that his voice was getting higher and faster. He couldn't control it.

"You're a cop? Is that it? That's how you get out of everything, and that's why you can't do it?"

"No. I'm not a narc."

"Then what is it? Just tell me. I don't care what the reason is. I won't tell anyone else. It'll still be your secret."

Gem shook his head adamantly. "I can't tell you, Bethany. I'm sorry to hurt your feelings. I never meant you to think I was going to live with you."

"Is it another girl?"

"No."

"Another guy?"

Gem stared at her.

"Just 'cause you like me, doesn't mean you can't like some guy better," Bethany pointed out.

"It's not another guy."

"If you can share an apartment with Joey, why not with me? If you want a separate room of your own, that's fine. I just don't understand the problem."

"Bethany, let it go."

"Even if we get one with a fire escape?"

Gem froze. "What?"

"Joey couldn't figure out why you wanted to switch rooms with him. The only difference I can see is that yours has a fire escape. So who's coming and going on the sly? You or a visitor?"

Gem licked his lips. "I don't want to talk about this anymore," he said hoarsely.

Bethany didn't say anything for a minute. She pushed it once more. "A separate room and a fire escape. You still wouldn't room with me?"

"I—I don't know."

"Maybe?"

Gem bit his lip. He tried several times to answer, but he couldn't.

He turned and walked out the door.

———

Gem paced anxiously, talking to himself.

"What am I going to do? She's too close to finding out. I gotta split... But after getting in with the gang for protection? Waste all that effort and start all over again somewhere else? ...What else am I going to do? She can't find out. Nobody can find out... Who says she will? ...She's too observant. She figured out about the fire escape. You think if we lived together, she wouldn't find out? ... What if she did? ...No one can find out! If people find out, I'm done for... She wouldn't tell. We could move in together and still be safe. I like her... I know I like her, but that's not really the point, is it? ...The point is, can she be trusted?"

Gem was silent for a while.

"Can she be trusted?" he repeated softly.

———

"Gem Johnson," the social worker repeated slowly. She was the first person from Gem's past that Riker had talked to who didn't remember Gem immediately. "The name is familiar."

"I'm told that you picked him up from a rest home. A mental treatment facility."

"This is a kid?"

"Yes."

She thought about this for a few minutes. "I vaguely remember one kid. Must be your Johnson. He was medicated to the eyeballs. But he wasn't one of my regulars. His worker was out of town at the time; I just subbed in."

"I see. Could you give me the name of his regular social worker?"

"Let me look it up on the system and I'll call you back."

"I can hold," Riker offered, suspecting he'd never get a callback.

She sighed loudly and put him on hold. Riker worked through some papers while he waited. Eventually, she picked up again.

"Mary Saunders," she said, and gave Riker a phone number. "She was Gem Johnson's last social worker before he disappeared. I take it you know his current whereabouts?"

"I do."

"He should be under a social worker's supervision, even if he's not in care. Give Mary the details when you call her and she can transfer his case to your local social services."

"Sure. Thanks for your help."

He managed to get Mary Saunders on his first try, which was unusual when trying to reach a social worker.

"I'm looking for information on a boy you used to supervise. Gem Johnson."

"Gem. Sure, I remember him. Where did you run into him?"

Riker briefly outlined the place and circumstances for her. He could almost hear her shake her head.

"Gem was always very difficult to keep tabs on. I take it you know he's supposed to be on medication."

"I gathered as much. What is he supposed to be taking?"

"I don't remember the list. It was about half a page long, a cocktail of about every antipsychotic, tranquilizer, antidepressant and anti-anxiety prescription you can think of. He was practically catatonic."

"Then how did he end up on the streets? Who stopped doping him?"

"He went to a reputable group home. They've not had a problem with medication schedules before or since. The head swears that he personally gave Gem everything on schedule. Gem must have been making himself throw the pills back up."

"So he disappeared from the group home?"

"Pretty much."

"Pretty much?" What did that mean?

"He actually disappeared from the hospital. There were allegations of abuse at the group home and he was at the hospital to be evaluated."

"Abuse of Gem?"

"That's what we were hoping to determine."

"Who made the allegations?"

"One of the other kids in the home. Said he'd seen things."

"Are you going to give me details or be cryptic about it?"

"If I say too much, I'm opening myself up for prosecution. Nothing was ever proven. We just have one unsubstantiated accusation."

"Accusation of what? What did they say had been done?"

"An accusation of possible abuse," Mary said evenly.

"Okay." Riker shook his head in frustration. She obviously wasn't going to budge an inch on the details. "I'll move on. How long were you Gem's social worker?"

"A couple of years."

"And you know his history before that?"

"Yes, as much as is on the record."

"What made him the way he was? The mental problems he had."

"We don't really know what causes anyone's mental illness. With Gem, there is a family history of mental illness. His mother had major problems. In and out of facilities for as long as we could track her. The grandmother also apparently had problems, better hidden. Managed to stay out of the system. We don't know anything about Gem's father but, considering the mother's circumstances around the time Gem would have been conceived, he probably had mental health issues as well."

"What was Gem diagnosed with?"

"He had different diagnoses over the years. None of the doctors could ever agree. Schizophrenia was the most common. But that's just a catch-all diagnosis."

"You don't think it was schizophrenia?"

"I don't know. I always thought there was more to it than that. But I'm no psychiatrist."

"So tell me about what Gem was like for the two years he was under your supervision."

"Unpredictable. At times perfectly reasonable and under control. Then another day, overemotional, violent, totally out of control. You just never knew what to expect from him."

"Could his unpredictable behavior be explained by abuse?"

"Most abused kids hold it together pretty well at school or under the eye of authority. There may be schoolyard fights, petty theft, but not full-blown meltdowns or psychotic episodes. They try not to do anything to set them apart from the other kids. Gem... the other kids knew he was unbalanced. There was no hiding it."

"Was he in foster care the whole time?"

"Oh, no. Gem spent very little time in foster care. He was usually with his mama or gramma."

"With their histories of mental illness?" Riker said with surprise.

"Once they're back on their meds, you're not allowed to discriminate. However much you might want the kid out of there. And we could never prove anything with the gramma."

"So he just kept having these episodes, getting medicated, going through his caregivers' episodes, being bounced into care for a week or two at a time..."

"Being picked up by police wandering the streets," Mary added, "or disappearing for days at a time. Yeah, you got the picture. And nothing we could do about any of it."

"Was he ever treated for multiple personalities?"

"Who told you that?" she demanded. "It was suspected at one time, but he doesn't show all the symptoms. No, the only reason he was ever treated for that was because it was trendy. Interesting fact for you, though, when he was little, he used to refer to himself as 'we' or 'Gem' instead of I or me. But that was just a developmental thing."

"Interesting. So how did you finally get him away from his family and into the rest home and group home?"

"His gramma relinquished. I don't know what precipitated it. There were not a lot of details."

———

Bethany had about decided that Gem was not coming back. She hadn't seen him for a week, and Joey said he'd packed his bag and disappeared. So she was re-evaluating her options and was surprised to find Gem on her doorstep again.

"Uh—hi, Gem. What's up?"

"You gotta come see." His smile was wide. He bounced up and down on his heels, unable to contain himself.

"See what?"

"Come on." He grabbed her hand.

Bethany hesitated, but was caught up in Gem's excitement and went with him. Gem took her a few blocks to a building of middle-class apartments. An older building with fire escapes. Bethany looked at Gem questioningly, but he just took her up to a vacant apartment. He brandished a key and let himself in. He grabbed her hand again and hauled her in. They dashed through the front room to the first bedroom.

"This one's yours," Gem declared breathlessly, manic. "You like it? Mine's next door. Want to see?"

Without waiting for an answer, he took her into his bedroom.

"Fire escape and all," Bethany observed.

"Yeah." He laughed. "Do you like it?"

"What changed your mind?"

Gem stopped and considered it for a moment. "I just talked myself into it," he said finally with a shrug.

"Are you sure it's what you want?"

"It's already paid for. We just gotta move your stuff over. And get a mattress for me."

"You could probably afford a whole bed."

Gem laughed in delight. "Yeah, I guess I could."

CHAPTER ELEVEN

THRASHER HAD INVITED GEM to come to his apartment. Or ordered him to appear. So Gem went. Thrasher gave him a beer, and they both popped the tabs on the cans and sat down in the broken-down furniture that made up Thrasher's entertainment room.

"I got a job I want you to do."

"Yeah?"

Thrasher nodded. He lit a cigarette. He didn't say anything for a long time, just smoking and staring off into space. "Somebody I want dead," he said finally.

"You don't need me for that," Gem said, shrugging. Thrasher usually took care of his own business. And if he wanted a hit taken out, he had the whole gang to choose from.

Thrasher smiled with his mouth, but his eyes remained steely and steady. "Ah, but this one is special. A cop. Needs delicate handling."

Gem bit his lip. "What cop?" he questioned, thinking immediately of Riker.

But it wasn't Riker. Gem tuned Thrasher out after the initial details, his thoughts drifting.

As a child, Gem had looked up to the cops, considering them his protectors. But as he grew up, they grew more suspicious of his activities and started to watch him and distrust him. So he responded in kind. By the time he ran away, he had considered them his enemies.

But when he had been in Raphael's shop, it had been different. Day in and day out, they had hoped for a raid. He and the other kids were on the side that needed protection. They talked disparagingly about the cops but prayed for them to come and set them free.

Gem had never gone back to hating the cops the same way after that. He saw there was a place for them, a need for the helpless to be protected.

Riker was another problem altogether. He wasn't just a beat cop keeping an eye out for trouble. He had taken a personal interest in Gem. He was on a mission to put Gem behind bars. He was a threat.

Maybe Gem should kill him too. Would that be too bold? Alibiing one cop's murder with another? Would that make it so that they couldn't prosecute him for either one? Or would they find a way around the logic?

"The boys have faith in you," Thrasher was saying. "They said you wouldn't have any trouble taking care of this problem for us."

Gem nodded, focusing back on the present and Thrasher's assignment. "Yeah," he agreed, "No problem."

———

Gem tossed and turned in his new room. New things made him anxious, and even though he knew the bedroom door was locked and the fire escape handy, he couldn't help being anxious.

Unable to sleep, he worked through his plans for completing Thrasher's assignment. He had decided to be more cautious instead of more bold. Taking care of Riker would have to wait until after his assignment was complete. He would work out a way not to leave any evidence so that nothing would tip them off that it was him. Of course, he would establish a good alibi too, just as he always did, in case they did manage to tie the murder to him and he needed one.

Thinking about murder alibis turned his thoughts back to Raphael.

He dreamed he was back in Raphael's shop, lying on the cold concrete floor. When he opened his eyes, his vision was blurry, but he could make out Honey sitting beside him, crying.

"What's wrong?" he croaked, trying to clear his throat.

"I thought you were dead when they brought you in here," Honey sobbed. "You're hurt bad, Gem."

"Rafe and his thugs," Gem explained the obvious.

"What did you do to make him so mad? We could hear him screaming all the way down here."

Everybody else in the room was staying as far away from Gem as possible, not wanting to draw Raphael's wrath by fraternizing with the enemy.

"Bit Sampson," Gem said, with a laugh that sent spasms of pain coursing through his body.

"You bit Sampson?" Honey repeated incredulously. Sampson was one of the regular Johns, nicknamed for his long hair and huge frame. The kids hated him passionately, but he paid Raphael plenty of money to look the other way and ignore the amount of abuse he inflicted on them.

"Bit him," Gem gloated. "He's gone to the hospital. Gonna need plastic surgery."

"Where did you bite him? No, no, forget it! Don't tell me."

"Let's just say I don't think he'll be comin' back here again!"

"It's a wonder Rafe didn't kill you," Honey breathed. "You're crazy, Gem. You're right crazy."

"So they tell me." Gem chuckled to himself, tears leaking from the corners of his eyes.

Honey held his hand softly in hers. "Does it really hurt, Gem?"

"No. I hardly feel it. I'm just floating way up there."

"Don't you die on me. I'll be so mad at you if you die."

"I'm not gonna croak. It ain't that bad."

"You're covered with blood and welts."

"I'm just floating...way up there," Gem murmured, euphoric. "Man, I fixed that Sampson good."

He drifted into another dream. Still Rafe's shop, but later, as he recovered from his beating. Still weak enough that Raphael could hold Gem himself without the help of his thugs. Instead, the thugs were holding Honey at the other side of the room.

"You crazy little whelp," Raphael growled in Gem's ear, his arm held tightly across Gem's throat. "I just got a call from another client who heard about Sampson and won't be coming back here. And Sampson—we'll be lucky if he doesn't lay charges and blow the whole operation! The cops are at the hospital every day, asking him questions. You want to ruin my business? You think I want to end up in prison?"

Gem just grinned. "I fixed Sampson, and I'll fix anyone else you put in the same room with me. You can't stop me. You don't scare me no more. I know how to get to you now."

Raphael reacted violently, pulling his arm tightly across Gem's throat so that he couldn't breathe. When Gem started to black out, Raphael released the pressure and shook Gem.

"Come on! Stand up; you're going to see what's going to happen. You think I can't control you anymore? Hah!" He motioned to one of the thugs standing with Honey across the room, who pulled out a machete and held it at her throat. "You like her, don't you? She's your special friend. She looks after you when you're hurt, huh? You like it if I cut her?"

"You wouldn't. She's no good to you scarred."

"Yeah? There's a hundred more that can replace her."

Gem didn't believe it. He stood and waited, no longer baiting Raphael, but offering no contrition.

Raphael nodded to the thugs. The one with the knife stepped back and slashed quickly, not pulling it across Honey's throat, but slashing it down her face.

Honey didn't scream at first. It happened so fast that she didn't know she'd been cut. Then the blood started to flow, and she squealed and covered her face. Gem ripped himself from Raphael's grip and went after the thug, trying to tear the knife from his hands. All he got for his effort was bloody gashes on his hands, which he saw but didn't feel.

Raphael laughed uproariously. "I can't control you anymore? Think again, little Gem. You'll do whatever I tell you to, now." He kicked the white first aid kit across the floor. "Your turn to play nurse now. You see if you can make her beautiful again."

Gem howled with rage. He kicked and screamed, waking himself up. He was disoriented, trying to figure out what had happened and where he was.

"Gem? Are you okay?" Bethany asked from the other side of the door.

Gem was embarrassed to have wakened her all the way in the other room.

"Leave me alone," he growled. "I just had a dream."

She went back to her own room. Gem pictured her going back to bed. The image of Honey before her accident was still in his brain. Honey had been pretty. Like Bethany. That same long, silky blond hair.

He had held Honey in his bloody hands, trying to see the damage, but at the same time trying not to look at her face, not to process it. The deep gash ran from her forehead, directly through the eye socket, down her cheek down to her chin. He couldn't tell the condition of her eye. She was crying and bleeding everywhere.

Gem opened the meager first aid kit. He pulled out a needle and thread shakily, looking at the horrible gash, ignoring his own wounds. It had to be stitched. He knew it did. She would bleed to death if shock didn't kill her first. There was, of course, no anesthetic in the kit. No painkillers. They didn't even have any access to alcohol. Gem swallowed. He couldn't sew her up with her squirming and crying.

Gem put his hand over her mouth and pinched closed Honey's nose. She struggled harder than he expected, slipping out of his grip. He had to lie on top of her, pinning her to the ground. Eventually, she stopped struggling, unconscious. Gem let her go and listened to her chest to make sure she started breathing again. Then he went to work, forcing his hands to stay rock steady, blanking his mind against what he was doing. He had a job to do; that was all there was to it.

After the sewing was finished, he bandaged her gently.

He pulled a blanket around her and cradled her like a baby.

———

Riker's research continued. Figuring out what had happened to Gem's mom and grandma was not easy. His mother had dropped out of sight a couple of years earlier and had not resurfaced. She could be dead or institutionalized as a Jane Doe somewhere. No way to know.

The grandmother was a little easier; she turned out to be dead, which was unfortunate. He suspected she was the one that could probably have told him Gem's secrets. Or at least something that would lead him to them. He looked for something that would indicate her cause of death, wondering briefly whether it was natural causes, or whether somebody might have helped her along. If she knew Gem's secrets, he might not have wanted to risk her being alive for people to call on. But he couldn't find any indications that an autopsy had been performed or that she had died of anything other than natural causes.

Riker's next step would be to try to track down family friends. That was not going to be easy. They had moved around over the years, through very transient areas where Riker wasn't likely to still find people who remembered them.

But he had to at least try. He was sure that Gem's secrets could be found in his past, if he could just ask the right people.

———

As he sipped his coffee, trying to get his engine revved up enough to face the day, Gem watched Bethany, pretending he wasn't studying her. He thought back to his dreams about Honey.

He remembered some time after the accident when Raphael brought Nickie in. Nickie ran a shop like Raphael, and they sometimes swapped kids. It was not smart to keep one kid in the same place for too long. That made it easier for the cops to track them. Even the location of the shops changed regularly. Unlike Raphael, Nickie was Albanian or something like that. He was blond, with a thick accent some mistook for Russian.

Nickie looked critically over the kids huddled around the room.

His eyes stopped on Honey, her head down and turned away from them.

"Show him your face," Raphael ordered.

Honey didn't move. Receiving a nod of permission from Raphael, Nickie bent down and grasped Honey's chin, forcing her head up. On seeing her face, he swore and let go of her like she was contaminated.

"She's *ugly!* Why would you keep her?"

Gem saw Honey's wince at Nickie's exclamation. The other kids were used to her scar by now and did not stare at it or refer to it. But to outsiders, the injury was grotesque. It was still red and only half-healed, even though Gem had long since taken the stitches out. Thankfully, the eyelid on the affected side had fused, so they did not have to look into an empty socket where she'd lost the eye.

"She's requested more than you might think," Raphael said, "there's some real weirdos out there." He gave a philosophical shrug. "But mostly, I keep her around to keep *that* one in line." Raphael nodded at Gem.

Gem watched Nickie's eyes go over him.

"He's got the look," Nickie agreed, licking his lips with an expression that made Gem's stomach tighten sickly.

The look. Girls had to look young and pretty. A figure was not an asset in a shop like Rafe's. Men who came to Raphael wanted little girls. Or boys with the look. Beardless, young, round-faced, with an aura of innocence despite their experience. Gem knew he had the look. It was the same look that used to make cops take him home to Gram instead of arresting him for loitering, trespassing, vagrancy, or truancy. Gem knew he had it, and would have done just about anything to lose it.

But what would happen when he did lose his look and was no longer useful to Raphael? Would Raphael let him go? Kill him? Promote him to one of the shops that offered older, more experienced kids? Gem half-wished that Nickie *would* deal with Rafe for Gem. Maybe Nickie would be less violent than Rafe. Maybe there would be a better chance of escape from his shop. Maybe the cops were closer to busting him.

"Gem?"

Gem startled from his reverie. He didn't usually daydream. He just put things behind him. But for some reason, Bethany reminded him so strongly of Honey.

"Sorry. I was thinking about something else."

"I noticed. What about?"

"Nothing. You don't have a sister, do you? You remind me of someone."

She jerked her head back slightly like he had slapped her. Her expression hardened, and she spoke firmly, a little too loud. "No."

There was something in her tone and manner that made Gem wonder if she were lying to him. He pondered whether to pursue it, but decided not to.

———

Bethany had intended to press Gem further about what he had been dreaming about, to see if she could figure out his secret. But he was probing too close to her secrets. She wasn't talking to anyone about her family, even him. She looked for a way to put the focus back on Gem.

"Uh—what is she like? The girl I remind you of?"

"She was special...really sweet... pretty..." Gem's voice trailed off. There was a note in his voice. He'd been in love with her, whoever she was.

"She was your girlfriend?" Bethany asked.

"No. Just a friend."

CHAPTER TWELVE

WORD GOT AROUND TOWN pretty fast that an undercover cop had been killed on the job, but details were slow in coming. As soon as they heard that it was Angelletti, an officer investigating gangs in general and the Rippers in particular, they started pulling Rippers off the street for questioning. Riker watched for Gem to be brought in. When he was, Riker went in to talk to him.

"Gem Johnson. I assume that you have your usual sterling alibi for the murder."

"When was it?" Gem returned, all innocence.

"About midnight last night. And don't bother telling me you were with the other Rippers. That seems to be the story of the day."

"Guess I was busy getting this," Gem said, gesturing to his black eye.

"And where'd you get that?"

Gem gave the name of a local bar.

"Who was the other guy?"

"Couple skinheads giving a girl a hard time."

"A working girl?"

Gem didn't answer right away. "Yeah," he admitted eventually.

"You sure got a soft spot for hookers, don't you?"

Gem stared Riker down and didn't answer.

"Was she someone you knew?"

"No. Just a kid I didn't like 'em giving a hard time to."

"Interesting. So your witness this time is a hooker again. Did you also know that Angelletti was killed in a whorehouse?"

Gem looked pained at the term, but he shrugged it off. "Did he frequent places like that often?"

Riker chuckled. "No, not as far as we are aware. But even if he did, we put it down as an undercover investigation, and that's the end of it."

"Yeah, that's convenient. I remember cops who—" He cut himself off abruptly, realizing that he didn't want to reveal his past.

Riker considered. "Cops who used Raphael's services?" he finished. He laughed at Gem's startled expression. "All the times we've met, and you didn't think I would check out your background?"

Gem shifted uncomfortably. "I know all about cops who use hookers," he asserted.

"You have a grudge against them?" Riker suggested.

"They're power hungry. They like games, and they like guns. And they like to see hookers hurt, whether they are on the giving end, or someone else is."

Riker face burned. "If you're referring to your last experience in our jail, I had nothing to do with that!"

Gem raised an eyebrow. "Sure," he agreed, "and I'm sure Angelletti wasn't in the habit of visiting whorehouses, either."

"Do you have any personal knowledge about that?"

"I didn't even know the guy was a cop. Why would I care what he was doing with his time? But if he was messing around, I can't blame whatever girl got tired of the power games and offed him."

Riker considered the details he'd been given about Angelletti's death. The madam said that he'd asked for a specific girl, who was occupied when he arrived. He waited alone. When she finished with her first client and joined him, the girl found him dead—shot through the heart with his service weapon, which he had removed and left in its holster on the side table. No fingerprints. Open window. Nobody heard the shot. The girl was hysterical. They had believed her story of an outside intruder, at least initially.

But Gem's speculation might fit too. The girl might be one of Angelletti's informants, which was why he'd asked for her by name, but it was just as possible that he simply frequented the house often and knew who he wanted.

Riker didn't know Angelletti personally, so he couldn't deny the possibility that Angelletti was into 'power games,' and might have pushed this particular girl a bit too far. It was worth looking into.

So was Gem's bar fight alibi.

———

Gem sat alone in one of the interrogation rooms while Riker went to make other inquiries. Gem knew he could make a fuss and get released since they had nothing to hold him on, but he was in no hurry. Let Riker ask his questions. He couldn't connect Gem to the murder. He didn't really even suspect him; he had just been brought in with the other Rippers. Gem had no more motive to kill Angelletti than anyone else. And he had an alibi.

Gem closed his eyes, drifting back in time.

He was sitting in a wheelchair in the hospital, locked inside himself. Ever since the home, he'd been there. Locked inside, under a foot-thick layer of ice he could barely see and hear through. They said it made him better, but that just meant it was easier to handle him. With help, he could walk, but he could hardly crawl on his own without assistance.

People walked by him like he wasn't even there. They didn't even look at him. He knew it was time to get out. Gem had been trapped for too long. It was the first time that he had been left unguarded, unattended.

Riker returned to the room, waking Gem from his reverie. "We're going to hold you until we've had a chance to verify your alibi."

"So you can put me in a cell again?" Gem sneered. He would call his lawyer this time. He wasn't going to put up with more abuse.

"We've got a bunch of the Rippers in custody." Riker offered. "I'll personally see to it that you are jailed with them."

Gem was surprised and suspicious. "You'd do that?"

"Maybe now you'll believe me when I tell you that last time I did give instructions for you to be put in a cell by yourself."

Gem considered it. He had seen Riker talking to the cop. The cop said Gem was supposed to get special treatment. Was it possible that one or both of the cops had intentionally done the opposite of what they were told? Or even that it was a mistake? Riker had made a show of being concerned the next day, even offering to take Gem to a doctor. Maybe that had been for real, not just show.

Riker took Gem to the cell block personally, as promised, and saw that he was put in a cell with others from the gang. He took the cuffs off of Gem's wrists and put his hand briefly on Gem's shoulder.

"I want you behind bars," he said, "but I'm not out to see you hurt or killed."

"Well then, maybe I won't have to kill you," Gem murmured, without turning his head to gauge the effect of his words or even if Riker had heard him.

He wasn't really talking to Riker, just voicing a thought out loud.

***

Riker was shaken.

He'd had threats made on his life before. Criminals had yelled and screamed threats at him. He'd heard it all. But Gem's matter-of-fact statement gave him a chill.

He knew that Gem was a cold-blooded murderer. A perp didn't set up alibis like Gem did after committing a crime in a fit of rage. The crimes that Gem committed were carefully planned and thought out. If Gem had plans to kill Riker, he was as good as dead if he didn't watch his back. Something about Gem allowed him to commit crimes no one else would dare to and to get away with it.

Riker knew he had to find out Gem's secret. And find it out soon.

———

In the jail cell, Thrasher gave Gem a friendly slap on the back. "I gotta say, Gem, I dunno how you do it, but you know your stuff."

Gem glanced around at the other boys and their surroundings. "I don't talk in the pen," he advised. "Too many listeners."

Thrasher nodded at his wisdom. "Too true, man. No honor anymore. Guy'll roll on you in a second, for a year off his sentence. Not to mention cops and wires. Good policy to have."

Gem was glad Thrasher was so philosophical about it. A lot of guys would have been offended. But Thrasher knew how it was, and he didn't push for an explanation of how Gem had done the job.

———

As always, Gem's alibi checked out. They couldn't connect the hookers involved on either end with Gem's old shop. But that didn't mean there was no connection.

Along with the cute black hooker Gem had defended, the bartender and bouncer also verified his alibi.

Riker thought back on the amount of money stolen from the bank and wondered if Gem's clever alibis were nothing more mystical than several large bribes. A little bit of cash greasing the right wheels, and he could get people to say whatever he wanted them to.

CHAPTER THIRTEEN

A TIRED-LOOKING WOMAN with gray streaks in her ponytail answered the door and looked questioningly at Riker.

"I'm looking for anyone who used to know Dee and Katie Johnson, who used to live in this building," Riker told her, the same as he had told every other occupant of the building who had answered their door. Few of them had lived there for more than a year.

The tired woman wrinkled her brow.

"Katie and Dee," she repeated thoughtfully, reversing the order that Riker had put them in. Riker nodded hopefully.

"Were they a mother and daughter?" she said tentatively.

"Yes, exactly. Could I ask you a few questions about them?"

She motioned him in. "It was an awfully long time ago. I don't see how I could be of any help."

"I don't know, but anything might help."

She herded Riker into a beat-up old recliner covered with years of filth. Riker sat down gingerly, breathing shallowly to reduce the smell of the place. He had seen evidence of rats in the outer hallway.

"I'm Peggy," she introduced herself.

"Riker." He tried to ignore the filth and the stench and concentrate on the conversation. "Dee was the daughter, and she had a boy named Gem, who would have been about three or four when they lived here."

Peggy nodded. "Yes, that's right... I used to babysit him occasionally when Kate went out. He was a strange kid."

"Oh?"

"He's the type you look at and think: he's going to be trouble, one day."

"Why? What kind of trouble?"

"You know, the kind of kid who kills neighborhood cats, and you know he's going to grow up to be a bad one."

"He killed cats?"

"He was too young to do that yet. I just figured he was the type."

"Oh, I see." Of course, he had no clue what she was talking about without more information. "What was he like?"

"Quiet, sometimes. He would sit in the corner, sucking his finger and watching everything, taking it all in. Or he'd be wild, screaming if you got close to him and racing around destroying everything. You never knew how he was going to behave."

"I've had others say he was unpredictable."

"Well, if he was in one of his quiet moods, you could pretty much count on him staying that way for a while. You didn't have to supervise him if he was like that. But if he was wild, you practically had to tie him down to keep him from destroying the house."

"Did you think he was emotionally disturbed?"

"Well, I didn't think he was normal..." She cocked her head at him and raised her eyebrows.

"Did you ever think he was abused?"

"They were right next door. Sometimes he would scream and yell like he was being murdered. I didn't like to get involved, but sometimes, I called the cops to check up on things."

"Did they ever find anything suspicious?"

"You tell me. They never talked to me about it. Sometimes he had bruises, but he hurt himself too. You never knew whether someone else hurt him or whether he did it himself."

"Did you see him hurt himself?"

"Yeah, I did." She nodded. "Hitting his head, scratching his face, things like that."

"How did he act around Dee and Kate? What did you think of them?"

"He was scared of them. That was obvious. Dee, I could understand. She scared me at the best of times. Kate seemed okay. A little distant, but I never saw anything to indicate she was mean to him."

"Tell me about Dee."

"It was so long ago... must be ten years... she was in and out of the psych ward all the time. You couldn't carry on a normal conversation with her. She'd say bizarre things, hallucinate, she didn't make sense. I shudder to think of her in the same house as a child, let alone raising one."

"I gather Katie did most of the raising."

"Don't you believe it. If Dee was home, it was her responsibility. Kate would even leave her alone with Gem."

Riker shook his head at the thought. "It's a wonder he's as normal as he is, and not walking around with a tinfoil hat to block alien transmissions."

"Is he really okay? I sometimes wondered if he'd even survive childhood."

"He's had a pretty rough life. I think his upbringing left some scars... Tell me—what did he do when he got in trouble? Was he pretty good at avoiding punishments?"

"No. He'd try to say he wasn't the one who made the mess, or whatever, but he still got in trouble."

"He must have learned that later. Did they leave him with you a lot?"

"No, not much. But sometimes if I knew he was left alone over there, I would go over and get him."

"How often did that happen?"

"A couple of times a week I'd go over and get him. I'm sure they left him alone more than that."

"He fended for himself at that age?"

"If they didn't tie him to the bed." At Riker's expression, she hurried on. "Not four-point restraints. One end of a rope tied to his wrist and the other end to the bedpost. He could roam around the room."

"I see. Did he talk much at that age?"

"Mostly gibberish. Not a lot of recognizable words."

"I see. Anything else? Anything you particularly remember?"

"No, nothing else." She shook her head. "I'm sorry."

"Do you know of any friends they had who might still be around? Or someone who kept in touch with them?"

Peggy thought about it. "No, I don't think so. People just don't stay long around here."

———

They were all out of jail, and Thrasher was drinking at his apartment with some of the other Rippers when he joined them. "Hey, Thrasher."

"Gem. Here's the man of the hour! How's the Angelletti investigation going?"

He shrugged. "They aren't getting anywhere," he said with a smile. "And they ain't gonna."

"They don't think it was you?"

"Right now they're investigating the poor girl who found him. I've got an alibi."

"I don't know how you do it, Gem. You're like a genius with alibis. What's the secret?"

"It's my secret," he said flatly.

Thrasher gazed at him. "Aw, come on. You can't give your pals some tips on alibis?"

"Don't get caught without a good one."

There were laughs from the Rippers.

"Yeah, but how do you arrange ones the cops can't bust?"

"Make it the truth."

Thrasher shook his head. "Drink up, on me. Maybe some booze will loosen your tongue."

He accepted the free drinks without argument. Even if he'd wanted to refuse—and he didn't—it wasn't smart to refuse a drink from a guy like Thrasher. Thrasher might act laid back and friendly, but he knew enough about people to know that Thrasher's sociability hid an intense, powerful inner personality. He knew all about people who were sweet and caring on the outside. There was his Gram, for one.

Her soft, sweet exterior masked an iron core few knew was there.

He could remember waiting for someone to pick him up from school. For the first little while, he just stood in front of the building, waiting. It was a long time before he realized that no one was coming. At first, he cried. He was only five or six. He still cried at that age. After a few minutes of tears, he realized it wasn't helping him. He could cry in front of the school all night; it wouldn't make his Gram come pick him up.

After he had settled down, he knew why she hadn't come. He'd cried on the way to school. Gram had told him that if he kept crying, she would leave him at school all night. So she had. He could try walking home. He wasn't sure he knew the way or could walk that far. But he didn't want to stay at the school all night, so he tried.

Other kids in the neighborhood were outside by themselves, so no one noticed one more who looked like he knew where he was going. As it got dark, he felt tears welling up in his eyes, and a lump in his throat made him want to start crying again. He didn't recognize anything around him anymore.

A woman stopped him as it started to get very dark. "Where are you going?"

"Home."

"How far is home? You're too young to be out here walking by yourself."

"I don't know."

"Do you know your address?"

"No."

"Come with me."

He resisted. "I'm not supposed to."

"I suppose not. Well, just walk with me to that phone, and we'll call a policeman."

He hesitated but trailed along behind her to the pay phone half a block away. They said at school that it was okay to talk to cops. And he had always been treated kindly by them.

The woman stayed with him until the police car pulled up. The cop who got out of the car shone his flashlight on Gem's face.

"How old are you?"

"Six."

"What's your name?"

"Gem."

"Jim what?"

"Johnson."

"Where do you live?"

"I don't know."

"Close to here?"

"I don't know."

"Well, you'd better come with me. I'll take you to Child Services until they can track down your folks."

He climbed into the squad car and let them take him to the Children's Home. He'd stayed at the Home before.

In the morning, Gram came to pick him up. She talked to the matron while looking at him. "I had to take his mama to the hospital again. I told the school. Someone was supposed to take him home and keep an eye on him. I don't know what happened."

He stood there, waiting for her to take him back to school. He could see the steel in her eyes. She'd shown him who was boss. He knew that if he disobeyed, she'd do it again.

"Come on," she told him, holding out a hand impatiently.

He took it reluctantly. Her hand was bony and dry, and she held on to him too tightly, crushing his fingers.

She pulled him out to the car, hauling on his arm.

———

Thrasher watched Gem covertly. The boy was gone, lost in his own world again.

Bethany would say he was in his quiet mood. Thrasher had talked to her again. Bethany wasn't owned by the Rippers anymore, so Thrasher couldn't give her orders, he could just request favors.

She said she hadn't found out anything significant. Gem had frequent nightmares.

She suggested that his personalities or moods were becoming more distinct. Sometimes she could tell the instant he walked into the room which personality was dominant. Thrasher was starting to be able to distinguish between them too, given some time. Not instinctively like Bethany could, but it was getting easier.

———

Riker found out almost by accident that Dee, Gem's mom, had siblings. There was nothing on Gem's Social Services record to indicate that he had aunts or uncles, but Riker had requested anything he could get on Dee and Katie, and there it was.

Dee had sibling twins who had died in infancy. There was also a brother who had committed suicide as a teenager. And another brother who had been put into foster care. Riker wondered whether he could be located.

———

Gem walked along the dim street, deep in thought. He was a little bit drunk and a little more stoned. He was feeling anxious, inexplicably worried that someone was going to find out about his past, about his secrets. He was so anxious about it that he'd had to take something to anesthetize himself.

A burly man stepped out of the alley in front of Gem and looked him over. Gem's stomach lurched.

"A little late to be out by yourself, isn't it?" the man slurred.

Gem swore and tried to step around him.

"Nice you're here, though, because I was hoping for some company tonight."

Gem tried to push past him. Most adults saw his gang colors and left him alone. But the big biker was probably in a gang of his own and didn't care squat about trouble with a juvie and his gang. He might even be carrying. Gem wasn't planning on sticking around to find out. The biker grabbed him as he tried to get by.

"Where do you think you're going? I said I wanted company."

"Lemme alone," Gem growled. "Find someone else."

"I don't think so. I like you. So come with me."

Gem struggled to free himself from the man's grip. He couldn't even reach his blade. Should've been carrying a gun.

Gem started kicking and struggling desperately, blind with panic and anger.

No rules.

Hit or kick whatever he could reach.

Bite and scratch.

Yell, swear and scream.

Kick up a commotion that no one could ignore.

Gem was consumed by blood-red fury. He was not going to submit to this man. Not again. Not here, not now. He refused to be shamed again. He was done with that scene once and for all.

Gem was aware of the people pouring out of the bar behind him. Hands pulled the fighters apart. He fought the hands, all the hands, fighting for his life.

Two-to-one, three-to-one, he was frantic and didn't know what the odds were anymore, only that he had to hurt them, to escape from them.

He fought until he was face down on the pavement, a couple of them kneeling on his back, arms, and legs, and someone with his boot planted firmly against Gem's face and neck, pinning him so solidly to the ground that he could no longer struggle.

He was defeated. Totally helpless. They could tie him up, beat him, and starve him until he was too weak and broken-down to raise a hand against them.

Again.

There were too many, and they were too strong. They could do whatever they wanted with him.

Sirens screamed in his ears. Gem didn't know whether to be scared or relieved. There were too many crooked cops. Too many cops who would look the other way or even take part in Gem's humiliation.

His captors did not scatter at the arrival of the squad cars and Gem despaired.

Crooked cops.

He heard the various voices around him but could not comprehend them. It was as if they were speaking a foreign language.

———

"What's going on?" Lucette demanded, getting out of his squad car. There was a big crowd, and he radioed for backup.

"These two were fighting," the bar owner explained, gesturing with a shotgun at the big, red-faced biker and the man under the pile of barflies. "Or... something. I don't know what happened, but the kid was screaming like a banshee fighting him off."

"He just attacked me!" the biker protested the first chance he got. "He's high or crazy; I don't know what. I didn't do anything but hold him off."

"Sure, you did. Move off, let me see him," Lucette told the pile of men on top of the kid.

"If we shift, he's going to start fighting again. He's nuts. Wouldn't stop."

The boy was muttering something in a low, desperate tone. Lucette motioned for his partner to cuff the biker and tried to make out what the boy was saying. At first, he thought it was something about the biker, but then it sounded like 'Riker.' He got closer to the ground to listen to him and was sure of it. He couldn't hear every word, just 'Riker' repeated several times, and something that sounded like 'straight cop.'

Lucette stood up and clicked on his radio. "Dispatch, is Riker in one of the units en route?"

There was silence for a moment. "Affirmative. ETA one minute."

Lucette walked to the curb and looked for the car. It pulled up a minute later. Riker stepped out.

"What's up, Lucette?"

"You know this junkie over here? I think he's saying your name."

Riker walked over and knelt on the ground to look. "Yeah. His name is Gem. Let him go. I'll look after him."

They protested. Riker motioned for the man with his foot across Gem's neck to back off. He reluctantly withdrew. Riker touched Gem's chin.

"Gem, it's Riker. Do you hear me?"

"Riker?" Gem croaked.

"Yeah. Now I'm going to get these yokels off your back. You stay still?"

"You put the cuffs on. You take me in. You're straight, Riker. I know you're straight."

"That's right. So hold still."

Gem didn't move. When he was released, Riker patted him down, then pulled Gem's arms back and cuffed him. He put Gem in his car and went back to find out what had happened. He got back in the car a few minutes later.

"Got yourself in an altercation with a drunk, I guess."

"You won't put him and me in the same cell." Gem's breathing was still ragged.

"No."

"You put me in with the Rippers last time. Some cops get a kick out of putting hookers and pimps in the same cell."

"You aren't a hooker anymore, and he's not a pimp."

"You think I don't know a pimp when I look him in the eye?"

Riker studied Gem through the grill. The boy was white as a ghost, his eyes so wide his face looked like a mask.

"Is that what you thought? No wonder you were so freaked out. Let's go to the station and talk. You're still pretty shaken up."

Gem said nothing. Riker drove in silence. He put Gem in an interrogation room and left him alone for a few minutes while he got coffee. Out of curiosity, he checked to see if the drunk Gem had tangled with had a record. He looked over Lucette's shoulder at the computer printout.

"Nice guy," Lucette commented.

"He really is another Raphael," Riker said. Gem had tagged him for what he was, all right.

"Who's Raphael?"

"An acquaintance of Gem's. One he's suspected of killing."

"From the witness's statements, I can't say I'm surprised. If the kid had a weapon handy, that guy would be in the morgue right now."

"He had a knife. Which means he was attacked, not the attacker."

"You believe the kid's story? With the state he was in?"

Riker shrugged. "Actually, I do. I've been dealing with him for a few months. If he wanted to kill this guy, he would plan it out and get away with it."

Riker went back to see Gem. He handed him a cup of coffee. Gem was not looking good. His face was swelling up with bruises. But even aside from that, he did not look well.

"Are you high?" Riker questioned suspiciously.

"Low," Gem contradicted. "Yeah, I'm stoned."

"Don't tell me you attacked that guy because you're hopped up on something."

"I took downers, not uppers."

"You're not acting down. You're jittery."

"That's why I took them," Gem said impatiently. He reached for the coffee.

"Maybe I'd better make that a decaf," Riker said.

Gem paused. "You got decaf?"

"I think I can track some down. Let me send someone for some." Riker stuck his head out in the hallway and sent a junior officer on the mission.

"You got any cigarettes?" Gem asked.

Riker hated sitting in a smoke-filled interrogation room and, of course, it was against city bylaws, but if there was a chance of getting Gem talking, he wasn't going to throw it away. He got out a pack of cigarettes and a lighter and put them down in front of Gem. Gem shook one out clumsily and put it in his mouth. He tried to light it, but couldn't get the lighter to work. Riker watched him getting more frustrated, and eventually pried the lighter from Gem's fingers. He thumbed the lighter, and it worked on the first try. Gem poked his cigarette into the flame and inhaled.

"Now, why don't you tell me what happened tonight?"

"That fat pimp propositioned me. I turned him down. He grabbed me, and I protected myself."

"He says you attacked him."

"Of course he does. What else is he gonna say?" Gem took a deep drag on the cigarette. "Why would I attack someone three times my size?"

"Because you're high."

"I couldn't even get at my blade. If I'd attacked him, I woulda pulled it and split his fat belly, not stood there trying to scratch his eyes out."

"What about him made you think he was a pimp? We've been watching him awhile and haven't been able to catch him at anything."

Gem shrugged. "The way he looked me over. The way a girl looks at a dress when she's deciding whether to add it to her wardrobe."

"You don't know anything about his girls or if he runs a shop like Raphael?"

"I never seen him before."

"Too bad. I wouldn't mind putting him away for something more than drunk and disorderly."

Gem's coffee arrived. Riker thanked the young officer and handed it to Gem.

"Your hands are shaking," he observed. Gem warmed his hands around the cup, then tucked them under his armpits.

"I'm cold."

"You're shivering. It's not that cold in here," Riker said, concerned.

Gem nodded, his teeth almost chattering. Riker took off his jacket and laid it over Gem's shoulders. Gem huddled inside it.

"It's probably the dope," Riker said. He took Gem's wrist and felt his pulse. He looked at Gem's face while he took it. "I'm going to take you over to the doctor."

Gem shook his head. "I'm okay. Just cold... and sort of nauseous."

Riker nodded. "I want to get you looked at."

He handcuffed Gem again and took him over to see the station's doctor. It was Dr. Stein, a woman. Tall, brunette, wrinkles at the corners of her eyes.

"Well, what have you got for me today?" she questioned.

"I'm no expert, but I think he's in shock."

Dr. Stein ushered Gem in and over to the examining table and looked him over while asking Riker questions. "He was in an accident?"

"No, a fight. But when I got there, he was practically incoherent. I wondered if the emotional stress..."

"Could be. What about drugs?"

"Downers. Can you be any more specific, Gem? What kind of downers?"

Gem shrugged. "Pills. Prescription."

"Tranquilizers?" she questioned.

"I guess."

"Your heart is racing. How were you feeling before that?"

"Hyped, worried, worked up..."

"Have you seen a doctor about these feelings of anxiety?"

Riker was interested in Gem's answer.

"I've seen plenty of shrinks about plenty of things. I've had lots of downers prescribed before."

"Were these prescribed to you?"

"No."

"Have you been drinking too?"

"Yeah."

"I suspect you're feeling the effects of mixing street drugs and drinking. Why don't you tell me about this fight tonight?"

Gem flushed. He glanced aside at Riker and shook his head. "Just a fight. Nothing to tell."

"How often are you popping pills?"

Gem shrugged. "I gotta have something to keep me cool."

"Well, you chill here for a minute while I talk to Riker."

Gem nodded and pulled Riker's jacket close while they went to the other side of the room to talk.

"Is he a psych case?" Stein questioned.

"Probably. Why do you ask?"

"You should have seen how much his pulse sped up when I asked him about the fight. And it was already abnormally fast.

Either he's got a heart condition, he's taken uppers instead of downers, or he's on the verge of a full-blown panic attack."

"Could be a panic attack. He never struck me as the type before, but I saw him after the fight. He was having a first-class meltdown. And he does have a psychiatric history."

"Well, to be safe, let's put him in the hospital for the night. I don't want to be responsible if he gets worse. I'll get the form for you."

Stein found one in her desk. They finished up and went back to Gem. "You're going to the hospital tonight."

Gem rolled his eyes. "I'm not sick."

"You know you are," Stein said firmly. "And I want you to get a consult to see if you need ongoing medication. No reason to be screwing up your system if an anti-anxiety pill will work for you."

Gem shrugged. "I told you I been through all that before."

"Well, try once more. There are a lot of new alternatives. Do you want to walk around with your heart jumping out of your chest all the time?"

Gem shook his head wordlessly.

"Then learn a lesson from tonight and take care of yourself."

CHAPTER FOURTEEN

RIKER TURNED ON THE radio. Gem sat in the back of the car, leaning his head against the side of the car, listening to the quiet hum of the engine. The adrenaline rush started to subside. His heart began to slow down, and his eyelids drooped. He'd taken downers and booze, and with the immediate danger gone, he was starting to feel them.

The hospital was not his favorite place. He'd had plenty of bad experiences in places like that. But doctors were usually kind, and he was taken care of. Institutions came with their own set of problems. But the hospital, for just one night, wouldn't be so bad.

The Home hadn't been bad, to begin with. Lots of rich nuts, most with no problem other than not wanting to face the real world. Gem had been lonely, but felt reasonably safe.

Then funding started running out. Instead of a private room, he was in a ward with the violent crazies. He kept getting in fights with the inmates and nurses.

Then he'd stopped seeing Schulz and started seeing a new, weird doctor. Suddenly they were doing hypnosis and regression, and they started giving him meds that made him hallucinate. Then meds to counteract the hallucinations and violent episodes. He was doped up until he couldn't do anything, then pronounced cured and kicked out.

———

Riker pulled into the specially marked police stall and opened Gem's door for him. Gem just sat there and didn't move.

"Gem, come on." He still didn't move or respond. Riker shook him. "Gem."

Shaking his arm had no effect. Riker pulled his arm a little harder. Gem slid his feet out and stood up. He still didn't look Riker in the eye. His face was blank. Riker shook him and spoke louder.

"Gem! Snap out of it. Come on!"

Gem did not respond, but he went with Riker when led. Riker took him to the admitting desk in emergency. The nurse at the counter motioned to the clip-boarded forms to be filled out, and Riker handed her the one the doctor had given him. She looked it over and typed on her computer while talking on the phone. She hung up the phone while pulling Gem's printout off the machine.

"You're going to be waiting for a while—" she started.

"He's changed since the doctor at the station saw him."

"Changed how?" she demanded.

"He's not responding to me at all. Checked out."

She stood up, studying Gem. "Gem, can you hear me?" she said loudly. There was no response. She reached over and pinched his arm. Riker winced, but Gem didn't flinch.

"He's been taking drugs?"

"Yes."

"I'll upgrade him. Go sit down, and a doctor will come get you."

Riker nodded and went over to the chairs. He sat down. Gem remained standing. Riker shrugged and didn't try to seat him. Maybe they would get a quicker response if Gem were more obvious.

———

The halfway house after the Home had been just as bad as the Home, in different ways. No more fights or hypnosis, but he was so drugged out that he could not protect himself against the abuse of the house parents.

But one of them had forgotten to completely close a door one day and another inmate had seen what was going on.

———

A white-jacketed doctor approached Riker and Gem, glancing over a clipboard. "This is Gem?" he questioned.

"Yes."

"Let's get him to an exam room."

The doctor took Gem firmly by the arm and guided him to a curtained exam area. "This is interesting," he said aside to Riker as he performed a swift exam on Gem. "Not at all typical for a drug overdose. Your admitting form says he has a psychiatric history?"

"I don't know any details, but he has been institutionalized."

"I'd suspect some kind of psychotic break, then. We'll order a tox screen and detox him if we need to. But I don't know if that will have any effect on this state. I'll order a psych consult." He paused. "Get a nurse to change him and lock up his clothes. And if you want to keep him in custody, put cuffs on him. You never know if this is put on, or how quickly he'll come out of it. You go to the john, and he's gone when you get back."

Riker nodded. That would be just like Gem. He'd disappeared from a hospital while supposedly in a catatonic state once before.

Riker wasn't going to let that happen again.

———

"Where's Gem been lately?" Rico asked Thrasher.

"I don't know. Bethany thought he was home a couple of nights ago, but he keeps the bedroom door locked, so she's not sure."

"It doesn't make sense, him disappearing like that. Where would he go?"

"Maybe he went on a bender or something," Thrasher said with a shrug, "I haven't seen him for a week."

Riker got a line on Dee's brother and was making arrangements to follow up when he got a call from the psych ward at the hospital.

"Hi, it's Marie," said the nurse he had gotten to know over the past week that Gem had been at the hospital. "Sleeping beauty has woken up."

"Great. Does he seem normal?"

"Some anxiety and restlessness, but not bad."

"I'll come up at the end of my shift."

He told Gordon that Gem was awake. "You want to go up with me?"

Gordon shrugged. "I don't know why you even want to. He's not being charged for anything. You don't need to see him for anything."

"I want to keep up with what he's up to."

"Go ahead. I don't need to be there."

Gem paced impatiently. He tried to stay away from the other patients. He refused to take any of the meds they wanted to give him. So far, he hadn't seen a doctor, only nurses, orderlies, and guards. He was too jumpy to sit down or stop moving.

He turned around and was startled to see Riker. "What're you doing here?"

"Checking up on you."

Gem snapped his fingers and slapped his legs, fidgeting. "Can you get me out of here?"

"You know I've got no say in that. The doctor will release you when he thinks you're okay."

"Gotta walk," Gem snapped, unable to stay still.

Riker walked beside Gem as he paced around the courtyard made available to the psych patients. Because apparently connecting with nature helped even if it was just a patch of worn grass enclosed by four walls of stone.

"You got a smoke?"

Riker had come prepared. He pulled one of them out and lit it for Gem. Gem smoked for a couple of minutes without speaking.

"It was a week?" he asked after a while.

"Yeah. Were you aware of what was going on?"

Gem shook his head. "No. Just dreaming." He paused. "Except I knew where I was when I woke up."

"Well, it's pretty obvious where you are."

"I knew you brought me here."

Riker raised his eyebrows. "Maybe you were conscious on some level. What's the last thing you remember?"

Gem thought back. "Some drunk trying to pick me up."

"You don't remember anything else?"

"No."

"The fight?"

"What fight?"

"With the drunk."

"No."

"Do you often have blackouts like that? Where you can't remember what happened?"

Gem shrugged. "Plenty of times."

"And has this happened before?"

"None of your business." Riker thought that was all he was going to say, but then he went on. "I been places like this before. For all kinds of things."

Riker nodded encouragingly.

"The doctors all think I'm screwed up. But I do just fine without their help."

"Even when you have to take downers to stay cool?"

Gem was startled. He looked at Riker. "What?"

"We had a bit of a talk the other day. You took downers before the fight."

"Yeah. They help better than the meds they give out at places like this."

"And then you end up in a trance for a week."

"That wasn't the downers."

"Do you know that for sure?"

Gem shook his head impatiently. "When am I gonna get out of here? I don't need to be here."

"I'm not a doctor. What did they tell you?"

"I ain't seen a doctor yet."

"Well, you should be seeing one before too long. Then they'll tell you what they think about you getting out of here."

"They can't hold me here without a court order."

"Not for long," Riker agreed.

———

Bethany called out when Gem unlocked and opened the apartment door. "Gem? Is that you?"

"Who else has got a key to this door?" He followed the sound of her voice to her bedroom.

"Come in here and tell me where you've been," she invited.

Gem went in. "What're you doing in bed?" he asked, looking at the clock. He'd never known Bethany to be in bed during the day. Not all by herself.

Bethany motioned to the crutches on the other side of the bed. "I wrenched my knee. The painkillers are making me nauseated if I get up."

Gem sat down on the edge of the bed. "Yeah? How's it feel when you're lying down?"

"Just fine. You want to join me?"

Gem grinned and slipped in beside her.

———

When Gem was relaxed and quiet beside her, Bethany probed for more answers. "So where were you for so long?"

"It wasn't so long."

"Well, where were you?"

"None of your business."

"You look like you lost weight."

"Maybe a little."

"Were you sick?"

"Yeah."

"Why didn't you come home? I would have taken care of you."

Gem shook his head. "I didn't want no one taking care of me." He sat up and reached for his clothes. "I take care of myself."

Bethany rubbed his back. "Sometimes, it's nice to be taken care of."

Gem stretched lazily, enjoying the massage. "Sometimes," he agreed.

CHAPTER FIFTEEN

RIKER WATCHED BOBBY, DEE'S brother, arrive home and gave him a few minutes to get settled before going up and ringing the doorbell.

The man did not look happy to be interrupted. He liked it even less when Riker flashed his shield.

"What's this about?" he demanded.

"I'm sorry to bother you, but I'm trying to get as much history as I can about your sister."

"My sister?"

"Dee."

"Oh, her. I can't help you very much there. I didn't really grow up with her."

"How old were you when you saw her last?"

"I've only seen her a few times since I left. I was only nine when I went into foster care. She would have been five or six at the time."

"So she probably hadn't started having psychiatric symptoms yet."

"I don't know what normal kids are like at that age. Maybe she was a normal five-year-old, or maybe she was already crazy. I don't know."

"Well, how about your mom? It would be helpful to get a little insight into her too."

Bobby shuddered. "I was happy to get away from her. The others were still under her spell."

"The others?"

"I have an older brother, too. And there were the babies."

"An older brother? Oh, the one who committed suicide."

Riker saw his mistake as soon as the words left his mouth. Surprise flashed across Bobby's features. "Suicide? Teddy? When?"

"He was fifteen, I think."

"Four years after I left. Over twenty years ago... and I never knew."

Riker nodded. "I'm sorry."

"Well, obviously, we weren't close after I was kicked out." He took a few minutes to assimilate the information. "Ma was nuts. She drove him to it. Woulda done it myself if I'd stayed there. She hated us. Parents are supposed to love their kids, but she hated us."

"Was she abusive?"

"She was *demonic*. She didn't hit us—she starved us, poisoned us, deprived us of sleep, locked us up, smothered us, all kinds of things."

Riker was surprised. "If all of these things were going on, how could Social Services not find out?"

"She was smart. They believed her lies. She rarely left a mark."

"Why did they move you to foster care?"

"She decided she didn't want me. Just like that. She had impulses, and that time it was 'I decided I don't want you anymore.' I was crushed, but it turned out to be the best thing that could've happened to me."

"When was the last time you saw your mother or sister?"

"It's been quite a while. Someone told me Mom was dead. Haven't heard from Dee for at least five years, and it was probably just a request for money. I never heard anything else from her."

Riker sighed. He'd come a long way to get nothing. "Did you ever meet Dee's son? Gem?"

"Yeah, she left him here for a couple of days. I called Child Protective Services to come to get him."

"What was he like? It's him I'm trying to get the background on."

"He wasn't too bad. Quiet while he was here, watched everything. Kind of disconcerting, the way he watched me."

"You didn't have any trouble with him?"

"I wasn't prepared to take care of a kid. I don't know the first thing about kids. He was only here for a couple of days. We didn't kill each other. He wasn't happy about me calling protective services on him."

"He wasn't violent or emotional when he was here?"

"No."

"How long ago did you say?"

"I don't know. Five years or more."

———

Riker assessed and reassessed the information he had about Gem.

There was no indication that there was anything special about Gem. He was mentally unstable, not a genius. The only solution he could find was the simplest one. Whenever he could, Gem used hookers as his alibis, trading on their shared experience. He backed them up with whoever he could buy with money from bank robberies or other big jobs.

Riker had just one more contact, an old family friend of Dee's. That would wrap up his investigation.

———

"Dee?" Rachel said, nodding. "Yeah, I remember Dee. She was pretty... freaky, sometimes."

Riker nodded. "I understand she had some major problems."

"Those poor babies; sometimes I wondered what would happen to them."

"Babies?" Riker repeated.

"The twins," Rachel said.

"Katie's twins?" Riker asked in confusion, recalling the dead siblings.

"No," Rachel frowned and shook her head, "I never knew Kate's twins. Dee had identical twin boys."

Riker stared at her, all the tumblers turning in sequence to unlock Gem's secret.

Gem.

As in Gemini.

The twins.

II

himself

CHAPTER SIXTEEN

A STUNNED RIKER EXPLAINED it to Gordon. "Dee had twins. Identical twins. That's how Gem could have unbeatable alibis. The witnesses' stories couldn't be broken because they were telling the truth. He *was* in two places at once."

Gordon rubbed his chin. "So what are their real names?"

"I don't know. I have to do some more research now that I know the truth. How could it be that none of the people that I talked to happened to mention that he was a twin?"

"Maybe no one knew."

Riker shook his head. "I talked to people who knew him as a toddler. They had to know."

———

Surveillance kept a close watch on Gem's apartment, trying to get tails on both boys. They had to have teams in front and behind the apartment, since one or both sometimes left by the fire escape.

They got some night vision pictures of the two of them together.

After watching their routines for a few days, giving Riker a chance to do some more research, they arrested the two of them separately.

———

"They must have been raised apart," Riker speculated. "I've talked to everyone who knew him when he was young, and no one knew he was a twin. One of them must have been raised by a family friend or some other casual arrangement."

"What about their names?" Gordon asked.

"No joy. There's only one birth certificate."

"What a bizarre situation. Did you notice that they have different personalities?" Gordon asked.

Riker frowned. "Do you think so?"

"I've been watching them while they've been questioned about the various charges. They have very different personalities."

Riker raised an eyebrow and waited for further explanation.

"What are we going to call them?" Gordon asked. "Gem 1 and Gem 2?"

"Seems like the only thing to do, right now."

"Okay then, Gem 1 is the brash one. He talks big, gets emotional quickly. Gem 2 is quieter, more withdrawn. He seems like he's the brains of the operation, and Gem 1 is the brawn."

"The split personalities! Everyone keeps saying that he'd be calm one day and wild the next. I thought it pointed to schizophrenia or bipolar or multiple personalities. But it was two separate boys."

"But... that would mean they were raised together," Gordon pointed out.

Riker stopped and considered. "Yeah... it would, wouldn't it?"

Riker and Gordon looked at each other, thinking through the implications of this statement.

———

It was Bobby who provided insight into what might have happened to the twins.

"I remember when ma's twins were born. She kept saying that they were evil, that one was a baby, and the other was a devil."

"How did she treat them?"

"She would feed one and lock the other in the closet. Things like that."

"Did she always neglect the same one?"

"The girl."

"They weren't identical?"

"No, boy-girl fraternal twins."

"But *both* eventually died," Riker pointed out.

"You don't understand my ma." Bobby shook his head. "Just because she thought the girl was the devil, that didn't mean she couldn't change her mind after the girl died and decide that meant the girl was the real baby, and it was the boy who was the devil."

"So you think that Katie would behave the same way toward Dee's twins?"

"Why not? Makes as much sense as anything."

Riker shook his head. "I can't fathom what you guys went through with her."

"You could never, ever even *begin* to understand," Bobby agreed. "And with crazy Dee trying to take care of those babies too? It's a miracle they survived."

CHAPTER SEVENTEEN

I THINK WE SHOULD put them together and see what happens."

Riker considered Gordon's suggestion. "I don't think we're going to get much more out of them while we keep them apart. They're sticking to their original stories."

"So shall we do it?"

Riker nodded. "Let's plan it carefully. I have a feeling we've got a pretty unique opportunity here."

———

Gem heard approaching footsteps. Inexplicable panic gripped him, squeezing his chest so hard that it hurt.

Then he saw Himself with the cop and understood. They had found his secret. Gem was silent as the cop opened the door and pushed Himself through.

The cop looked at Gem, grinning, then walked away.

Gem wasn't sure what to say. He had never imagined this might happen. He'd always been careful. No one ever saw Gem with Himself. He was careful.

"What's going on?" Gem demanded, unable to suppress the panic in his voice.

"They figured my secret out."

"How?"

"I don't know. I don't know how anyone could have found out."

Gem looked around the cell nervously. "Can't talk here. Could be bugged."

"Talk code," He suggested.

Gem immediately reverted to the 'babble' he had used as a very young child. It had been a while since he'd had to, and it was awkward for the first few minutes, but then it flowed, coming back to him like his native tongue. Which, of course, it was.

―――――

Riker walked into the room and looked at the two boys talking to each other on the monitor. Gordon, listening on a pair of earphones, shook his head and lowered the earphones to rest around his neck.

"No luck," he sighed, "we only got a few words, and then they switched to twin-speak."

"Twin-speak?"

Gordon switched the audio from the earphones to the speaker so that Riker could hear the babble.

"Sometimes twins communicate in their own language before learning English. Occasionally, they keep the language past early childhood for private conversations."

Riker listened in dismay to the twins babbling incomprehensibly to each other. "Unbelievable."

―――――

Mary Saunders, the social worker, had said that Gem referred to himself as 'Gem' or 'we' when he was young. She knew more about his history than any other person. It was time for Riker to meet her face to face.

Riker went to the Social Services office to meet with her. She met him at the reception desk and took him to a conference room to talk. She was a plain woman, her very red lipstick not hiding her mannish features. But she had a comfortable, pleasant manner that put Riker at ease.

Riker handed Mary a picture of the two boys together. It was a picture caught by the closed-circuit camera of the two of them cuddled up together asleep on the bunk, faces serene. Mary looked at it and sat down with a bang in one of the hard tubular chairs.

"What is this?" she demanded, staring at the print.

"You never once suspected there might be two of them?"

"Never! How could they hide that?"

"I understand Katie had a thing about twins. It was probably a matter of survival."

"But it isn't anywhere in the records; I'm sure of that."

"There's only one birth certificate. The deception must have started right from birth. I don't know what happened those first few years, but somehow by the time they were preschoolers, they knew they couldn't be seen together."

Mary shook her head, staring at the picture with her eyes wide in shock. "How could this be? It's impossible. How could such a young child fool everyone?"

"Normally, I'm sure they couldn't, but when Dee and Katie never gave any indication he was a twin, who would suspect?"

"I'll pull the old records. We'll have to go through them bit by bit, with new eyes, and try to figure out what was going on. This is going to be a big project."

"We're going to be doing the same on our end. We should get together occasionally to collaborate."

Mary nodded. "Two of them," she breathed, still staring at the photo. "It's incomprehensible."

———

Bethany wondered what was going on with Gem. No one knew exactly what he'd been arrested for. But they knew it must be something big. It had been a couple of days, and she figured he'd probably been transferred to juvie. But she went to the precinct anyway to see if he happened to be there still. She waited for a long time after asking about him at the front desk. The big woman at the counter told her to sit on a bench until she was called. It seemed like an awfully long wait, and she wondered if they'd forgotten about her. Eventually, she was approached by an officer whose ID tag said, 'Riker.'

"You're here for Gem?"

Bethany stood up. "Yes."

Riker motioned for her to follow him. "What's your name?"

"Bethany."

"And how do you know Gem?"

"I'm his roommate."

"I see. How long have you known him?"

"A few months. However long it's been."

"You close?"

Bethany shrugged. She didn't think she had to answer that. Riker didn't pursue it any further.

"I know you from somewhere," he said.

Bethany shook her head. She recognized him too, but she wasn't going to remind him how.

"Yeah, I do." Riker snapped his fingers. "You're the one 'owned' by the Rippers."

"Not anymore. Gem paid the debt."

"So Gem owns you now? That's why you're rooming with him?"

"No. I room with him 'cause I like him. Gem isn't like that."

Riker led her to a meeting room. Bethany was surprised not to be taken to the usual visiting area. Something was going on. Riker opened the door for her and shut it behind her.

———

Riker joined Gordon behind the observation glass to watch the reunion. Bethany stood inside the door, looking at the two boys.

"Hi, Gem," she said eventually.

"Hi, Beth," the one they had dubbed Gem 1 greeted.

"Hey, Bethany," Gem 2 said.

"I didn't know whether you would still be here. Figured you woulda been transferred to juvie by now."

She didn't make any comment about there being two boys. She didn't indicate which one she was talking to.

"She already knew," Riker suggested in a low voice.

"They haven't moved me yet," Gem 2 said.

Gem 1 paced, looking anxious and uncomfortable. Riker wondered if Gem 1 was the only one who took downers, or if Gem 2 ever got freaked out too. Had they both been medicated? Only one? Which had Riker taken to the hospital that day?

"Are you feeling okay?" This time, the question was directed at Gem 1.

"Yeah. Your leg feelin' better?"

"Under control now." She looked at Gem 2. "I haven't seen you for a while. Were you taking care of him when he was sick?"

Gem 2 shook his head. "Just lying low."

"You've lost weight too."

Gem 2 shrugged. Riker had noticed the weight difference between the two. They had also seen that Gem 2 was restricting his intake and Gem 1 eating more, to equalize their weights.

"Gem 1 was the one who was catatonic in hospital," Riker decided. "That's why his weight is lower."

Bethany looked toward the observation mirror awkwardly. "So, I guess your secret's out, huh?"

"Does everybody outside know?" Gem 1 demanded. "I don't want the gang and everybody to know..."

Bethany hesitated. Thrasher had asked her to find out about Gem. But she wasn't owned by the Rippers anymore. She owed more to Gem than to Thrasher. He had given Bethany her life back.

"They don't know yet... I won't say anything if you don't want me to," she agreed.

"Thanks."

They all stood looking at each other, saying nothing, all aware of the observers behind the mirror. Riker gave them a few minutes to restart the conversation, but an unspoken agreement had passed between the three, and they said nothing more. Riker went back and opened the door. The two boys were cuffed and removed from the room. Riker motioned for Bethany to sit down.

Bethany hesitated, then sat.

"You knew he was twins?" Riker questioned.

Bethany frowned. "I... wasn't surprised," she hedged.

"You're the first one."

She shrugged.

"Why weren't you surprised?" Riker persisted.

"It was like he had two moods. They were so different; I started thinking about them as two separate people. I never really thought, 'maybe he's a twin,' but it made sense when I saw them."

"And you can tell them apart?"

"I can usually tell as soon as he walks into the room."

"Do you see one of them more than the other?"

"I don't see much of the quiet one." She looked uncertain. "Do they have different names?"

"Apparently not. We're using Gem 1 and Gem 2."

"Which is which?"

"The quiet one is Gem 2."

"Gem 2 isn't around a lot. Not with the door open, anyway. They have fire escape access."

"So you knew someone was coming and going at night?"

"Suspected."

"You never asked about it?"

"We agreed to get a place together when he was quiet—Gem 2, I guess. Then Gem 1 freaked out about it later. I said I didn't care what his secret was. So I couldn't really ask him about the things that went on."

"Were there other things that were strange?"

Bethany shrugged uncomfortably. "With Gem, there's always something going on."

Riker studied Bethany. "You know more than you let on."

"I gotta go. I'm not in trouble or anything...?"

"No. I'll take you back up to the front."

"How long is Gem going to be here?"

"I'm not sure. It's been very educational having them around here."

CHAPTER EIGHTEEN

MARY FLIPPED THROUGH THE dusty files, trying to figure out whether to start at the beginning or the end. She began with the first file to look at the first complaint.

Gem—the twins—had been toddlers. A neighbor had made a complaint about prolonged crying. A social worker had followed up and seen no reason for concern. Complaints had been made regularly over the next year. Nuisance stuff that could never be verified. Suspicions. Gem had seen doctors regularly who saw nothing to be concerned about. There weren't deep bruises or broken bones—just bumps on the head, antibiotics for infections; normal kid stuff.

The first major incident was a near-drowning. Kate said it had been Dee, and that she was gone for good. She had refused to take Gem to the doctor, against the advice of the police and the social worker who followed up.

There had been worries about possible brain damage from lack of oxygen.

Riker started at the opposite end of the timeline.

He started with two columns, with Gem 1 and Gem 2 at the top. He had to figure out which boy had committed which crimes.

They had decided to prosecute using conspiracy charges since one boy had always alibied the other, but Riker wanted to know in his own mind who had done what.

Gem 1 had been the one catatonic in the hospital and was the one who had gotten into a fight with the drunk pimp. If he reacted like that to a pimp, he was probably the one who had been in Raphael's shop. But Riker couldn't see any way to prove it yet.

Riker didn't think that Gem had been in on the Angeletti murder. There was no evidence pointing to him.

But there was the bank heist. Riker would have to scrutinize the two tapes to see if he could find a clue which boy had pulled the heist and which had threatened Bernard.

———

Gem was finding being around Himself twenty-four hours a day difficult. It was comforting, but at the same time, it was stressful. He was used to taking great pains to hide his secret. Having it out in the open was unnerving.

Eventually, he was moved to juvie, as Bethany had predicted. Gem was still allowed to stay with Himself, in a locked cell without contact with the rest of the inmates. But he suspected it would not be long before they separated him and moved him in with the general population.

———

Gem had been removed from Katie's custody a couple of times for various cognitive tests while a preschooler. The results were inconsistent. Mary wondered if it was because two different boys had been tested.

One test had shown below-average cognitive ability. Pretty significant delays. But the next tests showed the opposite. Some minor delays, but on many of the tests, advanced intelligence. The tests only made sense if they were different kids.

He'd started school on schedule. Lots of truancy; he hadn't made it to school regularly. His marks had been low. Teachers had major problems keeping him under control. Social workers had visited him at school and had talked to Kate at home.

But they had been unable to discover the source of his behavioral problems.

———

The door opened and, instead of it being a corrections officer bringing him a meal, it was one of the administrators. Her name tag said only 'Schienberg.'

"You're free to come and go according to the day's schedule. Any trouble and you'll go to solitary. I don't want to hear your names mentioned in the daily logs unless it's for exemplary behavior." She studied her clip-boarded records with a stern frown. "You can't both go by the same name."

Gem looked at her steadily, saying nothing.

"Which of you goes by Gem?"

"I do," Gem and Himself said together.

She glared. "Pick another name." Gem shook his head. She pointed to him. "You're Gem." And to Himself. "You're Johnson. Got it?"

He didn't say anything. Schienberg nodded and walked back out, leaving the door to the cell open. Gem walked out, and He went in the opposite direction.

———

Gem wandered into the common room and looked around anxiously. It was immediately apparent that he was going to have to get in with a group. An organized gang, maybe. Or an unorganized group that watched each other's backs. Relationships in juvie were tentative, dissolving at the slightest provocation.

"Greenie on deck," someone commented, looking at Gem.

Gem folded his arms and braced himself.

"Who are you?"

"Gem Johnson."

"Yeah? What are you in for?"

Gem shrugged. "You know. Gang stuff."

"You're in a gang?"

"Rippers."

"Yeah? They got a few inside here."

Gem already had a backing, then. He nodded.

The boy looked him up and down. "If you're lying about being a Ripper, we'll know pretty quick."

"Yeah."

The boy nodded. "I'm Jordan," he said, sticking out his hand. Gem clasped hands warily, cautious of a trick. Jordan could shake hands with one hand and pull a knife with the other.

But Jordan didn't. Not this time.

CHAPTER NINETEEN

GEM WAS TAKEN TO the hospital for a series of tests. He objected, but they had subpoenas, which apparently meant that he didn't have any choice. He had a full day of x-rays, physical exams, CAT scans, and of course, the obligatory psychiatric interviews.

He hated the psychiatrists the worst of all. And this time, they knew his secret and asked detailed questions. Questions no one had a right to be asking him.

———

Jordan watched Gem covertly in the common room, wondering what was going through his mind. Word from the Rippers on the outside was that Gem had valuable talents. But the Rippers hadn't figured out that he was identical twins. Gem was going to have a harder time getting away with anything on the inside, where everybody knew his secret. A phony alibi wouldn't cut it anymore.

They had learned that Gem would not talk about being twins. Both twins went by the same name, and neither would admit to the other's existence. It made for some interesting conversations in the beginning, but eventually, everyone was learning to play along with him.

"Did you hear about the fight?" Jordan asked Gem as he moved farther into the room.

"What fight?" Gem questioned, immediately engaged.

"In the yard, tomorrow at exercise."

"Who?"

"Alliance against Others."

The Alliance included the Rippers and some other allies. "A rumble?" Gem asked.

"Well, as close as we can get in here. You gotta move fast and hit hard because it won't last long. CO's will have it broken up in no time. But it's something."

Gem nodded, understanding. "I'll be there," he acknowledged.

―――――

Riker carefully filed the medical reports that they had been able to gather. More information, more ammunition against Gem.

The x-rays taken while he was in juvie showed that it was Gem 1 who had broken his arm recently, and was, therefore, the one who had been in the drunk tank when Cairns was killed. Which meant that Gem 2 had been Cairns's killer.

Riker added it to his chart.

The x-rays also showed that Gem 1 had an old skull fracture a year or two old. Riker didn't know where he had gotten it, but it might be important information further down the line.

Both boys had plenty of older, healed breaks.

―――――

The brain scans had baffled the neurologist who looked at them. He would say little for sure other than that they were both 'abnormal' and that he would expect Gem 1 to be significantly impaired mentally. Riker didn't disagree. The psychiatrist had been very excited about his interviews with the boys.

"I doubt if there's even a word for their personality disorder," he enthused. "I'd like to have a chance to interview them again, maybe be part of their ongoing treatment."

"You'll have to arrange that with the facility. Did you learn anything from them?"

"Well, neither one was willing to give me any information, but just talking with them was fascinating. The one you call Gem 1; I would peg him as the most disturbed. I don't think he really even understands that they are twins. He never says, 'we' or 'us,' it is always 'I' and 'me.' He never used the plural once. When you ask him about his twin, or his other self, or other body, or anything, you don't get anywhere. He keeps denying it. But when I asked him about how he could have such good alibis, how he could be two places at once, he thought about it and said that he had 'a special gift.'"

Riker laughed. "A gift. Well, that's one word for it."

"Yes. He gets confused and emotional quickly. Very anxious."

Riker nodded. "Yeah. We noticed that. How about the other?"

"Gem 2 talks carefully, deliberately. I speculate that he is fully aware of their situation, but he sticks to Gem 1's story so that it is harder to tell them apart. Gem 1 talks naturally, he is more extroverted. He may be confused, but it doesn't stop him from forging on ahead. Gem 2 weighs every word, is painstakingly careful how he responds. I am sure he also suffers from some degree of personality disorder, but not nearly as badly as Gem 1."

"What would your diagnosis be?"

The doctor pondered. "I don't know. If I did not know their background and history, or that they were twins, I would probably end up diagnosing schizophrenia, for lack of something more specific. But I don't know if that would be accurate. There is also some hint of splintered personalities."

"Multiple Personality Disorder," Riker contributed.

"Right, MPD or DID but that's not quite accurate either. You see, when a child is abused that has a predisposition to MPD, the splintered personalities or dissociative state are for protection, to keep their sanity. The child cannot deal with what is happening to them, so it happened to someone else. But Gem is not like that. He can't remember because it *did* happen to someone else. In abusive homes with a number of children, the various children may take on exaggerated roles, depending on their predisposition. One, usually the eldest, becomes the protector. Another may be a perpetual victim. The youngest or most vulnerable child may be forced to stay in a subordinate role, never allowed to grow up emotionally."

The doctor stopped talking, considering.

"And then there's Gem," Riker said.

"Yes. He's neither one, but maybe a combination of the two. He doesn't have to create another personality to take the abuse. The other personality is already there. Both boys have developed certain parts of their personalities while neglecting others. Each one fills out the deficiencies in the other. They work as one full unit. Without each other, I don't think they could function fully."

"Gem 1 is more vulnerable, so Gem 2 becomes the protector. Gem 2 is more intelligent, so he is the planner and Gem 1 is the action man. Gem 1 is extroverted, and Gem 2 is introverted."

The psychiatrist nodded.

"Yes, exactly. Not two identities in one child, but one full identity in two children."

———

Riker opened the courier packet eagerly. It was photocopied medical documents, the hospital reports on the kids rescued from Raphael's shop. He flipped through, looking for Gem's records. There were pictures stapled to the top right corner of each chart. He saw the picture of the hooker who had admitted to knowing Gem in Rafe's shop, the one who had lost her contacts. She was just a child. Seeing her on the street with makeup and grown-up clothes a couple of years later, he hadn't realized how young she really was. Riker flipped quickly past. They were children, some of them shockingly young. They were all dressed in hospital robes that didn't hide how thin and frail they were. They had the hollow look of Holocaust survivors. Some had fat lips or black eyes.

One girl was different. She was dressed in a hospital robe like the others, but was lying in bed, intubated, her eyes closed. Surgical tape obscured part of her face but didn't hide an ugly, disfiguring scar. He glanced through the chart. She had extensive internal injuries. There was a time of death notation at the bottom. Riker turned to the next chart. He found Gem's and glanced over it.

Gem had been treated for a skull fracture and concussion. Riker smiled and noted it on his chart. Their x-rays showed that Gem 1 had a healed skull fracture. So he had confirmation it was Gem 1 who had been imprisoned in Rafe's shop, and therefore Gem 2 who had killed Rafe. He browsed the rest of the notations on Gem's chart. Gem had to be restrained and was calling for someone named Honey. Riker frowned and flipped back to the dead girl's chart. Honey.

What was their connection, and how had they both been injured so severely? Riker flipped through the other charts, skimming their diagnoses. There were some serious concerns—starvation, infection, active AIDS, plenty of STDs; but no other injuries like Gem's and Honey's. It wouldn't make sense for Rafe to put his assets out of commission.

Which led to the question: What had Honey and Gem done to infuriate Raphael to the point of nearly killing both of them?

CHAPTER TWENTY

GEM WAS SO HYPED up about the fight that he could not be still. He paced across his cell restlessly after lights out, wondering if he was going to be able to sleep. He talked to Himself, anxious.

"Who should my targets be? I have to go after the right people to get in tight with the Alliance."

"Are all the bosses going to be there? Or will they protect themselves?"

"I don't know. I don't know what usually happens."

"Then I have to have more than one target. Primaries and secondaries. Even if the bosses are there, they will be protected. I'll probably have to hit the others. People that give the Alliance a tactical advantage. People that the Other bosses rely on. Disable the bosses by disabling key men."

Gem nodded to Himself. "Yeah, that's it. That's a good plan."

Gem listed off some of the names that he could think of. He added a few more and then prioritized them.

Gem was surprised at some of the priorities in the end, but He had been watching and studying. Gem trusted Himself that those were the right priorities. Now Gem knew who to watch for in the yard, who to get close to when the time came.

Gem did sleep for a couple of hours before morning came. Then he had to wait until mid-morning before exercise. The tension in the yard was electric. Everybody was hyped and watchful. He was amazed that the CO's didn't sense it. It was obvious that something was going down.

Gem watched for a signal. He didn't know what protocol was usually followed, but from his observation of the Alliance leadership so far, he sensed that there would be a formal signal. It wasn't up to any of the lower-level gang members to throw the first punch. He was rewarded with the sight of King moving purposefully across the yard to talk to Hallem, the leader of the Others.

King started with insults and catcalls, and Hallem was happy to get things moving by throwing the first punch. The CO's were walking towards the boys to break them up when the air exploded around them. Gem spotted one of his priority targets and moved in. He was happy to be part of the rumble. It seemed like a long time since he had been in a good fight. Fighting was a good way to release built-up tension and anxiety.

He kept a careful eye on Alliance members around him in case someone needed a hand and watched for higher priority targets in case he got the chance to strike.

Jordan was right when he said that the fight would not last long. Alarms started ringing immediately. Before long, CO's were flooding into the yard. Gem did not think that they had much of a chance of halting the fight, but he did not take into account their experience in crowd control. This wasn't the first rumble in the yard. The CO's waded into the fighters with billies and pepper spray, aiming both for vulnerable faces and eyes. As soon as a fighter went down, covering his face, he was restrained with heavy duty plastic zips around wrists and ankles. The CO's moved quickly but deliberately through the fray, taking down the fighters as swiftly as possible.

The experienced juvies knew enough not to fight the CO's. When a CO approached, they would drop to the ground without needing further encouragement, allowing themselves to be restrained. Gem saw the merit of taking this action rather than getting sprayed or a broken nose. When a CO got too close to him, hit the ground. If the gang leaders were doing it, there was no shame in lying down instead of getting beaten. One of the CO's kicked him while he was on the ground, but Gem just lay motionless and was zip-tied and left alone. As things started to quiet down, those of them who hadn't been too severely injured sat up to gauge which gang had sustained the worse damage. It became apparent that some of the fighters on the ground were not getting back up. Questions rippled through the crowd. Who was down and who had taken them down?

The first question was answered quickly. Sheldon, Hallem's tactical man, was among those not getting back up. So was Richards, one of the leaders of the lesser gangs. The third was a young member of the Alliance, not worthy enough for them to even know his name. And who downed them? Gem knew that there were enough people in the yard that someone must have seen, and he kept his counsel.

Before long, members of both gangs were looking at him with new respect, eyebrows raised. *It was you? You downed Sheldon and Richards?* Gem just smiled and kept his mouth shut.

The CO's broke into two groups. One to look after the needs of the downed fighters, if anything could be done, and one to start clearing the restrained fighters out. They took the boys one at a time, frisking them for weapons, removing the leg restraints, and taking them back to their cells, asking questions along the way. It was going to take a while.

Eventually, one of the CO's grabbed Gem and pulled him to his feet. His toe sent a makeshift blade spinning across the concrete. The CO picked it up.

"This yours?" he demanded.

"I fought clean," Gem protested indignantly.

The CO twisted Gem's hands around to look at them. "Your knuckles aren't bruised," he pointed out. "You weren't bare-knuckle fighting."

Gem hadn't thought about that. "It isn't mine," he said lamely, knowing that no one would believe it.

"Yeah, right."

The CO motioned to another, who appeared to be in charge.

"Here's one of them," he offered, handing over the shiv. "One of the twins."

"Which one?"

"Who can tell? We'll charge them both like the cops are doing."

Gem was taken, not back to his cell, but to an isolation cell. He wasn't surprised. The CO shoved him in.

"You're marked now," he warned. "We all know that you stabbed one of those boys. We'll be watching you. Not just staff, but the Others too."

Gem sat down on the bare bunk to relax.

———

Bruno bagged the homemade knife and looked around for the other Johnson twin. He was on the other side of the group. Bruno approached him and lifted him to his feet.

"You got one too?" he demanded.

"One what?" the boy asked coolly.

Bruno didn't bother answering. He scanned the ground and started kicking the other fighters out of the way. A shiv identical to the first was under one of them. Bruno picked it up and bagged it, smiling at the boy.

"We got you both," he said smugly. He took a look at the boy's hands to be sure. They were a little scraped, but he still could have fought with his fists for a minute until he got his chance and then pulled the blade. Bruno passed the two knives off to one of the other CO's.

"See if those can be matched to the wounds," he instructed.

He cut the boy's legs free, patted him down in case he was carrying another weapon, and pushed him forward.

"Let's go."

The boy was studying the downed fighters from his new vantage point. Bruno shoved him harder.

"Yeah, they're both dead. The kid may make it, but the other two have served their time. Now let's go."

The boy allowed himself to be escorted down to the isolation cells.

———

Gordon hung up the phone just as Riker came back to his desk.

"That was juvie," Gordon said. "Sorry, I didn't know how long you'd be."

"What were they calling about?"

"Filing charges against the twins."

"Gem? What for?"

"Murder. A gang fight apparently."

"Which one?"

"Both of them went into it armed. Two kids killed. They're charging them each with both murders."

Riker shook his head. "They just don't get it, do they? They don't understand they can't get away with it anymore."

———

He was okay for the first day or two. He stayed calm and just thought and meditated and was fine. But after the first few days, isolation started to get to Him. He didn't know what to do with himself. The time dragged on and on.

Gem had been through worse. He had no call to complain about a few days in an isolation cell. Gem had suffered through all kinds of confinement. But He was climbing the walls in a juvie isolation cell.

He was sure that the CO was late bringing his dinner. The time dragged and dragged. When the key turned in the lock, He was out of the bunk and the two steps to the door. The CO swung the door open and, seeing how close He was to the door, the guard's hand moved to his holster.

"Get back, Johnson," the CO barked. "Go sit down on the bunk."

He didn't move. "How long am I gonna be in here?"

"Who knows? You getting cabin fever?"

He shrugged sheepishly, but still didn't move back to the bunk. He was starving for human interaction.

"Your twin doesn't seem to mind."

"Of course not," He snapped, and then bit His lip. He knew He should be more careful what He said. He wasn't supposed to let on that they were two separate people. But everybody knew already. And He was desperate for conversation.

"Why is that?" the CO inquired, looking curious and willing to shoot the breeze for a few minutes.

He knew Gem would be beside himself if He talked, but He couldn't help it. "Gem's been worse places."

"What's worse than this?" the CO gestured to the bare cell, windowless, with one bare bulb, an unpadded bunk, and a seatless toilet.

He thought of the Hole. A root cellar or crawlspace beneath one of Raphael's shop locations. Gem described it in graphic detail so that He could almost feel the grit of the dirt on his skin: four walls and a floor of cold, damp earth. No bunk. No light except for an occasional gleam through the crack of the trapdoor out of reach overhead. No toilet but the dirt beneath his feet. Food dropped through the trapdoor like Gem was a wild animal. As close and dark and quiet as a tomb.

Gem had been terrified and alone. He remembered with shame feeling his twin's terror, but being too afraid to do anything. He could have sneaked in at night, found the ladder to put down the Hole and brought Gem to safety. But He didn't. He was too afraid of being caught, of being found out and jailed there with Gem. So He stayed away from the shop and didn't take the chance of being seen.

Until the only options left were to kill Raphael or let Gem die.

"When we were little, our ma used to lock Gem up," He told the CO, electing not to tell him about the Hole. "Tie him up, lock him in a closet...worse than this."

"Yeah? She didn't lock you up too?"

"I learned how to untie the knots, stay away. Gem never did."

Sometimes He would untie Gem. Or take him food. He could have helped more, but He preferred to stay away. Avoid Ma's insanity and Gram's wrath. Look after Himself first, his twin only if things were getting too bad. Gem thought that He always helped if He could, but it wasn't true. He only put himself in danger if

Gem was in dire straits. He would ignore it when He felt Gem's feelings.

But since Rafe... that had changed things. The guilt of letting Gem suffer so long and nearly letting him die was enough to force Him to take chances, to ally himself with Gem more often. To be Gem's protector even when Gem had stupidly put himself in danger.

"So he got used to being locked up," the CO said.

He nodded. "And there's been other times too. In restraints in the hospital. Doped up on antipsychotics so he couldn't move. Things happen to him."

"So this," the CO motioned again to the isolation cell, "is a walk in the park for him. He's laughing."

He nodded again. "Yeah."

"You hungry, Johnson?"

"Uh-huh."

"Then go sit on your bunk, or I'll take this back out to the garbage."

He obeyed. The CO put the tray down on the floor and closed the door again.

———

Mike picked up the next tray off of his cart and opened the other twin's cell. They were side-by-side and probably didn't even know it.

The other Gem was lying on his back on the hard bunk, hands behind his head, like he was lying in the sun in a hammock instead of on a narrow bench in a windowless room. He raised his head when Mike opened the door and put the tray down, but didn't get up. As the other twin said, this was nothing to him. He was at the Ritz. They could probably leave him in there for a year, and he would still only curiously raise his head and put it back down again. Mike couldn't even tell that Gem's wrists were still cuffed together; he looked totally natural. They'd had to release the other twin from restraints the first day; he was so freaked out even though his hands had been chained in front and not behind his body, with a good length of chain that allowed for freedom of movement. For one that was bliss. For the other, torture.

Mike shut the door again and shook his head. When he was finished distributing lunches, he penciled two notes to the administration concerning the boys, put them in an interoffice envelope, and threw them in his outgoing mail.

CHAPTER TWENTY-ONE

T HEY TOLD RIKER THAT the twins wouldn't be moved out of isolation for a few more days yet, but if he wanted to check in on them, he could talk to the CO in isolation. Riker introduced himself to a laconic man named Mike and asked how soon the boys would be released.

"I don't call it. I can make recommendations, but it's them upstairs that decide who gets out when. Of course, they'll tell you they don't know either."

"They already did," Riker agreed.

"The one, I think he'll be out soon. Maybe even today. He's climbing the walls. The last thing we need is a kid who's prepared to throttle the first person he can get his hands on because he's so squirrelly from being locked up in iso."

"Which one is he?"

"We can't keep them straight. Need to put bracelets on them or something. Colored ear tags, maybe," he joked. "He's the smarter one. Usually calmer."

"Gem 2. He's climbing the walls? I would have thought Gem 1 would be."

"No way. He's been locked away so many times, he probably thinks he's in his mother's womb. He's more anxious when he's walking around free than in here."

"Who told you he'd been locked up before?"

"Number 2. Like I said, he's getting cabin fever. Wants someone to talk to." Mike lowered his voice, "We're not supposed to talk to them at all. But sometimes, when they're in here, and they start talking, you can learn a lot."

"And he told you Gem 1 had been locked up a lot before."

"Yeah. By their mama, and in the nuthouse, and so on. Number 2 says he learned how to escape when their mama locked them up, but Gem 1 never did."

"Really. Well, that's more than I ever got out of him. Can I see him for a bit?"

Mike pursed his lips. "I'm not supposed to do any more than give you a report," he said carefully, "But if you were to exercise your authority and say you wanted proof that they were both safely locked away here…"

Riker smiled. "I'm afraid I really do need to see," he said firmly.

"Well, then I guess I'd better show you."

Mike unlocked one of the cells. Riker stepped into the doorway. Gem 2 stepped towards him and looked confused. "Riker? What're you doing here?"

"Just checking up on you. Looks like you're doing okay."

Gem 2 shifted his stance. "I'm goin' nuts in here. I can't stand it. Couldn't you tell them to let me out?"

"I don't have any authority here." Riker turned as if to leave, then paused. "How much do you know about what happened to your brother in Raphael's shop?"

Gem 2 hesitated. "I know pretty much everything," he admitted.

"Yeah? What happened with him and Honey before they got out?"

The indecision in the boy's face was almost comical. He clearly felt he shouldn't talk about it, but he wanted to keep Riker there. "Gem and Honey were real close."

"Intimate?"

"In there? No way. They talked. Took care of each other."

"And what happened that last day?"

"I shouldn't talk about it."

"Oh. Well, I'll be going, then," Riker turned to leave.

"No, wait! I'll tell you, but you can't let him know that I said anything."

"Okay."

"Raphael used Honey to control Gem. Because Gem liked her. So if he got out of line, Rafe would hurt her. Rafe..." Gem motioned to his face where Honey's scar had been.

"He cut her?" Riker finished.

Gem 2 looked surprised. "Yeah. How'd you know?"

"I saw her picture. Nasty piece of work."

"Yeah, he was. So Gem behaved for a while after that. Didn't cause any major trouble. But then he got in a fight with a John."

"A fight over what?"

Gem 2 rolled his eyes over Riker's naiveté.

"Some guys like to get rough. When partners are into BDSM, they have safe words, so no one gets hurt—more than they want— right? It ain't like that in a place like Rafe's. You take what they dish out. No one's gonna come running if you scream. And if you get throttled, no one will know 'til it's too late. Gem wasn't too good at taking abuse."

"So he fought back in self-defense."

"Broke the John's nose, among other things. Guy had to be carried out. Rafe was furious. The John was a high roller. It wasn't the first time Gem hurt a good client. The time before; that's when Rafe slashed Honey."

"And this time, he beat her."

"With a pipe. In the chest and belly. Gem broke away from the thugs and went after Rafe, and got his head laid open with the pipe. Just about killed him. He woulda died if the cops hadn't shown up."

And that was when Gem 2 had taken action and killed Rafe, removing the threat and getting help for his prisoners.

"Why did Raphael hang on to Gem, if he was such a problem?"

Gem 2 considered his answer. "He was popular with Johns. Always in demand. He had a quality that men liked. Worth his weight in gold, if you could keep him in line."

Riker shook his head. "What a nasty business. Makes me sick."

Gem 2 studied him, shaking his head. "I don't get it."

"What do you mean?"

"What do you care what happened to Gem in Rafe's shop? What are you even doing here?"

"I thought you were enjoying our visit."

"I'm glad to have someone to talk to," Gem 2 agreed quickly, not in a hurry to end the interview. "I just don't know why you care."

"I want to get the two of you safely put away where you belong. But I'm not out for vengeance. If you belong in prison, that's where you're going. If you—or one of you—belongs in a mental facility, then that's where you'll go."

"No."

"No?"

"No more asylums. Juvie, fine. But not another nuthouse."

"Was it you in the rest home or your brother?" Riker asked curiously.

"Gem. Not me."

"So what happened there that was so horrible?"

Gem 2's brow creased. "They tried to... erase us... him, I mean. Take away what we... I... was."

"With drugs."

"Yeah. And hypnosis and stuff. They would change us... him... me... whichever you put in that place. They change you."

"That's the whole point, isn't it?"

"Don't try to change us."

Riker raised his hands with a shrug. "I have to do whatever is right. You enjoy your stay here. I'll pop by again if you're still here in a day or two."

"Don't go!" Gem 2 protested, stepping forward to stop Riker. "I'll tell you more."

"I've got other things to do. I only have a few minutes."

Gem 2 tried to stop him or get past him. Riker grappled with him for a moment. Mike came to his aid.

"You wanna be put back in cuffs, Johnson?"

Gem 2 backed off slightly. "No."

"Then go sit down."

Gem 2 was unwilling, but he didn't want to be handcuffed again either. He dragged his feet over to the bunk and sat down dispiritedly. Mike closed and locked the door.

"You want to talk to the other one?"

"It's worth a try."

He opened the next cell. Gem 1 was face down on the floor... doing pushups. He glanced up at Riker and then stared back down at the floor again.

"What're you doing here?"

"Just came for a visit. How's it going?"

"It's going just fine."

Riker watched him for a moment. "I hear you and your brother have been getting in some trouble."

Gem 1 grunted as he lowered himself toward the floor. "They say I stuck a couple of guys in a rumble," he acknowledged.

"You, or your brother?"

"I don't have any brother."

"So you killed both of them yourself."

"If that's what they say."

"Why did you do it? They look the wrong way at you in the shower?"

Gem 1 sat back on his knees, his face flushing dark. "What are you saying?"

"I want to know why you did it."

"You think they were scoping me out?"

"Well, you do seem to be awfully sensitive in that department."

Gem 1 scowled. "They were gang targets. Nothing personal."

"So you're in with a gang in here already?"

"Rippers are already here. I'm a Ripper."

Gem 1 leaned back on the floor and started doing sit-ups. "That all you're here for?" he questioned. "Because I got better things to do than talk to you."

Riker nodded. "That's all. Just talking to you and your brother."

Gem 1 kept up his sit-ups. It didn't seem to occur to him that his twin might say something he shouldn't.

As Riker approached the police station, he noticed a girl going up the stairs on crutches. He looked at her for a moment, trying to think of who she was. He couldn't get Honey's name out of his mind and shook his head. Then he remembered. He was associating her with Honey because they both had connections with Gem.

"Hey," he greeted, walking up to her, "I don't remember your name."

"Bethany."

"That's right. Bethany. You here to see Gem?"

"Is he still here?"

"No. He's in juvie now."

Bethany sighed and leaned on her crutches. "Well, then, there's no point climbing these stairs."

"No, I guess not. Do you know, you bear a striking resemblance to someone? You don't have a sister, do you?" She started to shake her head. "Or used to have," Riker corrected himself.

Bethany stopped shaking her head. "Used to have?" she repeated.

"She's dead, the girl you remind me of."

Bethany didn't say anything for a moment. "I don't have a sister," she said at last, voice firm. Subject closed.

"Just a coincidence, I guess."

"So will they let me see Gem in juvie?"

"Not today. He's—they're—in solitary."

Bethany nodded. "Okay, thanks."

———

Gem stretched his legs after getting out of solitary. He wanted to talk to the Alliance and see how his rep had improved. He looked for Jordan or one of the members he was more familiar with. Before he got far, Dixon, one of King's lieutenants, was approaching him.

"Johnson. He wants to see you."

King himself wanted to see him. Gem took it as a good sign. He followed Dixon to King's cell. King was sitting talking to one of his other lieutenants but finished up when he saw Gem, motioning him away.

"Johnson." King stood up and clasped hands with Gem. "I heard you got out of iso."

"Yeah." Obviously.

King sat back down and studied Gem. "You knew you'd get caught, didn't you?"

"I knew I might. Ditched the blade and thought I might not, but..." He shrugged.

"Why would you do two murders, knowing you'd get caught? And knowing that someone would see you?"

"For the Alliance."

King nodded briefly. "You picked good targets. They're already scrambling, weakened. We disable another man or two while they're off balance, and we might be able to get absolute control."

Gem was pleased. He'd been nervous, not wanting to take the risk without knowing for sure that the other gangs would be compromised. But he trusted Himself. He was smart.

"You took a risk you didn't have to, and you did a good turn for the Alliance. We won't forget it. Word on the outside was that you would be an asset, but I don't trust anyone's word 'til I see it with my own eyes. You're a good soldier. I'll be watching for opportunities to use you again. But don't take any chances in the meantime. Keep a low profile."

Gem nodded. "Sure. Thanks."

"You're going to have to watch out for the Others. We'll do our best to protect you, but they ain't gonna be happy to see you. You can expect them to try to get revenge."

"Yeah. I'll look out."

"Good."

King turned his attention to the next matter of Alliance business, and Dixon motioned for Gem to leave.

CHAPTER TWENTY-TWO

LOOKING AFTER HIMSELF PROVED more difficult than Gem had expected. He was frisked any time he went into a common room or entered or left the cafeteria. He took lessons from the older Alliance boys on places to hide a blade where the CO's would be less likely to find it frisking him casually. But then, of course, it was harder for him to get at if he needed it.

And he was getting strip-searched frequently. Gem didn't mind so much if the CO's were professional about it, and most of the more experienced ones were. But some of the CO's thought they had something to prove. Gem hated the ones who teased about his boyish physique—or worse, threatened to take advantage of him. So far, they had done nothing more than groping him under cover of a thorough search. But he saw the looks in their eyes and knew that one day, instead of a pair searching him as regulations said, it would be one of the CO's alone, and with a gun in Gem's face or back, he would be helpless to protect himself. He knew that day would come.

Gem hung around with the Alliance members who kept themselves armed. Those who hadn't been caught armed recently were not searched as often as Gem. One of the boys was nicknamed Colt for the revolver that he had somehow managed to get smuggled into juvie and often carried with him. Gem spent a lot of time around him, hoping to learn something of Colt's considerable talents.

Gem was jostled from behind in the cafeteria. He dropped his tray with a clatter, holding on to his plate with one hand and his utensils in the other.

Gem turned quickly to gauge the height of his attacker and threw the plate of hot food like a Frisbee into his face. Then he drove the fork forward with as much force as he could muster. He didn't even know who it was; he just moved as fast as he could to protect himself.

Gem stayed clinched with the boy, holding him tightly until iron hands pulled them apart. His hand was covered with blood.

The CO threw him to the floor and, with his knee in Gem's back, frisked and cuffed him. Gem could hear the other boy screaming that he was going to die, and doubted he'd be screaming so loudly if he were mortally wounded.

Gem was pulled to his feet.

"Who started this?" the CO demanded.

"He hit me from behind," Gem said, angry but in control.

"I never touched him! Maybe I bumped him, but I never hit him!" the other boy protested.

Gem let the CO take him back to his cell. They didn't put him in iso yet, but they would before long.

"You just can't keep out of trouble, can you?" the CO demanded, and shoved him in.

Gem sat down on his bunk to wait.

Schienberg entered the infirmary. She could hear Birks screaming two hallways away and had no trouble finding him. The doctor was trying to bandage him up. Schienberg shook her head.

"Let me see before you cover that."

The doctor peeled back the bandage and Schienberg looked at the ugly wound. It was still bleeding pretty badly. She shook her head.

"You'd better have him transported to the hospital. It's deep, needs stitches, and who knows what kind of bacteria was on that fork."

"I'm gonna die," Birks bellowed.

"If you were going to die, you'd at least be unconscious by now. Stop your yelling."

"It hurts!"

"They'll give you something at the hospital. Now quit being such a baby or I'll tell the other boys you were barely even scratched."

"Oooh," he subsided to a more reasonable moan.

"Do you think this was another gang hit?" Schienberg asked one of the CO's supervising Birks.

"Not likely. They're both Alliance. Probably just Johnson being too jumpy. Or it's something personal."

"I never did nothing to him," Birks whined.

"Well then, I suggest you avoid him in the future."

———

As Gem expected, he wasn't left in his regular cell for long. The door opened, and it was Schienberg and a CO the juvies referred to as Mutt. Gem didn't know his real name. Gem got to his feet, so they weren't towering over him.

"I want him moved back to isolation," Schienberg ordered. "Strip him first; I don't want any incidents downstairs because he gets a weapon down to the isolation block."

"Yes'm," Mutt agreed. "I'll make sure."

"You want to tell me what happened?" Schienberg asked Gem.

"He hit me from behind. I was protecting myself."

"Well, since he wasn't holding a knife to your back, I think a fork in the gut was a slight overreaction."

"How did I know he didn't have a knife?"

"I don't want to hear that you've attacked anyone else with a weapon."

Gem shrugged. "Then you keep everyone else away from me."

"How about I keep you in isolation, away from everyone else?"

Gem nodded. "Fine."

Schienberg shrugged and shook her head. "Look after him," she told Mutt and walked out.

Gem sized Mutt up. "If you touch me…"

"What will you do? You're unarmed; I have a gun. You're a hundred pounds sopping wet; I'm two-eighty. You're in handcuffs. What does that add up to? You've got nothing to threaten me with."

"I'll make a complaint."

Mutt snorted. "Juvies make complaints every day."

"You have to take the cuffs off for me to strip."

"So? What are you going to do?"

Gem calculated the distance to his bunk, where he had a shank. Mutt had to uncuff him, so Gem would be able to pick up the knife and fight if he could get to it. He didn't think Mutt would shoot him. He'd call for backup. If he did shoot, Gem figured he'd go for a leg, not a fatal shot, and the gunfire would bring witnesses.

"Are you going to behave yourself?" Mutt questioned.

Gem nodded.

"Good." Mutt unlocked the handcuffs. "Strip down," he ordered.

Gem obeyed, waiting for Mutt to look away for an instant, bored or distracted. Watching for his chance. The end-of-lunch bell rang, and Mutt glanced out the window into the hallway. Gem dove for his bunk.

The cell was so small, Mutt was on him in an instant. Gem struggled for the knife, but Mutt knocked it to the floor, holding Gem down, swearing furiously. "You stupid kid! What do you think you're doing?"

"Protecting myself," Gem said through gritted teeth, trying to wriggle out of Mutt's iron-hard grip.

"Protect yourself from what? What do you think I'm going to do?"

Gem looked back at Mutt over his shoulder. Gem, bare as a jay, bent over the bed, with Mutt behind him, using his weight to hold him down. What did Mutt think he was afraid of?

Mutt became conscious of their positions and the look in Gem's eye. He flushed, easing off his weight a little. "You think I'm going to molest you?" he said incredulously. "What would ever make you think that?"

Gem relaxed a little, hearing the sincere astonishment in Mutt's voice.

"I'm going to get up. I don't want you to move a muscle."

Gem nodded. Mutt got up and straightened his uniform. He picked up Gem's shiv.

"You got any other shanks in that bed?" Mutt questioned.

"No."

"Sit on your bunk."

Gem turned around and sat down. Mutt threw Gem's uniform to him.

"Get dressed."

Gem was happy to comply. Once dressed, he sat down again. Mutt leaned against the wall, studying Gem.

"Who's been messing with you?"

"No one."

"Then where'd you get the idea I would?"

"Some of the CO's..."

"They touch you?"

Gem shrugged.

"Threaten you?"

Gem nodded.

"Who?"

"If I tell you names, they'll come after me."

"Not if I have anything to do with it. But I can't stop them if I don't know who they are."

"I'm not saying," Gem repeated.

Mutt growled. "You ever been bothered in iso?"

"Not yet."

"I'm taking you down there now. Then I'll see what I can do about the situation up here."

"Don't use my name."

"I'm sure if you've been threatened, others have too. They won't know it was you."

Gem let Mutt take him down to a peaceful isolation cell.

CHAPTER TWENTY-THREE

"WE HAVE A PROBLEM," Mutt said, walking into Schienberg's office. She looked up.

"Johnson?"

"A certain anonymous inmate was terrified when you left him alone with me just now, that I was going to—uh, take advantage—of him."

"From what I understand, your anonymous inmate has had a lot of experience in that department. And we all know he's not exactly stable."

"He said he'd been propositioned by some of the security staff."

"And you believe it?"

"I saw the look on his face. He was afraid."

"I'm not saying he was lying; I'm saying he was mistaken."

"You don't think we need to worry about the possibility of anything going on here."

"I think there would be a rash of complaints if sexual abuse by the staff was an issue."

"There are always complaints. How do you tell fact from fiction?"

"You watch for patterns. But I haven't seen any patterns to indicate that we have a problem."

"Why don't you do a memo reminding everyone of regulations?

Two CO's for every strip search. No verbal harassment of inmates. That kind of thing."

"Everybody will know there's been a complaint. They'll get paranoid about an internal investigation."

"Better that than to actually have an investigation."

Schienberg studied Mutt for a long moment. "You think there's something to this?"

"I saw the kid's face. I know certain of my colleagues have said inappropriate things in front of me. And if anyone were to be harassed, you can bet Johnson would be right at the top of the list."

"Why him?"

"For the reasons you mentioned. And because he hasn't hit puberty yet. And because there's just something naive and immature about him."

"I assume he didn't name names?"

"Of course not. Would you, in his position? But I have my ideas. Like I say, people sometimes say things they shouldn't."

"And why haven't you brought any of these inappropriate comments to my attention?"

"I thought they were harmless. It didn't occur to me that kids might take them seriously or feel threatened."

Schienberg shook her head. "Let me get this straight. You think the inmates *are* in danger, or you think they *feel like* they're in danger?"

"I don't think any of the guys would follow through; I think they're just teasing. But if there's a possibility that just one of them follows through, we've got trouble on our hands. And if we've got kids here who think the corrections officers are a threat, then the CO's are in danger. Johnson had *another* shiv in his room and tried to pull it on me. You know we can't stop these kids from making weapons out of anything they can get their hands on. I don't like having to worry that they're going to be pulling shivs on me instead of each other."

"That risk is never going to go away. That's why you carry a sidearm."

"It won't go away, but normally these kids aren't going to attack someone three times their size without provocation. But if a kid thinks he's got his honor or his life to protect... he'll do it."

Schienberg sighed.

"I'll do a policy memo. And you are going to give me the names of anyone you've heard making borderline remarks. And you will let me know if you see or hear anything else after the memo goes out. No protests about ratting out your brothers. If we're going to do this, we do it right. No tolerance for harassing behavior. Verbal or otherwise."

Mutt gave a nod, acquiescing.

"And thank you for coming to me with this."

"Yes, ma'am."

"Sit down and write me a memo with those names. I want a paper trail showing that we're dealing with this."

"You're not going to mention my name or Johnson's to anyone."

"No. I protect my informants. You don't have to sign the memo."

"Thanks."

———

"Johnson."

He turned around and saw Jordan. "Yeah?"

"King, he was looking for you."

He nodded. "Where is he?"

"TV room."

"Thanks. You wanna walk with me?" He asked Colt.

Colt laughed. "You need protection to walk down one corridor?"

He shrugged and walked away. Colt trailed along behind him, snickering. When King saw Him, he started in without preamble. "Where do you get off disabling an Ally?" he demanded.

He was startled. *What* Ally? One of the victims at the rumble? "I didn't know he was an Ally," He said cautiously.

"Oh, come on. You spent half a day with Birks just the other day."

"Birks?" He repeated. "I never hit Birks."

King studied him for a minute. "It wasn't even you, was it?"

He formulated His answer. "Sometimes, I don't remember things so well."

"And you don't remember stabbing Birks with a fork, do you?"

"No... I don't remember that."

King motioned to Dixon. "Find out where the *other* one is."

"Prob'ly down to iso."

He waited to be dismissed. King looked at him and shook his head. "I don't know how you do it, man. I'd go nuts. You can go."

He took his leave.

It was easier when Gem was not around.

———

Mary had been going through a lot of records. There was no indication that anyone had ever suspected twins.

There was a transition period between his childhood school problems and his eventual running away when things started to escalate. There was still no proof that his problems stemmed from his home life, but the police began to enter the picture more and more often. The truants changed to loitering and trespassing charges. He started getting into trouble for shoplifting, drinking, and suspected gang activity.

His behavior at school became more and more bizarre. Teachers refused to let him in their classes because of the disruption.

Then finally, one day, his Gram called and asked them to commit him to the state institution. He went from there to the private nursing home, to the group home, and then disappeared, falling off their radar.

———

Bethany told them she wanted to see Gem. The CO in Visiting looked her over. "Which one do you want to see?" he asked.

Bethany shrugged. "It doesn't matter, really. Either. Both."

He pecked at his computer keyboard. "One's in isolation, so I guess that means you get the other one."

"Sure."

He directed her to the visiting area. It had recently been renovated. Once before she'd been there, and it had just been an open room with tables, where she sat down and talked, with the CO's keeping a close eye on her. Now it was like the higher security adult prisons. There were little cubicles with phones that never worked well, and they could record your conversation. Bethany went down to the end of the row as directed and sat down. At least with the two of them on opposite sides of the glass, unable to touch, she didn't have to submit to a search. She couldn't pass off a weapon with a pane of bulletproof glass between them.

Bethany sat down and waited. He was escorted to the other side by a CO and sat down. It was Gem 2. He touched the glass in front of him, and Bethany touched the other side. Almost like holding hands. Except they weren't. They both picked up the phones.

"Hi, Bethany."

"Hi. How're you doing?"

"Can't complain. Rippers are part of the Alliance here, so I got protection."

"Good. I was worried..."

"Nah, nothing to worry about." He glanced over his shoulder at the CO supervising, lowering his voice. "Security is all bent out of shape over something. I don't know what their problem is."

"And they're taking it out on you?"

"Not really. Just get that feeling that... pressure's building. Someone's gonna blow."

"Be careful."

"Yeah, I will. *I* don't cause trouble."

She understood the unsaid. Gem 1 did cause trouble.

"Riker said you were in solitary."

"Yeah. Well, I guess I caused a *little* trouble. But not to the CO's personally. Just, you know," he shrugged, "gang stuff."

"You okay? Being locked up in iso?"

"It freaked me out a bit," he admitted casually, as if it were long forgotten. "Sometimes... it doesn't bother me. Sometimes... it does."

"One of the CO's said you were still in iso," Bethany said carefully. Gem 2 appreciated her tact when it came to talking about his twin. He nodded, giving her a smile of approval.

"Not still, again. Yeah. I'm in iso again."

"But... now doesn't bother you."

"No. Piece of cake."

Bethany smiled, shaking her head at the bizarre conversation. "So you need anything?"

"Not that they'd let you bring! I'm okay. I'd rather be out, but it ain't so bad. I suppose I'll be behind bars for a few years, so I'd better get used to it."

"When do you go to trial? Don't you have any defense?"

"I don't even have a lawyer. Some public defender came by one day, but he was still wet behind the ears. Hasn't got a clue what to do. I don't know if they even have a trial date set."

"That isn't right. They've got to try you."

"Yeah, well, I haven't even thought about it that much. I guess I should care, but I figure it doesn't matter. They're going to convict me anyway."

"Why?"

"They know my secret," he pointed out.

"So, that should make it all the harder to prove. They can't prove which of you did what."

"They're charging on conspiracy; that means they don't have to narrow it down to one person."

Bethany frowned. "How long is—are you—in iso?"

"I don't know. A few days, at least. Why?"

"I want to help. But I want to make sure they talk to you if someone comes by."

She imagined a public defender trying to talk to Gem 1 about a defense. It would be hard enough for them to talk to Gem 2, when he had to be so careful what he said. But to talk to Gem 1, who didn't even understand that they were two separate people; that would be impossible.

"I don't see how I can defend this anyway," Gem warned Bethany.

"I know. But we have to try. If I can get someone here in the next day or two, and they talk to you... you'll try to help, won't you?"

He shrugged. "If you want me to. But I think it's hopeless."

"Okay. I'll see what I can do."

They looked at each other in silence for a few minutes, not sure what else to say. Bethany was going to say goodbye when Gem spoke up. "You need money."

"No."

"For rent, I mean. To keep the apartment. How do I give you access to the money?"

"Where is it?"

"Safety deposit box."

Bethany considered. "I don't know. I think you have to go in person, don't you? They check ID and everything?"

"Yeah."

"They won't let me at it, then."

"I'll ask the lawyer. There's gotta be a way to get your hands on it."

Bethany nodded. She pursed her lips, staring at him. "Gem..."

"Yeah?"

"How much money is there...?"

He shrugged. "Enough to keep you in the apartment until I get out, even if it's in fifty years."

Bethany paused to try to work that out in her head. Her eyes widened. "You have that much?"

"I don't spend much," Gem said with a wry smile.

"You don't have to use a public defender. You can afford to pay someone." Bethany's heart sped.

He thought about it. "I wonder..."

"At least a real lawyer would have a chance of getting you off. Maybe even get bail and get out of juvie until trial."

"And if I got out, I could raise *more* money."

Bethany nodded. "You could win."

He drummed his fingers on the table, then scratched his chin.

"Go ahead and get the public defender here," he said, "and let's see if I can get bail set without letting on that there's any money. Then we can surprise them. They won't set bail high or put a lot of time into building a case if they think they're just going against a public defender."

"If you do get out, you could just jump bail…"

Gem shook his head. "Shh," he warned, looking over his shoulder at the CO and indicating the phone by tapping on it. "They won't pass information on to the prosecutor about our defense, but if you talk about committing another crime, they could throw a wrench in the works."

Bethany nodded. "Sorry."

"Don't apologize. You're a big help."

CHAPTER TWENTY-FOUR

IN SOLITARY, GEM FOUND himself dreaming again. He dreamed of the period of time before his Gram committed him. Gem couldn't hack it at school. Not being able to do the work was the least of his problems.

The boy in a desk across the aisle from him kept looking at him. Gem was getting more and more agitated by the glances. He couldn't concentrate on the lesson. He wasn't even sure what class he was in. Finally, he stood up and confronted the boy, knocking his books to the floor with a crash.

"What're you looking at?" he demanded.

The boy's eyes widened in surprise.

The teacher stopped teaching. "Gem, take your seat," she told him firmly.

"I wanna know why he's lookin' at me!"

"Maybe because you're making a scene. Sit down or go to the office."

"He's staring at me!"

"Billy, don't stare at Gem, please. Gem, sit down."

Gem sat down slowly. The other students turned their attention back to the front of the room. The teacher tried to pick up her train of thought again. People kept looking back at Gem. Gem stood up and swept everything off his desk with a crash. "That's it!"

"Gem, go to the office!"

Gem stalked out of the room, but did not go to the office. He slammed his fist against lockers as he walked away down the hall, uncontrollably angry and confused. He didn't know where he was going or what he was going to do. He just knew he was angry and couldn't suppress it. Another teacher came out into the hallway.

"What do you think you're doing? You're disturbing classes!"

"What are you going to do about it?" Gem challenged.

The teacher approached him threateningly. "I'll take you to the office and get you suspended."

Gem swung wildly and his fist connected with the teacher's mouth. Blood poured out. Gem froze at first, staring at him, then he ran for his life.

Gem sat up with a gasp, his heart racing. He stared into the blackness, trying to remember where he was. It was pitch black. No light, no windows, but he could feel a blanket over him. It could only be jail. Gem closed his eyes and lay back down.

He was safe in isolation.

No one could hurt him there.

———

Gordon looked up from his computer when Riker got back to his desk. "New development for you."

"What's that?"

"Gem's hired a new lawyer."

"Hired?" Riker repeated.

"Yeah, hired. As in, not legal aid. He had his legal aid guy in a couple of days ago, but then today, a brand-new criminal lawyer shows up."

"Where'd he get money for a lawyer?"

Gordon shrugged. The answer was obvious. "The bank heist. Are the bills hot?"

"I already checked. They weren't marked, inked, or consecutive serial numbers. No way to trace them. But the lawyer has got to know the money is dirty."

"Sure. But if you can't prove it..."

Riker swore angrily.

Gordon shrugged and considered it. "He must have a partner."

"Yeah, his twin."

"No. An accomplice on the outside. Who is paying the lawyer? Gem doesn't have access to the money from juvie."

"The gang?"

"Would you trust one of the Rippers with the location of your loot?"

"The girl, then."

"Gotta be the girl," Gordon agreed. "And if she knows about the money, chances are she knows where it came from. She's a tough, streetwise kid. You think she's going to crack if we confront her?"

"No, but we can catch her with the money and remind her the bills are marked, and we can tell it's from the bank heist."

"But they aren't—" Gordon stopped and smiled. "Yeah, we could do that."

———

Bethany looked Gem over before speaking to him on the phone. She could see that this time, it was Gem 1. "Hey. You're back out of iso."

"Yeah. Just got out."

"Is everything okay? You look..." Bethany searched for a word other than scared. "You look worried."

Gem scratched his jaw. "I don't like being around all these people." He glanced over his shoulder. "The CO's..."

"Have they been bothering you?"

"I've only been out a couple of hours. They're... waiting. Something's going on. I don't know what they're planning."

Bethany nodded. "You said—uh, before—you said that they were uptight about something."

Gem shrugged, looking around again and then finally facing her and giving her his full focus. "I need something... a favor..." he trailed off.

"Sure, whatever you need."

"I can't give you any money, though."

"You already did. I can get whatever you need. Though, I don't know if they'll let me bring anything to you."

"I don't need something brought." Gem shifted anxiously. He looked down at his hands. "I wanted to buy flowers for a friend..."

"Oh." Bethany was unable to think of a response.

"For her grave," Gem finished.

Bethany was still. "Oh. I'm sorry. What do you want? Roses? Mums?"

Gem shook his head, his eyes distant. "Violets, if you can find them. Otherwise... anything. It doesn't matter."

Bethany could feel the blood draining from her face. She stared at him. She felt like she was looking at a ghost.

Gem frowned, uncomfortable with her gaze. "If you don't want to do it, you don't have to..."

"This girl—what was her name?" Bethany's voice was hoarse.

He drew in a deep breath and swallowed hard. "Her name was Honey."

The tears came too suddenly for Bethany to stop them.

Gem was confused. "You don't have to do it," he repeated in alarm.

"Is she the one you said I reminded you of?"

"Yes—but I told you we were just friends—and she's gone. I still—I still only have feelings for you..."

"No, it's not that. Honey is—was—my sister."

His jaw dropped. Now it was Gem who felt like he'd seen a ghost. "You said you didn't have a sister."

Bethany nodded. "Yeah. I lied."

They looked at each other, both brimming with questions.

"Did you... you knew she was dead?" Gem asked.

"Yeah. When did you know her...?"

Gem didn't answer right away. "Do you know about... before she died?" he said uncomfortably.

Bethany nodded. Gem searched her face.

"I told you about that place."

Bethany remembered. She swallowed. "You were there. You were with her when..."

"It was bad," Gem said, his voice low and rough, "it was really bad."

Tears flooded down Bethany's cheeks. Gem bit his lip, trying to keep his own emotions in check. His breathing rasped loudly over the phone.

"She's the reason I came here. I had to see where they buried her. I had to be near her."

"Then you're the one. You put the violets on her grave."

He swallowed, giving a tiny nod.

"Why did he do it?" Bethany sobbed. "Why did he do such terrible things to her? I know the trade. You don't disfigure your girls, and you don't kill them like that without a damn good reason!"

———

Gem put his face in his hands, the memories overwhelming him. He felt hot tears on his palms, but couldn't stop them. The pain was as fresh as if it had happened yesterday.

"Why?" Bethany demanded again. "What did she do to get hurt like that?"

"It wasn't her."

"What?"

"It was me. It wasn't her. Raphael did it because I liked her. He wouldn't mark me."

"What?" Bethany repeated uncomprehendingly.

"It was me," Gem repeated, voice breaking.

Bethany stared at him as if she'd never seen him before. Seeing him as a John would see him. Seeing him as a pimp would see him. "You," she repeated, with dawning comprehension.

Gem was miserable. It was his fault. He'd caused Honey to be killed, and because of that, he would lose Bethany too.

"You were with her," Bethany said.

Gem dreaded the next sentence. The accusations, the well-deserved blame, the break-up. *You're the reason she's dead.*

"I'm glad she had someone."

Gem looked at Bethany through his fingers at the unexpected

words. "I was the reason he hurt her," he said, in case she hadn't understood that part.

"You didn't want him to hurt her. You liked her," Bethany's voice was calm now, the tears gone.

"I *loved* her," Gem said, agonized.

"And she loved you, didn't she?"

"Who could love in that place? Who could look around that filthy, horrible place and love anybody?"

"You did," she pointed out.

"I'm not normal." He rubbed at his burning eyes. "I held her in my arms, like a baby. When he cut her. She was so small, so hurt. I stayed awake holding her, afraid if I fell asleep, she'd be dead when I woke up." Bethany didn't stop him. "I had to take care of her. Everyone was afraid to help, or he'd punish them too. No real medical supplies. I sewed her up, with a needle and thread. I never even sewed a button before. Prayed to God to help me do it. Never prayed before. Never since."

Bethany wiped at her eyes. "You loved her. She loved you. I'm glad you were together."

Gem tried to stop sobbing. "I loved her, and I killed her."

"You couldn't save her. But you saved me."

Gem swallowed, a hard, hot lump in his throat. "I gotta go. I gotta go; I can't do this."

He got up. A CO grabbed him by the arm, handcuffed him, and took him away.

CHAPTER TWENTY-FIVE

EARS STILL BLURRED GEM'S vision. He let the pressure of the CO's grip on his arm guide him.

"Aww, is Johnson crying over his girlfriend?" one of them taunted.

"Johnson is the little girl," another said.

"Lemme 'lone," Gem growled, blinking to clear his eyes and looking around to see who the CO's were.

Benny and Lo. Gem didn't trust them. He saw their eyes and knew he couldn't trust them.

"I think we'd better do a strip," Benny suggested.

Lo rolled his eyes. "He was just searched an hour ago."

"Policy manual says inmates known to use weapons should be strip searched after leaving the visiting room."

"That was when we had an open visiting room."

"Manual still says it. And the memo said we're supposed to be following the policy strictly."

Lo shrugged widely.

Benny took off Gem's handcuffs. "Let's go. Strip."

Gem glanced over at the privacy screen he was supposed to be allowed to use, but Benny shook his head, arms folded across his big chest.

"Right here. Right now."

Setting his jaw, Gem obeyed, while Benny stared at him and Lo looked off into space. He was clearly not happy, but not going to stand up to his partner.

When Gem was finished, he looked at Benny for instructions, but instead of the CO stepping him through the usual routine, Benny pushed him against the wall.

"Spread 'em, Johnson. Legs apart, you know the drill, little girl."

Gem reluctantly assumed the position. Benny ran light hands provocatively down Gem's back and sides.

"Smooth, soft skin any girl would envy," Benny sneered.

Gem's skin goose-bumped and his face and ears flamed hot. "Get your hands off me," he growled. "You're not allowed to touch me!"

The protest only encouraged Benny. Under the guise of frisking Gem, he took advantage of Gem's position. When Gem tried to move, he was pushed harder into the wall.

"I think I'd better do a cavity check too," Benny proposed. Gem tried to move, but Benny pressed his gun into the small of Gem's back and told him to hold still.

"Come on, Ben," Lo protested. "Only a doctor—"

"Policy manual says if repeat offenders are suspected of carrying weapons or drugs, a cavity search is permitted. Now, how often has Johnson been caught with a shiv?"

"I don't think..."

"Go get a coffee," Benny growled. Gem tried one more time to squirm out of his position against the wall, but Benny wasn't about to let him move.

"Ben..." Lo protested.

"I said go get a coffee."

Lo stood there a moment, then left.

Mutt saw Lo peering anxiously into the window of one of the search rooms. "Hey, Lo. What's going on?"

Lo startled and faced Mutt. "Oh. Hey. Benny's just finishing up with one of the kids."

Mutt looked at him with a sick, uneasy feeling in his gut. He elbowed Lo aside and went into the room. Gem Johnson was on his knees, naked, ghostly white, slowly picking up his uniform and holding it close to his body. Benny turned around as he disposed of a pair of bloody latex gloves. When he saw it was Mutt who had come in, the color drained from his face, but he kept his cool.

"What's up?"

"What the hell did you do to him?" Mutt demanded.

"Routine search. What's it to you?"

Gem didn't pay any attention to them as he robotically put on his uniform and rose unsteadily to his feet.

Mutt indicated the bloody gloves. "This is not routine. What did you—hell, you're fired. Get your stuff together and get out."

"You can't fire me!"

"You'd rather explain this to Schienberg?"

Benny swore and stormed out of the room. Mutt turned to Lo, who had followed him into the room. "What was your part in this?"

"I didn't do anything! I told him he couldn't do a cavity search. He told me to get lost."

"You were watching through the window. What did you see?"

"I went for a coffee. I just got back when you came along."

Mutt glanced at Gem standing there vacantly, eyes glazed.

"I didn't see," Lo insisted again.

"Why weren't you in the room to witness and provide backup?"

"I told you. Benny told me to scram."

"You should have followed protocol."

"How was I supposed to stop him? If I'd stayed in the room, I'd be fired too."

Mutt nodded. "And you don't think you will be? You could have gotten help if you couldn't stop him yourself."

Lo shook his head and walked out without another word. Mutt was left with Gem.

"Are you okay, Johnson?"

Gem didn't look at him or answer immediately. He acted like he was on a time delay. "I'm okay," he finally muttered.

"Come on."

Mutt took the inmate by the arm. Gem walked with his head

down, feet shuffling. Some time after they walked past Gem's cell, he stopped walking and refused to go farther. "No."

"I'm just taking you to the infirmary."

"No. I said I'm okay."

"I want the doc to check you out."

Gem shook his head adamantly. "The guys will see me. No one can know about this!"

Mutt understood. Gem couldn't deal with the reputation that he would get if the other inmates heard what was going on. He'd never survive his stay in juvie if he became a favorite target for the other boys.

"We'll make sure he looks after you in private. He won't say anything. No one will know."

"No."

"You could have injuries that need to be treated. I don't know what he did to you, what if he ruptured or punctured something? That's serious."

"He didn't do nothing. Just a routine search. Don't do this to me!"

"Gem. Come on. You have to get looked after."

"Then take me to the hospital. If you take me to the infirmary, it'll be all over juvie."

Mutt considered. "Come on with me, then. I'll have to talk to the administration."

Gem went with him to Schienberg's office, and Mutt sat him down in a chair, handcuffing him to an anchor for safety. Schienberg watched this process through her open door.

"What's up?" she asked when Mutt entered.

"What we didn't want to happen...? Well, it did."

"Because Johnson says so?"

Mutt shook his head and grimly described the scene he'd walked into.

Schienberg's frown deepened. She swore. "Where are Benny and Lo?"

"I couldn't get anything out of them. I told Benny he was fired,"

"You don't have the authority to fire anyone."

"That's what he said. When I suggested he talk to you about it, he left."

"And Lo?"

"If he's smart, he'll tender his resignation."

"Was he involved?"

"Just in turning a blind eye, as far as I can tell. Left Benny alone when he should have been standing up for Johnson's rights and protecting him."

She swore again. "We're going to have to get the police in. Report this whole damn mess to the authorities. That means all kind of monitoring and people sticking their noses into my prison."

Mutt nodded, saying nothing.

"And what does he say?" Schienberg nodded in Gem's direction.

"General denial."

"Why isn't he in the infirmary?"

"He won't go. Doesn't want the other inmates to know what happened. And I don't know that the doc could do anything more than refer him to the hospital."

"Bring Johnson in here."

Mutt nodded and retrieved Gem. Gem stared down at a spot on the carpet and didn't look at Schienberg.

"I hear you got hurt, Johnson."

"No, ma'am."

"You and Benny have trouble before this?"

There was a long silence before he answered. "No, ma'am."

"You want to go to the hospital?"

"Want to go to my bunk."

"You need a doctor. Are you going to the infirmary or the hospital?"

"Hospital, if I gotta."

"You gotta," Schienberg agreed.

Gem sighed. Schienberg nodded to Mutt. "Get me the form, I'll sign it, and you can take him in."

"You can't tell no one," Gem said in a low voice, barely audible.

"No one will know anything."

———

The doctor Gem saw at the hospital had a pleasant bedside manner.

"We're just going to scope you out," he said matter-of-factly. "We'll freeze the area to numb the pain, but you'll still feel some pressure. Then in an hour, you'll be out of here, provided you don't need further treatment."

"Okay," Gem agreed, his face flushed a deep red.

The doctor followed Gem's eyes to Mutt. "You won't be able to be there during the procedure," he warned Mutt. "Is that a problem, as long as he's secured?"

"No. I don't need to watch."

Gem's shoulders dipped down as he breathed out.

The doctor nodded, satisfied. "A nurse will be in to prep you shortly."

———

Doctor Sykes talked to Gem occasionally during the procedure. "How're you holding out there, pal?"

"Okay."

"Any pain?"

"No."

"Good man. You tell me if there is."

The doctor was silent for a while. "Have you had this done before, son?" he asked quietly, staring at the video screen.

Gem swallowed, trying to keep the memories from becoming real. He flashed back to it. Lying flat on some quack veterinarian's table, moaning in pain even after they shot him up. Raphael standing beside him, supervising to make sure he didn't say anything to anyone. Gem thinking he was going to die right there.

"Yeah," he admitted to the doctor.

"I'm seeing a lot of scarring from before. Everything seems to have healed up okay, though."

"Uh-huh."

"That must have been pretty painful."

Gem let his breath out in a slow hiss. "Yeah."

"It's not nearly as bad this time. But I suspect you already knew that."

"I told them it was nothing."

"Well, I wouldn't say nothing. But I don't see anything that's going to require surgical repair this time."

Gem remembered the waves of nauseating pain. So bad that he was throwing up yellow bile and felt like his guts were going to turn inside out. Rafe had thought he was faking the pain at first. Until he saw all the blood.

"Just about done. I just want to go a bit further to make sure there's no more damage further up."

"Okay."

The doctor finished up shortly. "Okay, you've been great. That's all I'm going to need to do. I'm going to have the nurse finish up and then take you back to your friend. You can get dressed and discharged right away."

————

The doctor went to talk to Mutt before Gem got there so he could speak in private.

"There was a good amount of trauma. But the worst of the bleeding had already stopped. He'll probably be pretty sore the next few days, may bleed a little off and on, but he should heal up without any medical intervention."

"So if no one had seen he was hurt, we never would have known anything had happened."

The doctor nodded. "This kind of thing happens in juvenile. Experimentation, power games, high hormone levels. Sometimes kids don't realize that they can do real damage."

Mutt hesitated. "This... wasn't done by another kid."

The doctor considered this. "You look out for this boy. He's been hurt enough already."

"Something you're not telling me?"

"He has a right to privacy. I can't tell you anything other than his current condition."

Mutt nodded. "If you can't say anything, you can't say anything.

I know he's got a pretty checkered past, if that's what you're hinting at. Is there a medical condition we should know about? Something that needs ongoing monitoring or treatment? AIDS?"

Sykes shook his head. "No. Just what I said. He's been hurt enough. Keep an eye out for him."

"I will," Mutt promised.

———

Gem went back to his cell and stood there for a minute. He turned around and looked at Himself.

"Are you okay?" He asked.

Gem nodded and hugged Himself tightly.

He stepped back eventually. "Someone else is here now," He said, gesturing to the bunk.

Gem looked around, uncertain what He meant. Then Gem realized that they must have changed bunkmates while he was down in iso. Someone else's things were there.

"When did that happen?"

"Few days ago."

Gem nodded.

"You sure you're okay?" He asked.

"Doctor sent me back. It's okay."

CHAPTER TWENTY-SIX

THEY HAD BETHANY UNDER surveillance so that she would lead them to the money. She must have kept a good amount out for expenses because so far, she had not retrieved anything from the hiding place. They knew the money wasn't at the apartment; it had been searched when Gem was arrested. She must have been carrying a lot with her, but she couldn't carry the whole take around. She'd lead them back to it sooner or later.

After she and Gem had a fight in the juvie visiting room and she left in tears, she had led her tails to Honey's grave. She'd cried and put flowers on the grave. Riker pondered this for some time. He looked again through the photos of the kids retrieved from Rafe's shop, wondering if Bethany had been there with Gem and Honey. But her face was not among the photos.

———

Gem woke up shouting, someone shaking his arm roughly.

"Johnson, Johnson! Wake up! Knock it off!"

Gem jerked his arm away. "Lemme alone."

"Leave you alone?" Scout demanded. "You're the one wakin' me out of a sound sleep in the middle of the night screaming bloody murder!"

Gem grunted. "I had a dream," he muttered, trying to calm the shakes and push the images of Rafe from his brain.

"Yeah, I figured. Why don't you get some pills from the doctor?"

"What pills?"

"Sleeping pills. So you sleep deeper. Don't dream."

Gem rubbed his eyes and turned over. "You think that would work?"

"I wish you'd try something that might give me a good night's sleep."

Gem sighed. "Yeah, okay. I'll try."

"Thanks," Scout grunted and lay down on the other bunk to try to get back to sleep.

———

"Did you hear about the new teacher?" Colt asked, bouncing on his heels, as jittery as if he were high.

"No. What about him?" Gem said.

"*Her*. Miss Foster. Some of the guys know her from when she taught at St. Pete's."

"Miss?"

"Yeah. She apparently had all the juvies there eatin' out of her hand. They all had the hots for her."

Derry heard Colt's conversation and came over.

"Miss Foster? Oh, yeah! I was at St. Pete's. I'll bet that she got love notes from every juvie in the place. In the middle of assignments, in her desk drawers, in her pockets... everyone, including me. One look into her baby blues and the hardest con turns to mush."

"What's she doing teaching in juvie?" Gem questioned.

"Breaking hearts, man. Who knows why she teaches here? She could get a job in a public school. But she starts teaching, and suddenly everybody's taking classes."

"She doesn't sound like the type that could handle a juvie class."

"That's just the point. She's a babe, and not a bit tough, but she does it."

———

He went to his school class strictly out of curiosity, wanting to see what all the fuss was about. The class was hyper, waiting for the new teacher to show up. When she came in, everybody took their seats and quieted down.

He had not expected to be affected by her. He had Bethany. He wasn't looking for another interest. But when he saw Miss Foster, he was smitten. It wasn't the physical lust that he had expected—though she was a looker—it was something intensely emotional, almost spiritual. He wanted to hold her in his arms, and he would knock the teeth out of anyone who as much as whistled at her. But it was more than that. He was deeply in love with her, even before she opened her mouth.

When she did speak, a collective sigh went up from the class, and they all sat spellbound like a class of first graders with a crush instead of the juvie-hardened cons they were. He'd never seen anything like it.

———

The doctor looked over Gem's medical records. "Which one are you?"

Gem gazed at him steadily. "Gem."

"Which one?"

"There's only one."

"They've messed up the records. They've got two files with the same name."

Gem shrugged. "That mean you can't give me sleeping pills?"

"Well, I'm not sure." The doctor looked through the two files. "You've got a psychiatric history? You've been prescribed anti-psychotics before?"

"So what? I'm not on anything right now."

The doctor fiddled with the bent corner of one of the folders. "I guess it should be safe, then..."

"What're sleeping pills gonna do?" Gem said reasonably. "I just wanna stop wakin' up all the time with nightmares."

The doctor nodded. He went to the locked supply cabinet and dispensed the pills to Gem.

"Now, you can only take them when you need them. It's easy to become dependent on them. Only take the prescribed dose."

Gem pocketed the bottle without reading the label. "How many?" he asked. "Couple pills?"

"Only one. And like I said, only when you need them," the doctor warned.

"Yeah, I got it."

———

Riker slammed his phone down. "That blasted new lawyer of Gem's!"

Gordon looked up from the form he was filling out. "What about him?"

"He's moved to sever the trials. Says he's only representing one of the boys, and he'll turn state's witness against his brother."

"For a reduced sentence."

"For immunity from conspiracy charges. If they can't use conspiracy, they'll never convict him of anything."

"Which one is he representing?"

"Gem 2. They're not sure, but Gem 1 would never admit he had a brother, forget agreeing to testify against him."

"Do we have anything concrete against Gem 2?"

"He's the one who killed Raphael. I know it was Gem 1 who got his skull cracked and was locked up, so he couldn't have killed Rafe, but they'll get around that somehow. We can't prove it was Gem 2 except by elimination."

———

King looked over his officers before giving them their assignments. "What's wrong with you, Scout?"

The boy smothered another jaw-cracking yawn. "Can't get any sleep. Bunking with Gem Johnson."

"He still keeping you up half the night?"

"Worse than ever." Scout rubbed the space between his eyebrows, wincing.

"I thought the doc put him on sleeping pills."

"He's been *worse* since he got hooked on those. Didn't you hear about Steiner?"

King squinted at him thoughtfully. "I saw he had a black eye...?"

Scout nodded. "Steiner tried to wake him up in the morning. Gem knocked him off his feet. That's what he's like when you try to wake him up from a nightmare. And if you *don't* wake him up, he just keeps going, yellin' and thrashing around. Keeps me awake all night."

King laughed. "I wish I'd seen little Gem knock Steiner down. That bull doesn't have a problem holding the biggest juvies down. I wish I'd been there!"

Scout covered another yawn. "Sometimes they switch, and the other one sleeps quieter, but that kid is gonna kill me with lack of sleep."

———

For weeks, Miss Foster was all anyone talked about. They mooned over her, dreamed about her, fought over her, and went to her classes. Eventually, the clamor started to settle down. Boys began to lose interest as she was no longer new. They got tired of attending school classes and being expected to do the work just to see her. She still had a large following, but the excitement died down.

"Gem, would you stay after?" Miss Foster said.

A ripple of whispers went through the class, and everybody looked at Him, wondering what He had done. Miss Foster didn't give detentions and individual attention outside class time was rare.

"Yes, ma'am," He agreed.

She went on with giving out assignments. When the buzzer sounded, He stayed in his desk, watching the others trickle out while Miss Foster wrote notes in her planner.

When they were alone in the room, Miss Foster brought her

stool over to his desk and perched atop it, looking at him thought-fully. A CO stood in the doorway, keeping an eye on things.

He looked admiringly at Miss Foster's crossed legs, then at her face. She was older than he'd thought. There were fine lines around her eyes and mouth. He gazed into her baby blues for a few moments before she spoke.

"How are you doing, Gem?"

He shrugged, surprised at the question. "Okay."

"I've been a little worried about your work."

"I do okay."

"*Sometimes* it's okay. Other times... you don't seem to have any idea what you're doing."

He grunted, not trying to explain.

"Gem... can you read?"

"Yes."

"I'm serious. Can you?"

He looked into her intense blue eyes. "I can," He insisted. "But..." He tried to form the words, "but *he* can't."

"Who can't?" Miss Foster asked, her forehead wrinkling.

He wavered under her steady gaze. "My... uh... other..."

She looked at him for a minute. "Your twin," she said finally, "they told me you had a twin."

He nodded. "Gem," he agreed.

"You two swap classes?"

"Yeah."

"You're going to have to stop that if we're going to help you."

"I can't."

"Why not?"

"I'm not—he—I can't explain it."

"Try me. I'm pretty quick."

"He's Gem."

She nodded. "Okay...?"

"And I'm Gem."

Miss Foster stared into His eyes. "You're not *both* Gem."

"Yes."

"You can read."

"Yeah."

"But he can't."

"Right."

"He needs to be in a remedial reading class. You don't."

"You can't separate me—my selves."

"Different people need different things. You two don't have the same needs."

"But I'm not different people."

"You and your brother are separate people with different needs."

"No."

There was a long silence. He shifted uncomfortably.

"You need help, honey."

He shook his head. "No shrinks. No doctors. I been through all that before."

"You know you're not the same as other kids."

"So? That doesn't mean there's anything wrong with me."

"No, but I do think you need help."

"I don't."

She was silent for a while, then shrugged resignedly. "Well, then I guess there's nothing I can do. You can go."

———

"What the hell was that?" Gem demanded, jolting Scout from sleep.

"Go to sleep," Scout groaned.

"No, I saw a flash. Like lightning."

"There's no lightning in here. You're dreaming." Scout dragged his blanket over his head, trying to block out the noise.

"I wasn't asleep!"

"You were asleep. You were dreaming."

Gem sat up. "What're you trying to pull? You're taking pictures of me in the dark!"

"You're nuts, man! I'm sleeping. No one's taking pictures."

"You're lying! I saw a flash."

Scout gave up and got out of his bed, furious. "Shut up and go back to sleep! Do I have to knock you out?"

Gem jumped out of his bed and shoved Scout into the wall. Scout banged on the door, shouting for a CO. Gem jumped him from behind, screaming, trying to get a chokehold on him. Scout kicked the door and yelled to get the attention of one the security staff. Gem pulled him away from the door, forcing Scout to concentrate on defending himself. Eventually, the door opened and light flooded into the room. Scout tried to push Gem away so that the CO's could grab him. For a few minutes, there was chaos. Then the CO's managed to get Gem under their control. One of them had a hand on Scout's arm to make sure that he didn't do anything. They took Gem out of the cell.

"What's going on here? What're you guys doin' starting a ruckus in the middle of the night?" Barker demanded, letting go of Scout's arm.

"He's crazy! I didn't do a thing. He thinks I'm spying on him or something."

"Can't you two get along?"

"Get along with that screwball? I didn't do anything; I was sleeping! He's paranoid. He's totally off his rocker!"

"No different than he's ever been."

"Yeah, he *is*. The doctor finally took him off those sleeping pills, and now he's gone nuts withdrawing!"

Barker shook his head. "What are they doing messing around with his meds? Well, you get back to bed. We'll put him in solitary and see if he evens out."

"And if he doesn't, you just leave him down there, okay?"

Barker chuckled. "We'll see about that."

CHAPTER TWENTY-SEVEN

HE STARTED GETTING SLOPPY. He knew it, but he was complacent. He'd spent so much time with the older Allies, He thought he was untouchable. No one would try anything while He was with a senior Ally; and he had been with them so long that He Himself felt he was a senior member, untouchable.

He wasn't going far. He'd been hanging around with Colt and was going to the rec room. A couple of hallways. He turned a corner and found himself facing half a dozen Others. He froze for an instant, then tried to turn and run. He got about three steps before being caught. He shouted for help until one of them put him in a chokehold so tight that he couldn't draw breath. He fought to free himself, knowing they weren't going to just take a swing or two and fade into the woodwork. They were serious. He and Gem had killed two of theirs. He would be lucky if none of them was armed.

His initial shouts did eventually bring the CO's, but not enough of them to subdue all the Others. He tried to endure the blows, speculating how much more He could take before blacking out. Then it was over, and He lay on the floor, drifting, waiting for the CO's to help Him up.

One of them took his pulse with firm, competent fingers.

"What do you think?" another asked.

"He's okay. But we'd better take him to the infirmary and make sure." He was shaken by the arm. "Johnson. Come on. Get up."

He could hear the buzz of conversation as a crowd started to gather. He listened for Gem's voice, but of course, Gem didn't come. Gem was still adamant about not revealing his secret. Old habits died hard.

"Come on," again the shake on His arm, rousing him. He tried to ignore it. A couple of them hauled him to his feet, and He was forced to open his eyes and try to take his weight.

―――――

"I have more news for you," the prosecutor advised Riker over the phone.

Riker sighed and closed his eyes. "I don't want to hear it. You made the deal with Gem."

"No, that's still in the works, depending on what he can give us. But I thought that you'd like to know he might be moved."

"Moved? Where? When?"

"One of them got jumped in the hallway. His lawyer wants him moved somewhere else. I think he also wants the two of them separated to build his case."

"How badly was he hurt in this fight?"

"Bruises, stitches, he spent one night in the hospital. He's back in juvie today."

"You don't believe he's going to testify against his brother, do you?"

"His lawyer says it will be easier if they're out of contact with each other. A physical separation between the two so that a psychological wedge can be driven between them."

Riker had to admit that made sense. "But it's Gem 2 who's talking about a deal, isn't it? I mean, he's the one we know is guilty of murder. He's the brains of the operation, the one who planned everything."

"Unfortunately, that's the way it works sometimes. But we want to get them both behind bars, and we might not get either of them if we mess around."

"But we know. We know they committed these crimes."

"Knowing it and getting a jury to convict are two different things. You know that, officer. Especially when there's as much confusion as there is in this case. The jury has to be one hundred percent sure, or we're going to lose them both."

———

A great Christmas present. Finding out that He was being transferred, but Gem wasn't. For His own protection, they said.

Gem was furious.

But Gem had been alone before, and in worse places. Gem would be okay.

And it meant less confusion. It meant that He didn't have to be so careful. He had more chance at a normal life. However normal life could be in juvie.

———

Bethany knew she was in trouble the minute the bank manager led her out to the front. A squad car with its lights flashing was on the street in front of the building. Looking around, she saw Riker leaning against the counter, smirking at her. The bank manager looked around.

"What's going on here?"

"Do you have any idea what she has in that safety deposit box?" Riker questioned.

"Of course not," the bank manager said, primly shocked.

"She's got money that was stolen from this bank, don't you, sweetheart? Gem had the nerve to hide the take at the same bank that he stole it from in the first place."

Bethany stood firm. "I don't know what you're talking about."

"Open up the box," Riker told the banker, "you'll see."

"You know I can't open it without a warrant."

"It has your own money in it. Money heisted from this bank a few months ago."

The man looked perturbed but stuck to his guns. "The bank has no authority to open it, and neither do the police."

"Well, I'll be back with a warrant, so keep it handy." He turned to Bethany. "You're under arrest."

"What for?"

"Accomplice after the fact. Bank robbery. You know what I'm talking about."

"I had nothing to do with any robbery."

"Turn around. Hands on the counter."

Bethany reluctantly turned around and let Riker frisk her. He pulled a thick wad of bills from her pocket.

"Well, well, well," he said. "Wouldn't it be handy if these matched the serial numbers of the stolen bank money."

Bethany's heart dropped to her stomach. She'd heard nothing of the bank robbery before this. Gem had never told her where the money came from. She knew it had to have come from somewhere. From something big. He obviously hadn't just 'come into some money' as he had claimed. And if the police could prove it—well, she had been handling hot money.

She swallowed hard and said nothing to Riker. He handcuffed her and took her out to the waiting squad car.

———

Bethany's eyes were wide and her breathing was rapid. She was pale and sweating as she sat in the conference room, waiting for them to take their best shot. Riker didn't think she would last long. She looked like she would collapse like a house of cards as soon as they applied some pressure. She was no bank robber. She didn't have the backbone for what she'd gotten herself into.

"Why don't you tell us what you know about the money before you're in too deep?" Riker suggested.

"I don't know anything about it." Bethany gave a wide shrug. "It's not my money."

"It certainly isn't. Do you know how long we can put you away for laundering money?"

"It's not my money," Bethany repeated. "I just have power of attorney."

Riker raised his brows. He hadn't thought about how she might have access to the money. "Gem didn't tell you where the money came from?"

"Why would he?"

"We're checking the serial numbers right now. If you want to make a deal, you'd better get talking before we get word back."

Bethany shook her head adamantly. "I don't know anything."

Riker studied Bethany for a long time. "You're in big trouble."

"It's nothing to do with me," Bethany maintained. But she looked worried sick.

Riker stood up. "I'll go see how they're coming along."

He left her there to stew. A few minutes by herself, and she'd be ready to talk.

———

"I'm not sure you had cause to arrest her," Gordon advised.

Riker shrugged. "You know what gets me? We can't trace that money. We've got it in our hands, and we can't do anything without a confession from her."

"She's hanging tough?"

"Yeah. Too tough. I need something else to use as leverage."

"We don't have enough to do what we're doing," Gordon pointed out unhelpfully.

Riker let Bethany stew for forty-five minutes before going back in to talk to her. She was drumming her fingers on the table, clearly agitated.

"Well, have you thought of anything to tell me?" Riker questioned.

"Yeah," Bethany said softly. Riker's hopes rose. "I want my lawyer."

Riker gritted his teeth. "Because you've decided not to cooperate, or because you want to work out a deal?"

"I want to get out of here. I told you I don't know anything."

"You're sure this is what you want to do?"

Bethany nodded.

"Fine. I'll take you to the phone in a few minutes."

———

Miss Foster leaned over Gem's shoulder briefly. "Can you stay after, Gem?"

"Yeah," Gem agreed, his voice low.

She watched him from the front of the room as they worked on their assignments. She knew that the twins had been separated, so she only had to deal with the one who remained. And this was the other Gem. Not the one she had talked to before. This was the one who couldn't read.

The class change bell rang, and the boys filed out, talking, throwing glances at Miss Foster as they dropped their assignments on her desk. Gem approached her desk and waited for the others to all leave.

"Gem, I want to move you into another class."

"Why?"

"You're not keeping up. I want to put you into a remedial reading course."

"What's that?" he asked suspiciously

"A class to help you to read better."

"I can read!" Gem folded his arms across his chest, jaw set.

Miss Foster put a basic reader in front of him. "What does it say?"

Gem stared at the words for a moment. "I don't got nothing to prove," he growled.

"Write your name for me."

Gem grabbed a pen from her desk and scrawled 'Gem' on a piece of lined paper in large, childish printing.

"Now write my name."

He hesitated, head twitching to the side. "I don't know how to spell it."

"F-O-S-T-E-R," she spelled slowly.

Gem printed it out painfully in block letters.

Miss Foster noted that his "R" was reversed. "Did you used to have trouble keeping up in school?" she questioned.

"Yeah, sometimes." His tone was unemotional. Uncaring.

"So you got your brother to do what you couldn't understand?"

"I don't have a brother."

"He could do it, but you couldn't. So he covered for you, and you never had to learn."

"I can do it sometimes. Sometimes I just forget what I'm doing."

"Like now."

He looked frustrated. "I could do it if I tried," he insisted.

"I think you need help. And I think I can help you. But you need to be in the right class, not one that's so advanced."

"I'm not going to any dummy classes. I'm not dumb."

"Of course not. A lot of the kids who don't learn to read as children are actually highly intelligent."

"Yeah?" He brightened.

"Sure. Are you telling me it's easy to keep people from finding out you can't read?"

"No, it ain't." His chin went up.

"Or to function in a world where everyone else can read?"

"No."

"So let me put you in another class. Then you can get caught up."

Gem scratched his wrist, thinking about it. "I guess," he said finally.

"Good. We'll meet for third-period class instead of the second period. Okay?"

"Okay."

———

Mary had gone to juvie to check on the boys and see how they were doing. She hadn't been told about Gem 2 being transferred out. On looking at Gem 1's administrative files, she was surprised to see Miss Foster's name. She and Susan Foster had gone to school together years before.

They got together for a bull session on Gem. Mary was happy to hear that the boys had been separated so that they couldn't do any more switching.

"Do you realize that this is the first time that we will be able to do proper educational testing with him? We have no idea what his aptitude is. For either of them. They did some neurological and psychiatric analysis when the boys were first brought here, but there's never been any comprehensive psychoeducational analysis."

"It's so bizarre—their story, what's happened to them. It's unbelievable," Miss Foster said.

"You're not kidding."

"He's going to be a challenge. I'm not sure he's quite all there."

"I'm quite sure he's not all there," Mary countered. They both laughed.

"Have you heard what he's been up to here? There are all kinds of rumors, though I don't know what is true and what is not."

"I know he's been in solitary more than he's been out, if the records I reviewed are correct. He's got quite a reputation?"

"You bet. I take it all with a grain of salt, but I know I have my work cut out for me if I'm going to help him."

Mary shook her head. "I don't know how you can do it, day after day, trying to straighten these boys out."

"One day at a time, the same as you."

<hr>

CHAPTER TWENTY-EIGHT

<hr>

H E MET WITH HIS lawyer in a conference room instead of separated by a pane of glass like at the other juvenile center. He shook hands with Lowther for the first time.

"Hey."

"Nice to finally talk to you like this instead of over the phone."

"Yeah," He agreed awkwardly.

"You ready to get down to business?"

"I guess."

"It's time to start talking. If you don't, there isn't going to be a deal."

"I have to decide now?"

"They're giving me an ultimatum. You start giving up details, or negotiations regarding the charges against you are off."

"What would I have to say?" He asked tentatively.

"You have to give them detailed information to use against your brother. Like we discussed."

"And then what happens to me?"

"If they can't use conspiracy charges, they have to prove that you, not your brother committed each crime. And they can't. So you get off."

"No, I mean Gem. What happens to Gem?"

"That's the brilliant part," Lowther said smugly. "You give them detailed information about him, so they think they have him dead to rights. But he'll never stand up to trial. He'll be ruled not competent in a flash."

"So I—we—go free."

"Yes. He will have to be institutionalized, at least for a while. No big deal."

It was the first time Lowther had mentioned having to institutionalize Gem. Up until then, He thought they would both be free again, like before.

"You can't put me—Gem—in a nuthouse."

"It won't work, otherwise."

"I know what they do in those places. I've been there before."

"Then you know it's no big deal. He'll bide his time in a forensic unit for a while, and then he'll be released."

"Gem won't be released! They'll mess with my brain, put me on drugs—him, I mean. They'll try to separate—us."

"You *are* separated."

"Not up here," He touched his head, "or here," hand over His heart. "Just because they keep us apart, we're not separated. I can still feel Gem. Gem can—feel—me. Hear me. But in those places... they try to block out the feelings and the voices."

Lowther frowned at him. "You keep talking like that, and you'll be in the nuthouse. No voices. No sympathetic vibrations, or twin telepathy, or whatever you're trying to get at. You have to make sense, or this won't work. You'll end up in the loony bin instead of free."

He looked down at the table. Being apart was more difficult than He had anticipated. He had thought He'd be able to distance Himself. Shut out Gem's feelings and act for Himself. But He could feel Gem reaching out. Wanting to know what He was up to—wanting to know why He was blocking Gem out.

"I can't testify against Gem."

"Don't start that again," Lowther warned. "If you're going to pay me, you have to work with me. None of this monkey business. Tell me something I can give to them. A hook. A teaser. Something to let them know we're serious about dealing. You're not hurting your brother. It's all part of a larger plan to save both of you."

"I can't testify against him. Not if it will put—him—back in that place." He shook his head. "I have to think."

"I'm going to leave you alone for ten minutes. Then you'd better start talking, and give me something good."

Mutt walked past Gem's cell and glanced in the window. Gem was there, pacing jerkily, muttering angrily to himself. His behavior had been getting more bizarre every day since the twins' separation. Pretty soon, they would have to transfer him to some psych ward.

Mutt opened the door silently and listened for a moment to Gem's chatter.

"No—no—I can't do that—don't do that—don't talk—don't tell anybody anything—don't talk—don't tell them..."

"Johnson," Mutt interrupted in a quiet voice. "Are you okay?"

"Get out of here!" Gem screamed, turning to face him. His face was a mask of rage. "Everybody leave me alone!"

"Okay, okay," Mutt agreed, backing off. "I'll leave you alone."

Mutt shut the door again. He started to walk away, then changed his mind and stopped to lock the door. He wasn't sure whether he was protecting Gem or protecting the other inmates from Gem, but Gem was not stable. He couldn't be around the others.

Riker slowly hung up the phone scowling about the call. "What the heck is he up to now?" he growled.

"Gem again?" Gordon guessed.

"Gem 2 has confessed. In detail. To everything."

"For what deal?"

"No conspiracy charges against his brother."

"That was the deal before, wasn't it?"

"No. Before it was no conspiracy charges against himself. Now he's going to take the full rap."

"What's he up to?"

"The prosecutor said Gem's lawyer was against it, so Gem dumped him."

"So he just wants to protect his brother?"

Riker shook his head, trying to puzzle it out. "I don't know. I just have this awful feeling that we're not going to get either one of them."

———

Gem hadn't wanted to go to dinner, but he had skipped so many meals that the security staff insisted and took him to the cafeteria. Schienberg had been hearing about his increasingly bizarre behavior and was watching him to see it for herself.

Gem seemed to be in another world. He took the tray that was put into his hands and walked mechanically down the counter to get his meal, but he might as well have been blind. He was bumped forward by the person behind him and halted by the inmate in front of him. When he reached the end of the counter, he stood there as if lost. One of the CO's went over, took him by the arm, and led him to a seat. Schienberg watched him for a moment longer, then turned to leave.

She whirled back around at a strangled scream.

Gem was standing up again, his hands at his throat. "No!" he shrieked. "No, stop it! No, no, no!"

He made ghastly gagging and choking noises, falling to his knees and then into a fetal position on the floor.

"What happened?" Schienberg demanded when she reached the CO's at Gem's side. "Who did what to him?"

The CO's tried to pry Gem's hands from his throat to assess the damage, but his hands were clamped down too tightly. He choked and gagged, lips turning blue. It seemed to last forever, until he lay still, unmoving, without a sound. The CO's pulled his hands back. Gem's throat was covered with red imprints from his own fingers.

"Is there something in his throat or windpipe?" Schienberg questioned urgently. "A piece of food?"

Mutt, bending close to the boy's face, shook his head. "He's breathing freely now."

They all looked at each other in confusion.

"So this was just some sort of psychotic episode?" Schienberg suggested.

"Maybe he did have something in his throat, but it dislodged when he fell."

"Maybe." Schienberg stared down at him, trying to make sense of it.

————

Riker climbed back into the car with a couple of steaming coffees, laughing. He saw Gordon's grim expression and stopped. "What's wrong?"

"I got a call... Gem was found hanging in his cell. They just cut him down and declared him."

Riker felt the blood drain from his face. "Which one?"

"Gem 2. That confession now qualifies as a dying declaration. Gem 1 is cleared, as long as they honor their deal with Gem 2."

Riker's brain wouldn't process this. His mind went immediately to Gem 1, alone in a separate facility, unaware of what had transpired. He was going to be destroyed by the news.

"Has he been told?"

"I don't think so."

"We'd better get over to juvie before he hears it through the grapevine."

————

At juvie, they got the runaround to start with, but were eventually referred to a woman named Schienberg.

"We need to talk to Gem Johnson."

The heavyset woman looked at him with a stony expression. "You'd better come with me."

She escorted them to the infirmary, where Gem was being loaded onto a gurney by two paramedics.

"What happened?" Riker asked.

Gem was semi-conscious, making whimpering and groaning noises. His hands were cuffed behind his back, so the medics had lain him on his side, securing him to the gurney with straps across his torso. Schienberg pulled his uniform down where it was bunched around his throat, revealing purpling bruises.

"What happened to him?" Riker repeated. "Who hurt him?"

"As close as we can tell, he tried to choke himself to death. He's being transferred to psych at the hospital for evaluation."

Riker stared at her in disbelief. "His twin just hung himself," he said.

Gordon made an abortive motion toward Gem, warning him about revealing it to the boy so bluntly.

"I think he already knows," Riker said.

They all looked at each other.

"He knows," Schienberg agreed. She brushed Gem's hair back from his eyes gently. "We're sorry, Johnson."

The paramedics took Gem out, sobbing quietly to himself for a loss that only he could understand.

Gem had suffered through all kinds of torture and isolation.

But he'd never before been alone.

III

alone

CHAPTER TWENTY-NINE

ON THE SIDEWALK IN front of Thrasher's apartment building, the Rippers were talking loudly; there was excitement in the air. They quieted when Bethany approached.

"What is it?" Bethany asked, looking around at them.

No one would say anything. They just looked at each other, avoiding her eyes. Bethany felt her stomach tightening.

"What's going on?" she persisted.

They looked to Thrasher for guidance. Thrasher indicated Dietrich. "D, take her for a walk."

Dietrich looked awkward, but nodded. "Yeah, okay."

He stood up and motioned for Bethany to walk with him. Bethany walked beside him, folding her arms across her roiling stomach.

"What's going on, D?"

He didn't answer right away. They walked in silence. Bethany waited. "It's about Gem," he said finally.

"Gem? What's happened?"

Dietrich hesitated. "You guys have been pretty close."

"Yeah."

"I'm sorry... he hung himself in his cell."

Bethany gasped. "What?"

"Yeah."

"Which one?"

"I dunno. The other one's flipped out and gone back to the nuthouse. I'm sorry, Bethany. I really am."

Bethany grasped Dietrich's arm for support, squeezing hard. "Gem is dead? How could that be? How could he do that to his twin?"

Dietrich just shook his head. "I don't know."

———

Riker had been by the hospital to visit Gem several times, but each time, he had found Gem so drugged up that it was impossible to talk to him or get anything coherent out of him. Even if Gem opened his eyes at Riker's persistent shaking, he stared right through him, making no response to Riker's questions or comments.

It was a week or two in before Riker arrived when there was a doctor around so that he could talk about Gem's state and course of treatment. He knew from his searches into Gem's history that keeping him doped up was a method that had been used in the past to control his behavior.

"He's been so heavily sedated," Riker said. "That can't be good for him. When are you going to start reducing the sedation so that he can interact?"

Dr. Ives looked at Riker, scratching his jaw with the top of his pen, making an annoying rasping sound. "And where did you get your medical degree?"

"I'm not claiming that I know how to treat him. I'm just asking. At some point, won't you have to back off the sedation enough that he can actually deal with his issues?"

"Believe me when I say that we have been keeping on top of it, Officer Riker," Ives said slowly, crisply enunciating every word. "Johnson's condition is very grave. The loss of his twin has been devastating to him."

"I know. I know how close they were to each other, how intertwined with each other they were. It would have to be extremely hard on him."

"If you don't want a second suicide on your hands, you're going to have to let me treat him as I see fit."

"So how much longer does that mean?"

Dr. Ives clicked his tongue and slid his pen into his lab coat pocket. "Mr. Riker, why don't you come with me?"

Unsure of where it was leading, Riker followed Ives to his office.

"Have a seat." Ives gestured to the chairs in front of his desk, and Riker sat. Ives sat on the other side of the desk and spent a few minutes tapping away on his computer. There was a big LCD screen mounted on the wall where they could both see it, and Ives turned and looked at it as a video loaded.

On the screen, Riker saw Gem sitting in a room. A bare cell with just the bed that he sat on. His wrists were held in place, fastened to a belt at his waist. His eyes were dark bruises. He was giving a constant, low moan and, as Riker watched, he threw his head back into the wall behind him. He banged it several times, a steady, rhythmic tattoo.

"He's coming out of sedation," Ives narrated.

Riker became aware that the moan was changing, getting louder, broken by sobs and occasional choking. The banging too was changing from a steady beat, getting louder, harder, so that each crash made Riker wince. Hospital staff moved into the frame, pulling Gem away from the wall, where he left a red smudge. They laid him down on his side. Gem struggled and shouted, incoherent but sounding like he was in severe pain. Riker watched the staff transition him from the wrist restraints to full four-point restraints connected to the bed.

No longer able to bang his head, Gem howled, twisting his head back and forth from side to side. Riker waited for the shrieking to stop, for Gem to tire and start to settle down again, but he didn't. Dr. Ives put the video on fast play, the counter in the corner of the screen stretching from minutes to hours, with staff members popping onto the screen for an instant to mark a notation on his chart, then disappearing again as the minutes sped by.

Eventually, Riker saw Dr. Ives himself on the screen, standing beside the bed. Normal play mode resumed. They could once again hear the recorded sound. Gem, so hoarse he could barely make a sound, still fought the restraints. Riker watched Ives prepare a needle and jab it into the flesh of Gem's thigh. Riker winced, but Gem made no sign he had even felt it. Gradually, the animal-like moans faded away, the writhing body movements slowed, and Gem lay still.

Riker let out his breath, realizing that he had been holding it. He sat there for a moment staring at the frozen picture on the screen.

"How long?" he said finally.

"How long will he continue to injure himself or fight the restraints? Until he's too exhausted to continue, or we sedate him again."

"How long until he starts to show improvement?"

Ives shook his head, expression grim. "Maybe tomorrow. Maybe never. The brain is an unpredictable thing, Mr. Riker. This boy was already unstable. He was deteriorating even before his twin's suicide. They should have had him here and in treatment before the crisis occurred. Maybe then we could have avoided total collapse. But that didn't happen. I'm no fortune teller. I can't tell you when he will begin to show improvement." Ives looked at the screen and shook his head. "We're trying antidepressants. Mood stabilizers. Antipsychotics. Whether they will make any difference in the long run, or whether this will run its course, I don't know. We can't do grief counseling or therapy when he is in this state. The sedatives are for his own protection, but as far as when we will be able to start weaning him off of them... your uneducated guess is as good as my experience. No one can tell what will happen."

"You're saying it could be permanent? He could be permanently... broken?"

"I've studied the neurological and psychological testing that was done when the twins arrived in juvenile detention. No one has ever seen anything like this before. The boy's entire identity was based on their twin relationship. I don't know whether he'll ever be able to function independently. Or to get past this grief."

Riker stared at Gem's image frozen on the screen.

———

Ives escorted Riker back to the ward. Riker slowed as they approached Gem's room. He knew that Gem would be there and that his condition would be the same. Ives's video had demonstrated that. But he had come all the way to see Gem and felt compelled to look in on him. Ives seemed to expect that and stopped in Gem's doorway.

Ives looked in at his patient. "That may be the best therapy for him right now," he said quietly.

Riker peered into Gem's room. As expected, Gem was lying on the bed, unmoving. Beside him was Bethany, half-sitting and half-reclining, cuddled up close to Gem and holding his hand. She was whispering to Gem, but Riker couldn't hear what she was saying.

She saw them in the doorway and sat up. "Oh. Hi."

Riker and Ives moved into the tiny room, crowding together.

"Hi," Riker greeted. He motioned to Gem. "He's the same?"

Bethany brushed Gem's hair back from his face. Her eyes glistened. "Yes."

There was an awkward silence. Ives busied himself, checking Gem's pulse and looking at his eyes. Riker doubted there was any need. Gem's condition was not likely to have changed since the last time he had been looked in on. The video had shown a staff member at Gem's bedside several times an hour. He was probably being monitored every fifteen minutes.

"Can he hear me?" Bethany asked. "When I sit here and talk to him, does he know I'm here?"

Ives held Gem's wrist and looked at her.

"I believe he knows you're here," he said. "Maybe not on any kind of conscious level, but his brain is still processing everything going on around him. Trying to deal with it."

Bethany shook her head. "Poor Gem. I just... can't imagine what it must be like for him." She swallowed. She looked at Riker. Her eyes were red and swollen even now, weeks into Gem's confinement. "I lost my sister... and that was bad enough. It still tears me up to think of what she went through and that she's gone forever. But Gem... it doesn't even compare to what he had with his brother."

Riker nodded. "They had something that I don't even know how to qualify. Telepathy? Empathy? Psychosis?"

"They were one. And now... a big chunk of him is just gone."

"You hear about twins dying within hours or days of each other. I always thought that was incredible. But with Gem, I can understand... how impossible it must feel for him to go on without... his brother."

Bethany took Gem's hand again and squeezed it. "I told him... I'm here for him." She sighed. "But I don't know if it's enough."

Dr. Ives gave her a little pat on the shoulder. "You're doing all you can. And we'll do everything we can for him."

Bethany nodded. She lay her head back beside Gem's again. Feeling like he was intruding on an intimate moment, Riker backed out of the room. Ives did as well.

"Thanks for all you are doing," Riker told him, offering his hand. They hadn't exactly started out on the right foot, but Riker understood better now what Ives was dealing with. He wasn't just using chemical restraints to keep Gem from causing trouble, like had been done at the group home. He was doing the best he could to bring Gem back over the lip of the precipice, to give him time to decide there was something worth living for. Just like Bethany, Ives was doing the best that he could with a limited understanding of how to best help Gem.

CHAPTER THIRTY

WHEN BETHANY LOOKED IN on Gem, she found him moaning and moving around on his bed. She went back out to the nursing station.

"Is Gem okay?"

The nurse put her finger on the document she was reviewing to keep her place, and looked up at Bethany. She gave a thin-lipped smile.

"The doctor is trying to reduce the sedatives. So he may be restless."

"Are you bringing him out of it?" Bethany's heart pounded as she considered the implications. She knew how Gem had reacted to the removal of sedatives before. She didn't want to see him hurt. But being buried so far beneath the surface by the drugs was not good for him either.

"No. Just lightening it. Seeing if we can keep him stable at a reduced dose. We've been changing it very gradually."

The nurse's eyes flickered to the wide LCD screen on the wall, where frame after frame showed the interiors of the various rooms in the ward.

"He looks fine. Someone will be checking on him in a few minutes."

"Okay. Just wanted to make sure..."

The nurse nodded and looked back down at her paperwork, ending the conversation. Bethany went back to Gem's room.

"Hey, Gem." She sat on the bed next to him and took his hand, as usual. "Doing any better today? The nurse says they're changing your meds."

Gem gave a low moan. Bethany searched his face. Was he in pain? Aware? She looked for any change in his expression—anything to indicate what was going on inside his brain.

"Shhh," she soothed. "It's okay. You're going to be alright. It will all work out in the end."

He rubbed his eyes. Although they were open, she still couldn't see any awareness there. He seemed just as distant as ever.

"Do you want to hear about what's going on with the gang?" Bethany suggested. It was better than trying to talk to him about his twin, or about the crushing grief that he was going through. "They're looking at Thrasher for that cop murder a few months back. Angelletti. I guess someone spilled something about Ripper involvement. They figure he might have hired someone to take care of it."

Gem's head went back and forth like he was shaking his head or trying to see through a thick fog.

"Nnnn... noooo."

Bethany stared into Gem's blank eyes. Even though she knew it wasn't really an answer to what she was saying, she continued as if it were. Like she would talk to a baby or a cat, pretending they were answering so that she could continue with a conversation.

"No? He didn't hire anyone? I don't know. No idea if he had anything to do with it. Not like he would tell me that kind of thing."

She waited until his next moan.

"He does tell me things sometimes. He knows I'm discreet and that I wouldn't tell anybody." She chuckled. "Even you, now. I know you won't be repeating it to anyone, but that's how good I am at keeping confidences. I won't even tell secrets to you while you're catatonic."

Gem pushed himself around weakly. Bethany helped him into a sitting position. "Is that better? Is that what you want?"

"Nnnnoooo…"

Bethany stroked his hair, smoothing down the wispy curls. "It's nice to see you getting up. Pretty soon you'll be running around this joint, making all kinds of trouble."

He grasped her wrist and pushed her hand away. Bethany let her hand hover for a moment, then tried again, touching his hair. Again, he reflexively pushed her away.

"Are you in there, Gem?" Bethany whispered. "Can you hear me?"

His lips twitched. She could see them form 'no' again, but he didn't say it aloud.

Bethany startled when a nurse entered the room. "Oh, I see you have a visitor, Mr. Gem Johnson," said a diminutive black woman with an island accent. "And how is our boy today?"

Bethany moved to the side so that the nurse could examine Gem.

"Did you sit him up or did he do that himself?" the nurse questioned.

"A bit of both. I helped him."

The woman was still for a moment, monitoring Gem's pulse. She dropped his arm back to the bed and picked up the clipboard she had set down. "A bit faster than I would like," she told Bethany. "I don't think the doctor wants him waking up yet."

"No. Not yet."

The nurse scribbled her comments on the form. Gem rubbed his eyes again, then reached over and grabbed Bethany's hand. Not pushing her away this time, but holding it like she held his for hours when she came to visit. The little nurse's eyes widened, and she wrote more down.

"How are we feeling, Mr. Johnson?" she inquired in a loud voice as if he were hard of hearing. She gave his other arm a bit of a shake, and then a pinch that made Gem pull away. He didn't let go of Bethany's hand, but waved his other arm at the nurse, as if swatting at an irritating fly.

"Nnnoooo… sssstop…"

She pulled out a light and flashed it in each of his eyes,

frowning when Gem swiped at her and blinked and squinted his eyes in response.

"The doctor's going to want to change his dose. He's too close to the surface," she said crisply. She looked at her watch with a scowl.

Bethany knew that the doctor didn't make his rounds very often. It would probably be several hours before he was there to authorize any further changes to Gem's treatment protocol.

"We'll have to use mechanical restraints until he can change his orders."

"No," Bethany objected. "Why would you have to do that? He's not fully awake. He's not hurting anything."

"No guarantee he'll stay that way. We need to restrain him for his own protection. If he tries to harm himself—"

"Please, no. Can't you wait and see how he does? Maybe he'll be okay this time."

"We really cannot take the chance."

"I'll stay with him," Bethany promised. "I'll call someone if he starts doing anything that might hurt him. If I'm with him, maybe he'll be okay."

The nurse looked at Gem and then gave Bethany a long look. "You need to call someone even if it seems minor. Scratching his face or hitting his head with his fist. Anything."

"I will," Bethany promised.

"And he hasn't shown any violence toward anyone else while he's been here, but the records show that he has been violent in the past. You don't know if he might come after you if he wakes up fully."

"Gem wouldn't do that."

"Don't judge him by what is normal or sane. His actions don't need to be logical. He could hurt the person he loves the most."

"No..." Bethany said with a regretful shake of her head. "The person he loves the most is already gone."

"Please be careful," the nurse advised. "I don't want either of you to get hurt. It's better he's restrained until the doctor is here to determine the best course of action."

"I'll be okay. I'll call if he needs anything."

The nurse shook her head and walked back out again. Bethany looked at Gem. There was still no awareness in his face, despite his actions. It was all reflexes. Even his hand holding hers. She gave it a little squeeze.

"I know you're in there, Gem. Please come back to me. I promise I'll help you."

His head went back and forth. She waited for some sign that he understood or was trying to reach her.

———

It was hours before the doctor got there, and Bethany was exhausted from her vigil. But she stayed at Gem's side, watching every movement and making sure he didn't injure himself.

Ives walked in, adjusting the stethoscope around his neck. "I understand our patient is a little more awake than expected."

Bethany nodded. "He's been pretty active. He hasn't really woken up... but he's so close."

"That's progress." Ives began a cursory examination of Gem, listening to his heart, looking in his eyes as the nurse had done, and testing his reflexes. Gem pushed him away irritably. "Yes, very good," Ives acknowledged. "Can you let him go? Move away?"

Bethany let go of Gem's hand. While she was reluctant to do so, it was also a relief. She'd been tense and sitting in the same position for too long. She got up off the bed and stretched her sore muscles.

Gem grasped in the bedsheets beside him as if searching for something he had dropped. He grunted, looking around him with more consciousness than Bethany had seen in him since his twin's death.

"Be—Beth..."

"I'm still here," she assured him, thrilling at his attempt to form her name.

"Nnnooo...."

His hands clenched into fists and drilled into his eyes. "Bethany," he said clearly.

"I'm here, Gem."

Ives pulled Gem's hands back from his face. "Gem," he said firmly. "Gem, I need you to listen to me. Can you hear me?"

Gem flailed, pulling back out of Ives's grip.

"Gem."

Bethany moved back toward Gem.

"No," Ives held up a hand to prevent her from getting closer. Gem's movements grew more frantic.

"Bethany!"

She wanted desperately to comfort him, but she obeyed Ives and stayed back. Gem's head slammed back against the wall with a crash. Ives reached forward to move or restrain him, and Gem fought off his hold. Gem turned his head toward Bethany, his eyes intent.

"I'm here," she repeated.

Gem reached out both hands toward her. Bethany moved forward. Ives allowed her to get closer again. Bethany took Gem's hands, held them for a minute, and then moved closer to hug him.

"Gem. It's okay."

"No," he shook his head. His eyes were dark and haunted. "No." He stared at her. "I died."

Bethany squeezed onto the bed beside him. She held him close, trying to comfort him. "No, you're alive. You're still here." She kissed his head. "You're alive."

Tears squeezed out of his eyes. Ives took Gem's wrist, and Gem didn't pull away.

"You are still alive," Ives agreed. "And we're here to help you. Bethany's here to help you, and my staff and I are here to help you."

Gem closed his eyes and held his face against Bethany's shoulder. He shuddered.

"I died," he repeated. "I'm not here."

"You are here," Ives said. "You still have a life to lead."

"He means his twin," Bethany whispered. "He says 'I' for both of them. He doesn't... he doesn't differentiate between them."

Ives considered this. "You have experienced a great loss," he told Gem gently. "We are here to help you with that. It was your brother who died. Not... you."

"I died," Gem repeated, his voice hoarse.

"Gem died," Bethany said. "Your brother. Yes."

"I am not here."

"You are here. Your brother is not here," Ives clarified. "You can continue to live without him."

Gem drew back from Bethany and just looked at Ives with his dark, hollow eyes. Bethany knew there was no way that they could understand the depth of his loss and how desperately alone he felt without his twin.

———

Riker found Gem, not in his bed, but slumped in a wheelchair in his room, a strap holding him in place to keep him from sliding out to the floor. Riker thought at first that this was just a measure to keep Gem from getting bedsores and that his condition was no different.

"Gem?"

Gem's head lifted at Riker's greeting, and Gem looked directly at him. Riker was startled by his reaction.

"Oh, you're awake. Hi. How are you feeling?"

Riker looked into the bruised, dark hollows of Gem's eyes. Gem rubbed a hand across his forehead. He stared at Riker as if he were trying to remember who he was.

"It's Riker. You remember me?"

"Where am I?" Gem demanded. "I'm not here."

Riker sat on the edge of the empty bed.

"You're at the hospital," he said slowly. "You're here to get better. Do you remember what happened?"

Gem's eyes went around the room. He looked at Riker again.

"At juvie?"

"You're at the hospital. You remember when you were at juvie before you came here?"

"Where am I?" Gem asked plaintively. "At juvie?"

Riker stared at him helplessly, at a loss as to how to get through to Gem. Gem put his hand to his throat. The bruises had long since faded, but Riker still remembered them as clearly as if it had just happened. A tear traced down Gem's cheek.

"You remember," Riker said. "You... miss him."

"I can still feel it," Gem said. He ran his fingernails down his throat as if trying to find the noose to loosen it and pull it off. "Don't let me die!"

"You're not dying. It's gone. It's not there anymore. I promise."

Gem stared at him. He blinked a few times, more tears running over his pale cheeks. "It's too late." His voice was as hollow as his eyes. "I'm dead."

Riker couldn't deny that a part of Gem had died. The boys had been more a part of each other than even conjoined twins. They were psychically bound together.

The neurologist had said that he was surprised that Gem could even function with the abnormalities they could see on his CAT scan. The psychologist had said that each filled the other's deficits. Together, they had formed one complete personality.

So how was Gem to function without that other half?

"I can't imagine what it must feel like," Riker said. "It must be like a soldier who has lost a limb. Or two. To be missing that part of yourself."

Gem's eyes fixed on Riker. "Myself," he whispered.

Riker nodded. "Yourself."

Gem put his hands up to his face, sobbing.

———

Riker was still there when Ives did his rounds. Ives looked over the record of the fifteen-minute intervals since he'd been there last.

"He's been crying for a long time," Riker said. "Can you give him something to settle him down?"

"Aren't you the one who was so concerned about getting him off of the sedatives in the first place?"

Riker shifted uncomfortably. "Well, yes... of course... but I just wanted to be sure... It can't be good for him to be so upset."

Ives shook his head. "On the contrary. It is very good. He needs to feel the loss before he can process it and grieve properly. He's not trying to harm himself now. Tears are the best we can hope for."

Riker looked at Gem's red face and eyes. Then Ives blocked Gem from Riker's view as he conducted his examination.

"Do you want to lie back down?" Ives asked.

Gem nodded his head, snuffling. The doctor unbuckled the strap that kept Gem from sliding right out of the chair and helped him transition from the wheelchair to the bed, Gem shuffling his feet and leaning on the doctor for support.

"There. Do you want to sleep, or do you want to visit some more?"

"Sleep."

"Alright. We'll see you another day, Mr. Riker?"

Riker stood up. "Yes. I'll be back. Do you think..." Riker dropped his voice to a whisper. "Do you think he's getting better? He'll be okay?"

Ives gave a slight head-shake. "It's a long road. He's barely taken one step. Let's take it one day at a time."

CHAPTER THIRTY-ONE

W HAT EXACTLY IS IT you expect to accomplish?" Gordon asked after Riker recounted the details of his last visit to Gem. Gordon shuffled through the papers in his in-basket, seeing what was getting urgent. He threw most of it back. "Under the deal that the DA made with Gem 2, Gem 1 is immune from any of the charges relating to Raphael's death and the crimes committed while he was with the Rippers. Are you hoping to uncover other charges?"

Riker stared at Gordon. "What?"

"Why are you going to see him? Do you expect him to confess to other crimes?"

"No. This isn't about charging him with anything. This is about... helping him deal with his loss."

"He isn't anything to you. He's not family or a friend. He's just a kid. A gang banger that up until now, you were doing everything you could to put behind bars."

"He *is* locked up. He's where he belongs. I'm just trying to help him."

"Because..."

"Because he hasn't got anybody else. He doesn't have any family. Who knows what happened to his mother. Buried as a Jane Doe somewhere, I suspect. His grandmother is gone. His brother is gone. He doesn't have anybody. Just... me. I feel sorry for him."

Gordon picked up his coffee and had a sip. "You're doing a lot more than I would ever be inclined to do. And he does have someone. The girl. Bethany."

"She's doing whatever she can for him too, but she's just a kid. Hopefully, we can get through to him."

"And what? Cure him? So that they release him back out onto the streets?"

Riker hadn't even considered what would happen to Gem if he got better. In the back of his mind, he had thought that once Gem was better, he'd be sent back to juvie again. But of course, that wasn't true. The ink was dry on the deal with the DA. When Gem was well enough to be released from the psych ward, he wouldn't be going back to juvie again. He would, Riker suspected, go straight back to the Rippers. And he would continue the course of violence he had followed before.

"I hadn't thought of that."

But that day was a long way off. Like Dr. Ives had said, Gem had a long road to go down, and none of them knew how quickly he would complete the journey or even if he would finish it.

———

Gem was a little better every time Bethany went to see him. A little more life returned to his eyes. A little bit more purposeful movement. His eyes weren't looking quite so dark and hopeless as they had in the beginning. He had lost a lot of weight, but he was starting to eat again. Starting to be more aware of the passage of time and the rest of the ward around him. He was no longer confined to his room but was able to frequent the common areas and, if he wanted to, visit with the other patients.

"Gem...?"

Gem had been watching the TV, but at Bethany's call, he turned his head. He looked at her wistfully. How long had it been since she had seen him smile?

"Bethany. You came."

"Of course I did," Bethany confirmed. "Where do you want to visit? Here? In your room?"

Gem looked around suspiciously at the other patients. "Too many ears," he observed. Bethany didn't reach over to help him get to his feet, even though he moved like an old man with an inner ear problem. Still getting his sea legs. She stood back to give him room and then walked beside him, letting him lead the way.

"You're looking a lot better," she told him.

He looked at her, his mouth moving, but nothing coming out. Eventually, he spoke aloud.

"I haven't... seen myself... for a long time," he said. "You say... I'm looking better?"

Bethany hesitated. It was the slightly stilted language that she had come to recognize as an attempt to communicate with her about his twin. He wasn't talking about not having a mirror to look at his own face. He wanted to know how the other Gem was.

But he knew that his twin had died. Those first few days after awakening, he had repeated it over and over again. *I died. I'm not here. I died.*

"Gem..." Bethany touched his face, trying to make it clear that she was talking about him, not his twin. "*You* are looking better. You are not looking so... worn."

He touched her fingers, then touched his face, like it was something foreign and unfamiliar. He explored it with tentative fingers.

"My face."

Bethany nodded. "Yes."

He dropped his hand. "I need to see myself," he said urgently. "I have to make sure... I'm okay." He looked around the corridor. "I... can't... find myself... here."

"No." Bethany felt tears coming to her eyes. She swallowed, trying to keep her voice calm and reassuring. "Your twin is not here. Gem... he died. You know he died."

"I am still here," he insisted. He touched his face again, with both hands, this time, squeezing and pressing it to prove its solidity. "I am here. But... it's empty. Where... is... *me?*" he pleaded.

Bethany hugged Gem. She kept a tight rein on her own emotions. She had to be strong for him. She had to help him find his way through.

"You are here. But he... your other self... is gone."

"No."

"Yes, Gem. You know it's true. They said you felt it when he died. You felt him pass out of this world."

"No! No. I am still here!"

"He is in your heart. He'll never leave you completely because he will always be in your heart. The two of you shared something... very special. A bit of your souls."

"Not gone!" Gem insisted. He shoved a laundry trolley sitting in the hallway, making it ricochet off the wall with a loud crash. "Not gone. I can't live. Not without... myself." He grasped at Bethany's words. "My soul!"

Nurses and orderlies were coming to see what the ruckus was about. Bethany tried to wave them back, knowing they would just upset Gem more.

"Gem... when Honey died, I felt the same way. I didn't think I could live without her. I didn't know how to go on without her. Even though we had been apart, knowing she had died just about killed me. I said it couldn't be true. I didn't want to believe it. I kept going to sleep, thinking that maybe when I got up in the morning, it would all just be a dream. But whenever I woke up in the morning... she was still dead."

"I am not *dead!*" Gem howled. He punched the wall, and Bethany heard the sickening crunch of the bones in his hand against the cinder block. The wing had been solidly built with psych and violent patients in mind, not with drywall that would be destroyed by a few blows.

The orderlies and nurses descended on Gem. He was no match for all of them at the same time. Especially not with his dominant hand out of commission. In just a couple of minutes, they had restrained him, jabbed a needle into the back of his thigh, and carried him back to his room. Gem was not completely unconscious, but lay there moaning, unable to respond to anything around him.

One of the orderlies began to connect the four-point restraints. "Just until we can treat his hand," he assured Bethany.

"What happened?" an Asian nurse asked Bethany, stepping too close to her, inside her comfort zone.

Bethany took a step back and held up her hands, trying to maintain some distance, physical and emotional. "We were just talking... He says his brother's not dead. But he knows he is."

"He is in denial. It's normal."

"It's normal? None of this is normal. Gem is not normal. He's... special. You can't understand the kind of relationship he had with his brother."

"He still has to go through all the stages of grief, just like anyone else."

Bethany looked at Gem, unable to move in the bed. She wiped her eyes. "You take care of him, please. He's very important to me. I want him to come back to me."

The nurse nodded. "We will do our best."

CHAPTER THIRTY-TWO

DIETRICH COULD SEE BY Bethany's eyes that she had been crying again. She'd obviously been up to the hospital to see Gem. He passed her a beer. Bethany startled, looking away from the TV she'd been staring at in a trance. She looked for a minute at the can he was holding in front of her face and eventually took it.

"Thanks, D." She gave him a wan smile. "I guess I could really use something tonight."

She didn't have more than a sip of it, though, before setting it to the side.

"How is he today?" Dietrich asked. Not because he wanted to know. Gem was, as far as D knew, broken beyond repair, and of no further interest to the Rippers. But because he knew it was the only thing that Bethany would be able to talk about and he wanted to talk to her. Until she had talked about Gem, she wouldn't be able to move on to any other topic of conversation.

"Not good today," Bethany said. "I mean... I guess he's getting better... he's moving in the right direction... or at least moving. But I don't know... I really don't know how he's going to get over this."

"From what I hear... he's not. So why are you still hanging out with him? He's where he belongs. With all the other nut jobs. Let them take care of him."

"I can't just leave him there, without any family or friends. That would be cruel."

"It's not doing any good, you going back there all the time. Is it?"

"I don't know... I think he's happy to see me. He knows who I am. He tries to talk to me about how he's feeling."

"But he can't do anything for you," Dietrich said. He touched her hand. "Don't you want... someone who can return your affection?"

Bethany pulled her hand away from his. Slowly, not like she was offended or disturbed by his touch. It just wasn't what she wanted.

"I'm not looking for reciprocation right now," she said. "I know it's going to take a long time before he's all better. Before he can get out. If he ever can."

"Then why not focus on someone who is available? You don't need to shut yourself off from the world, just because Gem is off his rocker. Live your own life until he's better, or forget about him."

Bethany shook her head. "I'm sorry," she apologized. She knew he would rather she turned her attentions to him, and she was trying to let him down gently. "Right now... I need to be there for him."

"Can't you be with him and still... take care of your own needs too?"

She shook her head.

Dietrich sighed. "Then why exactly are you still hanging around with the Rippers?" he demanded. "Sunnyboy's debt's been paid. You're not seeing anyone else anymore. Why haven't you moved on?"

Bethany stared at him, a crease between her eyebrows. She looked truly bewildered. "I... don't know. I never thought of what else to do."

"Go back to school. Get a job. Marry the nutcase and have nutty little babies." Dietrich shrugged. "What's the point in hanging around with a bunch of bangers on their way to jail or the morgue when you could actually have a life?"

As Bethany drew closer to Gem's room, she could hear him shouting. That wasn't unusual lately. Everything seemed to set him off. Dr. Ives was working on mood stabilizers, but Bethany understood that it would take days or weeks for the drugs to reach their full effect. Then they might find that they didn't work and had to be scrapped. Then they would try something else. She knew it was a slow process and wished they could just find the magic cocktail that would work and allow Gem to move forward.

"It's your fault!" Gem was shouting.

Bethany peeked in the door and saw that Riker was there. He didn't appear to be bothered by Gem's accusation. Whatever was going on, he was taking it calmly.

"If you hadn't arrested me, it would never have happened!" Gem pointed out. Bethany swallowed. There was only one thing that Gem could be talking about.

"I *had* to arrest you," Riker said. "That is my job. To get criminals off the street. I can't just stand by and let juvies rob banks and drug stores and terrorize and murder. You know the law. You knew you were breaking it and could get arrested for it. You both knew."

"You're not supposed to arrest me when I have an alibi," Gem maintained, his tone aggrieved.

"I broke your alibi. I did what I had to, Gem. I'm sorry for the choice that your brother made, but it wasn't my doing. I would much rather see the two of you behind bars than him dead and you here." Riker shook his head, mouth twisting into a grimace. "I can't understand why he would make that choice. I know why he wanted the deal. He wanted to keep you out of prison. But suicide..."

Gem choked, his face red with fury. "It's not fair! You took everything I had!"

"I didn't make that choice. Your twin did. He could have chosen to fight the charges. Or to serve his time. He didn't have to do what he did."

But Gem was not listening, completely shutting out everything that Riker was saying. He didn't accept that his twin's death was beyond Riker's control.

"It was you!" He threw a punch at Riker, hitting the cop square in the chest with his casted hand. "It was you! Your fault! You couldn't leave me alone!"

Riker shoved him back. "You're mad. I get that, Gem."

"Now you can't fix it! You can't take it back!" Gem's voice broke. He threw another punch at Riker, again connecting, and again being pushed back.

"He's dead," Riker agreed. "That's way outside of my jurisdiction."

Gem gave an incoherent cry of frustration, pelting Riker with both fists. Instead of pushing him away this time, Riker grabbed Gem and pulled him against his body, restraining him in a bear hug so that Gem was unable to keep hitting.

"No!" Gem cried. "No, no, no!" He gasped for breath. "You took everything I had!"

Riker saw Bethany standing in the doorway. He jerked his chin, inviting her in.

"Bethany's here," he told Gem. He carefully transferred Gem into Bethany's arms. "Don't hit her. This is Bethany."

Gem let Bethany hold him. "It's not fair," he moaned.

"I know, Gem," she whispered. "It's not fair. You two should have had a long life together. A chance at happiness."

Gem sobbed. Bethany held him and stroked his cheek tenderly. Riker moved toward the door.

"Back in a couple of days," he advised Gem. "Better practice your boxing skills before then."

CHAPTER THIRTY-THREE

BETHANY FOUND GEM SITTING quietly in his room. He was sitting in a wheelchair staring out the window and, at first, she thought that he had been sedated again.

"Gem?"

He didn't flinch or turn to look at her. Bethany sat on the bed and looked at his face, trying to analyze every line of his expression.

"Are you okay, Gem? Can you talk to me?"

"I can't *hear* myself," Gem said distantly, staring out at the skyline, not turning his eyes toward her or acknowledging her. "No matter how hard I try... I can't hear myself think."

Bethany reached over and touched his fingers. He folded his hand around hers. But he still didn't turn his head.

"It must be really quiet in there," she suggested.

Gem closed his eyes for a minute, then opened them again in a long, slow blink. "Where am I?" he whispered.

"He is still in your heart," Bethany said. "I believe that. He couldn't ever leave you totally alone."

Gem put his other hand over his heart, feeling and listening. He shook his head.

"I am hollow. Empty. I died and all that is left is this body."

Bethany squeezed his hand. She didn't say anything, letting him process it. What could she say? The medical staff was doing every-

218

thing they could to help him. And she couldn't claim to understand what he was going through, even if she had lost Honey. It wasn't the same. She couldn't comprehend the enormity of what he had lost.

Still with his hand over his heart, Gem whispered to Bethany. She couldn't make out every word, just enough to follow the progress of his thoughts. She listened without interrupting.

"I could always hear myself. Distance didn't matter. I could always hear, as clear as I'm talking to you... Not words, exactly... Thoughts. Feelings. Sometimes... I tried to block it... when things were bad... so bad it hurt myself..." His grip tightened on Bethany's hand, giving her a sharp shot of pain. Just a taste of the agony he was going through. "I always protected myself... myself protected I..." Gem sniffled. He choked. It was a long time before he could go on again. "Why...? Why did I do it?"

"I don't know." Bethany let go of Gem's hand to wipe away a tear that overflowed and trailed down his cheek. "I don't know what he was thinking. He wanted to protect you. To protect you from having to be in prison for the rest of your life."

"Without my soul?" Gem wrapped both arms around himself. Like he was cold or trying to hold himself together. "This *is* a prison."

"He made a deal to keep you out of juvie," Bethany said. Had anyone bothered to explain this to him? Had Riker told him about the deal? Had Gem been told of it ahead of time, by his lawyer? Or if Gem and his twin truly did share thoughts, did Gem already know all of this on an instinctual level? "He confessed to Raphael's murder, and Cairns's, and the robberies, so that they couldn't prosecute you for them. He wanted to save you."

Gem rocked back and forth slightly. "I didn't want to be here," he explained, his voice strained. He swallowed hard and licked his chapped lips. Bethany looked around for a cup of water to hand to him. A lot of the meds made his mouth dry. Not to mention the emotional upheaval. "I wanted to be free. I didn't want to come back here."

"He wanted you to be free, and safe, like before," Bethany agreed. "And you weren't safe in juvie, were you?" He hadn't explained to her all that had happened to him in juvie, but she knew some of it. And she knew enough about places like that to guess at how he had been victimized. Again. "He didn't want you to be hurt anymore."

"Why couldn't I stop myself?" Gem put his hands over his eyes, shaking his head.

He spoke hoarsely, his voice rising above the rasping whisper, and it brought tears to Bethany's eye to hear the anguish in his voice. She rolled her eyes up toward the ceiling, trying to avoid breaking down. She needed to be strong for Gem. She couldn't think of his twin, and how she would miss that quieter, more thoughtful personality. She only had one Gem now, and she couldn't think about what it was she had lost, because his loss was so much greater.

"I tried. I told myself. I begged. I tried to stop myself." He shook his head. "Why couldn't I stop myself?"

Bethany rubbed Gem's arm. He was too far away for her to hug him, sitting isolated and inaccessible in the rigid wheelchair.

"He made his own choice. So that you would be free to make your own choices."

Gem slumped, hands in his lap, staring out the window once more. Bethany sat quietly, letting him think it through.

How could Gem 2 ever have thought that Gem 1 would be able to continue without him? How could he have thought that his twin had any chance at a normal life without his other half? Was it weakness rather than altruism that had led him to commit suicide? Was he afraid to spend the rest of his life in prison? She'd always thought him the stronger one. More logical. The protector. But maybe he was just as frightened and victimized as Gem 1, trapped and unable to see any way ever to escape. Maybe it had been too much for him and he had taken the only way out that he could think of.

"If I can get out of here, maybe I can see myself again."

Bethany looked at Gem. He had to know the impossibility of ever seeing Gem 2 again. But who was she to judge how he might be able to reconnect with that side of himself? Bethany saw Honey in the funniest places sometimes. She was comforted to see violets springing up in an untended garden. To brush her own hair until it shone, remembering Honey's identical, long, blond hair. Honey had been beautiful. And sometimes Bethany felt like Honey was there, beside her, keeping her company. Maybe it would be the same for Gem. Perhaps even more so. Who was she to judge?

"Maybe you can."

Gem's eyes left the scene outside his window, and he looked at her for the first time on that visit, shocked at her agreement. Bethany took his hand again as his eyes searched her face.

"He'll find a way to be with you, Gem. Just like Honey."

Gem's fingers left hers and found the hair hanging in a sheet by her face. She was sure he too saw Honey's hair when he looked at her. He stroked the long, silky strands.

"I took care of her," he whispered. "She was my friend."

"I'm glad you were with her. Especially in the end."

He choked up and started to sob. Bethany let her own tears fall. She hadn't had anyone to share her mourning for Honey. The only family they had possessed had disowned them both, abandoning them to live or die on the streets. Now she could mourn Honey with Gem, the only other person who had truly loved her.

————

They eventually moved on to other topics, Bethany trying to lead Gem from thoughts of his loss to the future they might share.

"I'm moving out of our apartment," she told him carefully, unsure how he would take the news. "I was thinking... it's time for me to make a break from the Rippers. As long as I'm right there, they're going to keep coming around, even if I say no..."

Gem's brows drew down.

"You know they won't leave me alone as long as I'm right there, accessible. Especially without you around."

Gem shook his head. "I don't want you getting hurt."

"No. I need to do better at taking care of myself. Protecting myself. I'm not alone on the streets anymore."

She left it hanging, leaving the thought unfinished for Gem to jump in. She held her breath.

"You have the money..." Gem said. He seemed to be having problems forming the thoughts. He wasn't the planner. Not the one who would normally have dealt with financial issues. "That money is yours, whatever you need."

"Until you get out. Then we can spend it together. Like before."

She didn't feel obliged to argue and say that she didn't want to take money from him. They were together, and he wanted to take care of her and make sure she was protected. She wouldn't be reckless with it, but she would take what she needed. And she'd find a job. Something honest. Gem would get better, and maybe he could find a job too.

The courts were trying to get their hands on the money since Gem 2 had confessed, knowing it had come from the bank heist. But since they had arrested her as an accessory and then had not been able to hold her, Bethany had been dividing it up and moving it around, hoping that if they ever managed to get a subpoena for it, they would not be able to track it all down. If she and Gem could both get jobs, they could survive even if the police got the heist money.

Gem rubbed his forehead. There were lines of fatigue around his eyes. She knew he needed to sleep. He still wasn't strong.

"*When I get out,*" he repeated. "You think I'm going to get out?"

"Yes. You'll get stronger. And better. They won't keep you here forever."

He didn't say anything to that. Bethany wasn't sure if he wanted to get better. Moving on might feel like a betrayal of his twin. Moving on meant that the loss didn't matter. That he could recover from the devastating blow.

"I'm going to find a place closer to the hospital. So that it's easier to come to see you. If you only get out for day visits to start with, or if you're in an outpatient program, you can come back here easily for treatment."

"I'm still a juvie," Gem pointed out. "They don't let minor patients live on their own."

"They'd probably try a group home or treatment center," Bethany admitted. She saw a shudder go through Gem's body. His eyes widened in alarm. "But you wouldn't have to stay there. We'd get you out of there, and you would come live with me. At our apartment."

"I don't know." He rubbed his forehead again. "I... I just can't think anymore. I can't... I can't make it make sense. Like I used to."

"It's okay. We'll work it out. I just wanted to let you know. That we wouldn't be with the Rippers anymore."

Again, she held her breath. Saying that *she* wouldn't be with the Rippers was one thing. She had the right to make that decision, and she sensed that Gem was relieved by her decision. But suggesting that *Gem* wouldn't be with the gang anymore was a lot more daring, and he might completely flip out over the thought.

Gem just sat there, not reacting. Bethany stood up.

"You're tired." She bent down and kissed him on the cheek. "You want to lay down?"

He nodded and rubbed his eyes with one hand. Bethany restrained herself from helping him get up and settle into bed. He needed to do things for himself. He wasn't that frail. The more he did for himself, the better he would feel.

The more he would heal.

"Okay. See you soon, Gem."

CHAPTER THIRTY-FOUR

RIKER STOPPED AT THE nursing station after checking Gem's room and finding it empty. Gem didn't seem to be in any of the common areas.

"Where's Gem?"

The nurses all knew Riker on sight, and he was familiar with all the regulars. The redhead looked up from her work and smiled at him.

"He's just at group therapy." She looked at her watch. "He shouldn't be long now. They finished five minutes ago."

Riker nodded. He leaned against the desk, waiting for Gem's return.

"He's doing group therapy now? That's progress."

She gave a little shrug. "I can't really talk to you about his treatment..." She chewed on her lip. She knew that Gem didn't have any family. His only regular visitors were Riker and Bethany. They were his new family. "He's going to group, but he's not contributing anything at this point." She shuffled the folders on her desk. "Dr. Ives wants him involved in as many different programs as possible right now. To keep him busy and keep him from just sitting in his room all day."

"That makes sense." Gem had not been very animated during Riker's last few visits. His anger and animosity toward Riker had faded. Gem no longer yelled and tried to hit him. Now, it was like he didn't care. Like he wasn't able to feel anything at all. "What about the meds? Isn't he on antidepressants?"

"Of course. But not everyone reacts the same way. Sometimes they don't work. And in teenagers, they can cause suicidal ideation, so that's something else we have to watch for. Meds can't replace good therapy and the desire to get better, to overcome challenges."

"He's come a long way."

"Yes," she agreed, "but he still has a ways to go. And to keep going, he has to want it."

Gem and a couple of other patients were escorted through the big double security doors back into the ward. They split up to go their different directions. Gem saw Riker standing there and didn't say anything.

"Hey, Gem. You want to go to your room? Or the common room? We could walk around if you like."

Gem looked around. "I don't care."

"Why don't we walk?" Riker was mindful of what the nurse had said. They wanted to keep him from just sitting around.

Gem stood there for a moment. Riker motioned for him to join him. Gem peeled his feet off the floor like they had been pasted there and moved to Riker's side with a sigh.

"Group therapy today?" Riker said.

"Yeah."

"How's that going?"

"Sucks."

Riker chuckled. "How is Bethany?"

Gem thought about it. "She's good," he said finally. "She comes and visits, like you."

"She seems like a nice girl."

"Yeah." Gem stopped at the back of the common room and stared at the TV playing quietly at the front of the room. He didn't look at Riker.

"What are you two planning on doing when you get out of here?" Riker asked. "You should do something nice together. Take her out somewhere special for all she's done for you."

Gem didn't move or speak. Riker nudged him.

"Gem. Did you hear what I said?"

Gem grunted.

"You should plan something," Riker prodded.

Gem shook his head. "I'm never getting out of here." The words came slowly. "Didn't you know?"

"What do you mean? When you're better, you'll get out."

"I'm not getting better," Gem said. "I already died."

"Your twin died," Riker said. He didn't know how many times they had covered the same ground. "But you are still alive. He would expect you to go on, to live, and experience life fully."

Gem stared at the TV. They couldn't even hear what was being said by the two-dimensional characters on the screen. But Gem appeared mesmerized.

"He didn't want you to die. He wanted you to go on. To live a full life with Bethany." Riker didn't know why Gem 2 had done what he had. But this seemed as likely an explanation as any.

"I can't. I'm already dead."

Riker grasped Gem's shoulder. "Are you okay, Gem? Are you... thinking of killing yourself?"

Gem shook his head. Riker wasn't sure which question he was answering. If either of them.

"You're getting better," Riker encouraged. "I think you should be working on a plan for what you want to happen when you get out. Even if it's just something little."

"You're not my doctor," Gem snapped. "Quit acting like one."

"I didn't know I was. Is that what they're telling you?"

Gem nodded morosely. He brushed his shaggy hair back. He was in need of a good haircut. "Don't want to get better. Can't..." He grimaced. "I can't leave it behind. Don't want to. I... want it to hurt."

"Why?"

For a long time, Gem just stood there, gaze distant, much farther away than the muffled TV.

"I don't want to fill it up," he said in a hoarse voice. "Don't want to fill the emptiness." He put his hand over his heart. "That space... stays."

Riker contemplated this. "You're never going to forget him," he said. "Even if you move on and find something to do with your life, and love and laugh again. That's not a betrayal. You'll always remember him and what he was to you. But someday, maybe it won't hurt as much."

Gem turned his head to look at Riker. "Why would I want it to hurt less?" he challenged.

Riker couldn't find an answer.

CHAPTER THIRTY-FIVE

RIKER ARRIVED AS GEM and Bethany were packing the few personal possessions he had acquired while at the hospital into a limp duffel bag. Bethany was smiling, her face aglow. Gem seemed less certain about getting ready to go. He was looking well. Not quite back to how he had been before the separation from his brother, but he had advanced through the darkest parts of his grief. Maybe it was the chemical cocktail they now had him on. Maybe it was the therapy or the long talks. Or maybe it was just the passage of time. He had finally come to acceptance and was poised an inch away from taking the steps to move on with his life.

"Hi," Bethany greeted, seeing Riker before Gem did.

"Hi. All ready to go?" Riker asked.

Bethany looked at the bag and looked at Gem, raising her eyebrows. Gem picked up his luggage like it might contain a live snake.

"Suppose there's nothing stopping me," he said.

"You're moving into Bethany's place?"

"It's *our* place," Bethany said. "It's always been our place."

"Okay. Your place. Social Services is okay with that? They didn't insist on... adult supervision?"

"Monitoring," Gem said, and lifted his pant leg to show off a tracker strapped to his ankle. "Have to keep it on, come back for therapy, keep taking the meds." His face twisted and his anxiety showed momentarily through the studied calm. "Still in prison, even if I'm not in juvie anymore."

There were minor charges pending against him. Things that hadn't been covered in the deal with Gem 2. Riker knew that Dr. Ives had been in contact with Social Services, emphasizing how important it was that Gem keep coming back for ongoing treatment. Chances were, he'd never be able to live completely independently. If he ever broke up with Bethany, all bets were off. It was doubtful he could live outside an institutional setting without that support.

"It's to keep you safe," Riker said. "They know how vulnerable teens can be on their own."

Gem and Bethany exchanged glances. They both had more experience than they wanted in that respect. Gem could and probably would brag and bluster about how tough he was and how he could take care of himself, but he'd still been victimized. By Raphael. And by others, if Riker guessed right.

"Listen... I know you probably have all kinds of plans now that you're getting out. But there's one thing I wondered about... You don't have a job yet, do you?"

Gem snorted. "Because people are lining up to hire crazy juvies, right?"

Riker shrugged. He handed a pamphlet to Gem. It had gotten slightly crumpled and dog-eared in Riker's pocket, where he'd had it the last few times he had come to visit Gem. But the timing had never seemed right. Gem's eyes flickered over the front of the pamphlet, titled 'Night Rescue Foundation,' with a picture of an open doorway on the front. He showed it to Bethany and handed it to her.

Bethany looked at Riker, then down at the brochure. She read the title to Gem, then unfolded it and scanned the inside.

"A charity dedicated to ending child sex trafficking," she read aloud to him.

Gem's face flushed. He and Bethany looked at each other, faces guarded.

"I'm way out of that business," Gem growled. "Why would you give me that?"

Bethany didn't echo the sentiments, but it was in her face. Riker swallowed.

"They're looking for spokespersons," he explained. "People who know something about the business and can talk about it to at-risk children and potential donors."

Bethany clued in before Gem did. "A job? They would pay Gem to talk to people?"

Riker nodded. "It's not a lot. But it's an honest living. And you could help keep other kids from going through what you did."

Gem scowled at Riker. But he wasn't arguing, and he didn't blow up. He would need time to think about it and to talk it over with Bethany.

Bethany gave Riker an appreciative look. She didn't say anything to Gem about it in front of Riker. There would be a private conversation, or a series of conversations, between her and Gem. She had a feel for how to discuss things with Gem. An instinct for when to push and when to back off. Riker had only grown in his admiration for her over the months that Gem had been in hospital. She was still just a kid herself, but she had slipped into the role of both partner and caregiver for Gem and was more mature than most of the grown men and women he knew.

"I'll just put it in here," Bethany said and slipped the brochure into the duffel bag. "We'll look at it later."

EPILOGUE

"G EM ...?"

Gem realized that he had been staring at Bethany, lying in bed beside him, and she had caught him at it. He felt his face flush. But why wouldn't he stare at his girlfriend? Bethany was one of the most beautiful girls that he had ever seen, and it was hard to believe that the two of them were together. How had he been lucky enough to get her?

In the last few weeks, several people had commented on how radiant she looked. Bethany explained to Gem that there was even a term for this. Her *pregnant glow*. People didn't know her secret, but still commented on how well and happy she looked. She wasn't showing, and from what she had told him, wouldn't for a few more months. But she had known she was pregnant even before she missed her period.

"Have you thought about names?" he asked her.

A smile spread over Bethany's face. "You don't think it's bad luck? To talk about names this early in the pregnancy? It's my first one; a lot of women miscarry the first time."

"You don't want to talk about names?"

"Yes..." Her eyes sparkled. "I do!"

Gem couldn't help smiling. His stomach tightened. Those slivers of happiness still made him feel guilty. "What do you think of Honey, if it's a girl?"

"Oh…" Bethany put her hand on Gem's cheek, looking into his eyes. "I would love that."

Gem nodded. He felt a pang of sadness. It wasn't the agony he had suffered at the hospital or the months of oppressive depression. It was just a hurt that he knew would never go away. Not even with the birth of a new baby.

Bethany stroked Gem's hair, curling a lock around her finger and then pushing it back behind his ear. "How about Thomas if it's a boy?"

"Thomas?" Gem repeated. He shrugged. He hadn't ever known a Thomas. It didn't mean anything to him. But every name didn't have to be something special.

"Thomas… it means twin," Bethany explained.

Twin. Gem's heart gave a hard throb. He took a few breaths, waiting for the pain to settle again.

"I like Thomas," he agreed, his voice giving an unexpected crack. "Honey if it's a girl. And Thomas if it's a boy."

Bethany nodded and smiled her happiest, most brilliant smile. A smile Gem couldn't help returning, even if his own was tinged with sadness.

"You know," he said, "it could be both. My Gram had boy-girl twins. They say twins runs in families."

**Did you enjoy this book? Reviews and recommendations
are vital to making a book successful.**

**Please leave a review at your favorite book store or review
site and share it with your friends.**

Don't miss the following bonus material:
Sign up for mailing list to get a free ebook
Read a sneak preview chapter
Other books by P.D. Workman
Learn more about the author

Sign up for my mailing list at pdworkman.com and get Gluten-Free Murder for free!

PREVIEW OF RUBY, BETWEEN THE CRACKS

CHAPTER 1

Ruby lay in Chuck's arms, listening to his deep, regular breathing. She wondered fleetingly what he did the nights she didn't see him. Sometimes it was almost a week between visits. Sometimes she saw him almost every day, but sometimes it was a long time in between.

Ruby shifted to move her arm, which was falling asleep. Chuck stirred, and the hair on his arm tickled her cheek. Ruby stroked his arm with one finger, sighing. She felt safe. The nights that she ended up alone, when she couldn't find any company, were the hardest. Cold, alone, scared... Ruby's heart pounded faster just thinking about it. Ruby turned over restlessly to face Chuck. He stirred drowsily, and his eyes opened a slit.

"Are you still awake?" he murmured.

"Mmm-hmm."

"Go to sleep. It's gotta be two in the morning."

"Three-thirty," Ruby told him.

"Mmm. Come here."

He pulled her close to his chest. Ruby tucked her head under his chin and closed her eyes. He rubbed her back for a couple of minutes before he fell asleep again. After a while, Ruby finally fell asleep as well.

Ruby awoke in the morning to an empty bed. Chuck's side was cold and empty. Ruby stretched out her sleep-cramped muscles, slid out of bed, and pulled on her t-shirt and shorts. She wandered out to the kitchen, yawning.

"Hey," Chuck greeted. "You're actually up."

He was all ready for the office. Showered, dressed, curly hair perfectly coiffed. His blue eyes were bright and alert. He smiled at her and took a sip from his coffee mug.

"Yeah," Ruby smothered another yawn. "What time is it?"

"Almost nine. I'm on my way out," he glanced toward the door.

"Mmm. To work?"

"Yeah, precious. Some of us have jobs," he teased.

"I would if anyone would hire me."

"Well then, go to school," Chuck suggested.

Ruby laughed, wrinkling her nose.

"Uh-uh. What am I going to do at school?"

"Whatever the other kids are doing."

Ruby just shook her head.

"You look after yourself," Chuck said, smiling as he looked her over, "and don't forget your jacket."

"Yeah, yeah." Ruby rolled her eyes. She glanced around and picked the jacket up off of the back of the couch.

"Seriously." Chuck's voice took on a more severe tone. "Last time you left a pair of earrings on the sink. Be more careful."

"You already told me," Ruby huffed. "Sorry, okay?"

Chuck tugged at his shirt cuffs to get them a perfect half-inch below his suit jacket.

"All right, Ruby, let's go."

Ruby put her arms around his neck and pulled him in close for a good-bye kiss.

"I'll see you around," he said softly.

"Yeah. You gonna be there tonight?" Ruby questioned, picking up her backpack.

"Maybe."

Chuck rarely committed. Sometimes he'd pick her up, and sometimes he wouldn't. He never knew ahead of time. Ruby wondered if he met someone else the other nights, policing her as carefully as he policed Ruby, to make sure that she didn't leave any sign of her presence. He had his reasons, but Ruby always wondered if he was doing more than just trying to guard his reputation. Why was it so important that there were no signs in his apartment that he had a girlfriend?

They separated in the hall, Chuck going one way and Ruby the other. Ruby wandered to the coffee shop down the street and sipped a fresh cup of coffee slowly. The boy behind the counter always paid her plenty of attention, and Ruby often wondered what kind of guy he was. He was high school or college-aged, she wasn't sure which. She'd never seen him at the high school, but she didn't hang around there very much, he might go there and she just hadn't seen him.

"Running a little late today," he commented.

"Yeah," Ruby agreed. She wasn't sure what it was about her that interested him. She never did her makeup before she got there. Sometimes, like today, she didn't even have her hair combed yet. It was just a halfway point for her, between Chuck's apartment and wherever she decided to go next.

"Doing anything special today?" the boy questioned, with an interested smile.

Ruby shrugged.

"No."

He probably was intrigued because most girls Ruby's age would really be flattered by the attention of a guy his age and fawn all over him, but Ruby really didn't care. He was actually younger than the guys she usually went with. There were only a couple of guys under twenty that she really liked. He might be a better catch than the guys Ruby's own age, but he wasn't very interesting.

"What are you taking in school?" he asked.

"I don't usually go."

"Oh. Where do you go?"

Ruby shrugged.

"Around."

She put down her mug, and he moved to refill it. Ruby shook her head and waved her hand.

"No, thanks."

Ruby got up and went to the lady's room. Unzipping her knapsack, she dug for her lipstick and other makeup. She brushed her teeth before putting on the lipstick, and brushed her hair into order. Her blond hair was straight and fine and she rarely bothered to curl or style it. She pulled it back in a pony and put an elastic around it to keep it in place. She packed her bag again and moved on.

Ruby wandered through a couple of the arcades and hangouts that she usually found company at, but things were strangely quiet. She eventually gave up, and with a sigh, decided to try the school. She arrived halfway through the morning, and joined up with a couple of the girls she knew.

Kate was plain, with no figure, a girl who desperately wanted to be popular, but no amount of makeup or trendy clothes would make her so. She didn't have the personality to join the 'in' crowd. She didn't have the money, the manner, the superficiality.

Marty was a different story. Her name was really Martha, but she preferred the less feminine form. Ruby liked her better than Kate, because Marty was more boyish, more like the guys that Ruby usually spent her time with. Of course, Marty would never be mistaken for a boy. Unlike Kate, she was an early bloomer; her figure already well-developed and she had a head of wild, dark curly hair. Marty had an easy manner, the type that attracted people to her, but didn't really care for a lot of friends or attention.

Ruby felt at ease with the two of them. They were undemanding friends, and she could spend a day with them every now and then and not have them grill her on where she'd been and what she had been doing.

"Hey, Marty," Ruby greeted, and she nodded to Kate.

"Hi, Ruby. You're just in time for math."

Ruby wrinkled her nose.

"Oh, joy. What are we doing?"

"Algebra."

Ruby shook her head. They arrived in class a couple of minutes before the second bell, and Ruby and Marty talked and watched Kate trying to flirt with Robin, the boy who sat in front of her, who she'd had a crush on for a couple months.

"He's never even going to notice her," Ruby commented, watching Robin answer Kate casually, oblivious to her body language.

"I don't even know what she sees in him," Marty commented. "Or in any guy."

"Any junior high boy," Ruby agreed.

Glancing over at them, Robin noticed Marty looking at him, and his manner changed instantly.

"Hey, Marty! How about you, what'd you think of the homework?"

Marty shrugged, and rolled her eyes at Ruby. Robin didn't seem to know how to take Ruby, and didn't say anything to her.

"Did you get A-8?" Kate asked Marty.

"Yeah."

"Can I see it?"

Marty got out her book and passed it across. Kate stared at it for a moment, and scribbled the answer down in her book. The teacher walked in and looked around. He appeared surprised to see Ruby sitting there.

"Are you still in this class?" he questioned.

"Yeah."

"Where have you been the last couple of weeks?"

"Sick." Ruby shrugged.

"You have a note from your doctor?" he demanded.

"No."

"Your mom?"

"I don't live with my mom," Ruby pointed out.

"Where do you live?"

"Foster care."

"Do you have a note from your foster parents?"

"No. You can call my social worker if you want," she suggested.

He hesitated for a moment, then shrugged it off. Too much bother.

"You're going to have a lot to catch up on. Can you get the notes from one of your friends?"

"Uh-huh."

"Okay," he moved towards the middle of the front. "Kate, do

your own homework. If you don't have it by now, it won't do you any good. Anyone have any questions from the homework last night?"

Ruby stretched her legs out and looked around the room, tuning the teacher out.

———

At lunchtime, Ruby and the other girls went over to the senior high half of the school to look for some guys to join up with. Kate would never have been able to interest any of the guys by herself, and Marty didn't really care to, but Ruby had something that attracted the older boys.

"It's because you look so much older," Kate said. "They don't think they're dating a kid, then." She sighed. "I don't look a day older than I am. If I at least had a body like Marty..."

"You're welcome to it," Marty grumbled. "I sure don't want it. But that's not what makes the guys like Ruby. She's almost as flat as you are."

"You just look... more mature," Kate told Ruby.

Ruby shrugged.

"There's Brian. Let's see what he's doing."

Brian looked happy to see them. Tall, slim, with longish hair, he had a handsome face and was almost always smiling and relaxed.

"Hey, girls," he greeted cheerfully. "Looking for some action?"

He put his arm around Ruby's shoulders and gave her a quick hug.

"Got any plans?" Ruby questioned.

"Nope. You wanna go to my place and order a pizza?"

"Sure."

A couple of Brian's friends and Kate and Marty all agreed, so they headed for his house. Brian broke out a couple of six-packs when they got there, and they lounged around drinking and watching kid's shows on TV while they waited for the pizza.

It was almost one when the pizza delivery man got there, but nobody really cared. Missing the first class after lunch was no big deal. In another hour, though, most of them were done eating and getting set to go back to school. Ruby didn't move from her spot on the couch beside Brian.

"You going back?" she asked Brian.

"Not if you'll stick around," he said, giving her a squeeze and kissing her on top of the head.

"Good. I'll see you guys around," Ruby told Kate and Marty.

"Okay. See you later," Marty agreed.

The others went back to school. Tanner, one of Brian's friends, stuck around for another hour watching TV with them. Then he got bored, and suggested they all go somewhere.

"The arcade?" Brian suggested.

"For a while," Ruby agreed. She knew how it would go. They'd play for a while, but Brian would be off his game from drinking for three hours, and he'd get frustrated.

Ruby played a few games herself, but the games or the booze were giving her a headache. She watched Brian play for a while, but he wasn't getting anywhere near his high scores and she could see his frustration mounting.

"Why don't we go shoot some pool," she suggested.

Brian slammed his hand down on the control panel and let the game end. He turned to face her.

"Yeah. Let's blow. I'm totally useless at this today."

Tanner had disappeared at some point. The pool hall was more relaxing. Ruby and Brian shot a leisurely game together, without caring who got the better shots or who won. Brian cajoled a jug of beer out of the management, and they smoked and drank and shot into the evening.

"You know, your friends are sort of strange," Brian commented.

Ruby smiled.

"Yeah, I know it. They're misfits, like me."

"That Marty—she gives me the creeps. I get the feeling she's got a voodoo doll somewhere with my name on it."

Ruby pictured it, and laughed.

"Don't mention it to her, she might think it's a good idea," she giggled.

"She hates me, doesn't she?"

"It's not you. She doesn't like any guys. I think she's got a short-circuit somewhere."

Brian looked thoughtful.

"No, it's more than that. She doesn't look at the other guys like she looks at me. I think it's because you like me. I think she's actually jealous."

"Jealous?" Ruby repeated, surprised. "Nah. If she was jealous, why go back to school? She could have said: 'let's go somewhere' and we could have gone somewhere without you. She could'a' skipped one afternoon of school to do something with all of us. We would've done something with her."

"She doesn't ever get you to herself, does she? Just the two of you?"

"Well, not much..." Ruby admitted. "You're nuts, you know? Marty isn't like that, she just doesn't like guys."

"Maybe... but I don't know."

They dropped the subject.

———

"I gotta be getting home," Brian commented, looking at his watch.

"It's not that late," Ruby protested.

He gave her a couple of gentle kisses, softening the parting.

"I know. But I got things going on tonight," he apologized.

"You gotta go home? Right now?"

"Sorry."

Ruby shrugged.

"All right."

"You want me to drop you off somewhere?" Brian suggested.

"No. I'll hang around here a while."

Brian took a glance around.

"I get nervous, you hanging around places like this by yourself," he said.

Ruby looked over the crowds.

"They're just kids, Bri'. And it's not like it's a gang hangout or something."

"I guess," he agreed reluctantly. "You look after yourself, though."

"Sure. See you 'round."

"Okay, babe."

He kissed her again briefly, and left. Ruby hung out there for a while before going to the bar where Chuck would meet her if he was picking her up. The bouncers knew her, but they never let her in because she was too young. If she was a few years older, they might have bent and let her in, but as it was, she had to stand outside. If it was cold out, they'd let her stand inside the door periodically to warm herself up, but otherwise she stood outside with the hookers, watching for Chuck.

"Hi, Ruby," Betty greeted cheerfully.

"Hi, Betty."

"How're you doing, girl?" Grace questioned.

"Good. Chuck ain't been by, has he?"

"Nope. You expecting him tonight?"

"Maybe. Saw him last night, so maybe not."

"Does he ever pay you anything?" Grace demanded.

"No. It's not like that," Ruby protested with a laugh. "I like to be with him."

"He's taking advantage of you."

"No, he's not. Any time I felt like that, I'd just stop coming here," Ruby pointed out.

"She's just too young to know the difference," Betty interposed. "She thinks she loves him."

"No..." Ruby said, frowning, "I just... like being with him. I don't like being alone."

"Well, you could get company that paid a lot better than that," Grace grumbled.

"Aw, leave her alone. She's better off not getting into this business."

Grace lit a cigarette, and they were quiet for a while. A car pulled up in front of the bar. Betty went up to talk to the driver.

"Hi, honey."

The man indicated Ruby. Betty glanced over at her.

"Oh, she's not interested, honey. But Grace or me..."

"No. Her."

"She's not working."

"I'll make it worth your while," the man said to Ruby, holding up a wad of cash.

Ruby shook her head.

"She's just waiting for her friend," Betty explained.

He screeched his tires when he pulled out, and shot down the street. Betty went back to stand with Ruby and Grace.

Grace shook her head.

"You stand there in shorts and a tee and sneakers and get more pick-ups than we do. I just don't know what you do."

"She's young. Men like'em young," Betty said.

"I started at her age, and I never got the attention she does."

Betty looked at Ruby and shrugged.

"Some people just got what it takes."

Ruby watched for Chuck's car. If he didn't show up, she'd have to try and find somewhere else she could spend the night. But she wasn't going to take up a new profession to do it. An hour passed, and Ruby knew he wasn't going to show up. She said goodbye to the girls, and started to walk away. She got about half a block down, and a red convertible pulled up beside her.

"Hey, sweetheart."

"Not interested."

"Slow down. How'd you like to make a little cash?"

Ruby stopped and looked at him. A small, ferret-faced man in a red convertible. She'd seen him before, but she couldn't remember where. He was well dressed, but she got a bad vibe from him.

"What're you going to pay me for?" she demanded.

"To work for me," he said vaguely.

"Doin' what?"

"Leave her alone," Betty said, catching up to Ruby. "Ruby doesn't need any help from you."

The man looked at Betty.

"Stay out of it, Betty. This doesn't concern you."

"Ruby's my friend, you'd better believe it concerns me. Ruby, you ever met my boss?"

"No. Guess I haven't."

"Well, he's a snake, so stay away from him. You see this rat, you go the other way."

"Thanks."

Ruby turned and walked away. She could hear the pimp getting after Betty as she walked away, but Ruby didn't look back. The last thing she needed was to get involved in that scene. She went back to the pool hall, but no one that she knew was around. Ruby stayed there until the small hours of the morning before admitting to herself that her choices were either sleeping on the street or going home. She left the pool hall and started for home. Halfway there, a squad car pulled up beside her.

"Hi," the police officer said, through the open window.

"Hi there," Ruby acknowledged.

"A little late to be out wandering, isn't it?"

"I'm on my way home."

"How about if I drive you?" he offered.

"Yeah, okay."

"Hop in."

Ruby got into the squad car and shut the door. He pulled away from the curb.

"What's your name?"

"Ruby."

"Where do you live, Ruby?"

She gave him her address.

"Good. The name's Brown. What were you doing out so late?"

"Just hanging out." Ruby shrugged.

"There's lots of crazies out there. You shouldn't be out alone."

"I know."

"Your folks know where you are?"

"No."

"You do this often?"

Ruby shrugged.

"No. Not a lot."

Brown didn't say anything else. They pulled up to the house a few minutes later. Ruby glanced at the cop to see if he was going to insist on escorting her in and talking to her parents, but he was relaxed and didn't move to get out.

"Thanks for the lift," Ruby said.

"No problem," Brown took a business card out of his pocket. "If you're ever out late alone or need something, you call me. I'd rather be a taxi for a couple minutes then find you dead by the road somewhere."

Ruby took the card from him.

"Hey—thanks. That's cool."

She got out and went up to the house. The key was on a ring on her knapsack, and she waved at Brown and let herself in.

———

Ruby, Between the Cracks, Book #1 of the *Between the Cracks* series by P.D. Workman can be purchased at pdworkman.com

ABOUT THE AUTHOR

Award-winning and USA Today bestselling author P.D. (Pamela) Workman writes riveting mystery/suspense and young adult books dealing with mental illness, addiction, abuse, and other real-life issues. For as long as she can remember, the blank page has held an incredible allure and from a very young age she was trying to write her own books.

Workman wrote her first complete novel at the age of twelve and continued to write as a hobby for many years. She started publishing in 2013. She has won several literary awards from Library Services for Youth in Custody for her young adult fiction. She currently has over 60 published titles and can be found at pdworkman.com.

Born and raised in Alberta, Workman has been married for over 25 years and has one son.

Please visit P.D. Workman at pdworkman.com to see what else she is working on, to join her mailing list, and to link to her social networks.

If you enjoyed this book, please take the time to recommend it to other purchasers with a review or star rating and share it with your friends!